SEVEN

- heroes in hot water
- malicious magicians
- trials by terror
- superb stories of
  swords and sorcery

Here are Conan, Fafhrd, Eric of Melnibone

   . . . Ningauble of the Seven Eyes,
   the Gibbelins, the cannibal wizard of
   Hercynia . . .

   and other famous heroes and horrors
   locked in rousing combat to the death
   —and beyond.

THE SPELL OF SEVEN

STORIES OF HEROIC FANTASY

selected and with an introduction by

L. SPRAGUE de CAMP

Illustrated by VIRGIL FINLAY

PYRAMID BOOKS ▲ NEW YORK

THE SPELL OF SEVEN

A PYRAMID BOOK—First printing, June 1965
Second printing, December 1969

ACKNOWLEDGMENTS

"Bazaar of the Bizarre," by Fritz Leiber, originally published in Fantastic Stories of Imagination for August, 1963; copyright © 1963 by Ziff-Davis Publishing Co.; reprinted by permission of the author.

"The Dark Eidolon," by Clark Ashton Smith, originally published in Weird Tales for January, 1935; copyright © 1934 by Popular Fiction Publishing Co.; reprinted by permission of Arkham House, Publishers.

"The Hoard of the Gibbelins," by Lord Dunsany, originally published in The Sketch (London) and in The Book of Wonder (London: Heinemann, and Boston: John W. Luce, 1912); reprinted by permission of the Dowager Lady Dunsany.

"The Hungry Hercynian," by L. Sprague de Camp, originally published in Universe Science Fiction for December, 1953; copyright © 1953 by Palmer Publications, Inc.; reprinted by permission of the author.

"Kings in Darkness," by Michael Moorcock, originally published in Science Fantasy No. 54, 1962; copyright © 1962 by Nova Publications, Ltd.; reprinted by permission of E. J. Carnell, agent for Michael Moorcock.

"Mazirian the Magician," by Jack Vance, originally published in The Dying Earth (New York: Hillman Periodicals, 1950); copyright © 1950 by Hillman Periodicals, Inc.; reprinted by permission of Scott Meredith, agent for Jack Vance.

"Shadows in Zamboula," by Robert E. Howard, originally published in Weird Tales for November, 1935; copyright © 1935 by Popular Fiction Publishing Co.; reprinted by permission of Otis Kline Associates, Inc., agent for the estate of Robert E. Howard.

PYRAMID BOOKS are published by Pyramid Publications, Inc.

444 Madison Avenue, New York, N. Y. 10022, U.S.A.

CONTENTS

*To my fellow enthusiasts
for the art of heroic fantasy:
the members of the Hyborian legion.*

INTRODUCTION

Wizards and Warriors

HOW WOULD YOU like to escape to a world of wizards and warlocks, warriors and wenches—a world where gleaming cities raise their shining spires against the stars, sorcerers cast sinister spells from subterranean lairs, baleful spirits stalk through crumbling ruins, primeval monsters crash through jungle thickets, and the fate of kingdoms is balanced on the bloody blades of broadswords brandished by heroes of preternatural might and valor? A "purple and golden and crimson universe where anything can happen—except the tedious"? And where, moreover, nobody ever so much as mentions the income tax, the school dropout problem, or the virtues and faults of socialized medicine?

In other words, do you feel like saying: "To hell with the world's problems for a while! Let's read something for fun"? Then you should read heroic fantasy, like the stories in this volume and its predecessor, *Swords and Sorcery*.

These are stories laid in an imaginary world, superficially somewhat like ours, but a world where magic works and machinery has not been invented. Sometimes this world is that which the story-teller imagines ours was like in prehistoric times. Sometimes he fancies that it will exist in the distant future, when the sun has dimmed, science and civilization have decayed, and magic has once again come into its own. Sometimes the scene is a world in another universe parallel to ours, where the laws of nature are different.

For its ultimate inspiration, heroic fantasy goes back to the saga, the epic, the legend, and the myth. In fact, some modern writers like James Stephens have rewritten the legends of some particular cycle (in Stephens' case, the Irish Cuchulainn cycle) in modern novelistic form. Other writers, however, prefer to invent their own settings and characters.

After the murder of the medieval romance by Cervantes with *Don Quixote* (1605-15), heroic, romantic, and fantastic fiction were rather unpopular for over a century. In the late eighteenth and early nineteenth centuries, however, the use of the supernatural in fiction revived. At this time, fantasy reëntered the main stream of literature through three channels: the oriental fantasy narrative, the Gothic novel, and the child's fairy tale. The oriental influence on European fantasy began with the translation into French by Antoine Galland of the *Arabian Nights* and other eastern extravaganzas.

Books for children were practically invented in the seventeenth century by John Bunyan. For many decades, they consisted of grimly moralistic tales with much uplift but little entertainment. Then writers like Andersen and the Grimms began to record the folk tales that existed in oral peasant tradition. Later, other writers like Lewis Carroll and George MacDonald began composing original works in the genre.

The English Gothic novel began with Horace Walpole's *Castle of Otranto* (1764), inspired by similar works that had been appearing in Germany. It was followed by a flood of Gothic novels in England and Germany, all rife with crumbling castles, ruined monasteries, lecherous tyrants, imperiled virgins, impoverished young heroes of noble birth, secret passages, trapdoors, eldrich legends, and of course ghosts, sometimes fake and sometimes made of authentic ectoplasm.

While the Gothic novel bloomed, Walter Scott launched the modern historical novel with his *Waverly* (1814) and its many successors. People had previously written stories laid in a period long before their own. Homer's *Iliad* and Xenophon's *Youth of Cyrus* belong in this category. Such writers, however, made no special point of the differences between their own times and those of which they wrote. For the most part they were not aware of these differences. When they were, they tended to slight them.

Scott, on the other hand, discovered not only that the past *was* different from the present but also that this difference could be turned to account. The costumes and customs of a bygone age had an entertainment value in themselves. To an ordinary man in any civilization, harassed by the petty everyday needs of a drab existence, life in an earlier century seems more colorful and dramatic than that of his own contemporary world. Hence Scott looked back to the High Middle Ages. The medievals, for their part, looked back to Rome, the Romans to Greece, and the Greeks to the great days of Crete and Mycenae.

Scott's novels, in fact, were so influential that they touched off a whole wave of medieval romanticism. This movement reached its climax in the Eglinton Tournament of 1839. Lord Eglinton, a likeable and extravagant young peer, and his friends, at enormous expense, staged the last genuine medieval tournament on Eglinton's Scottish estates. Alas for romance! It poured.

In the 1880s, William Morris created the modern genre of heroic fantasy by combining the antiquarian romanticism of Scott and his imitators with the supernaturalism of Walpole and *his* imitators. Morris wrote a number of novels laid in an imaginary medieval world. Most of these stories strike a modern reader as rather dull. Nevertheless, some of Morris' techniques, such as his artful use of archaic language, have passed into general use in the genre.

After Morris, other British writers like Lord Dunsany and Eric Rücker Eddison developed the heroic fantasy further. The appearance of the magazines *Weird Tales* and *Unknown Worlds* encouraged a number of American writers, in the 1930s, to try their hands at fiction of this kind.

In the decade after the Hitlerian War, interest in heroic fantasy shrank, until such fiction bade fair to become a casualty of the machine age. The cause, however, was the trend of the time, in main-stream fiction and also in science fiction, towards stories with a strongly subjective, sentimental, psychological slant. In such tales, the anti-hero was often a wretched little twerp who could never do anything right. Instead of providing the reader with a heroic model with whom he could for the moment identify himself, giving himself a warm glow of vicarious heroism, the writer presented his reader with a protagonist so ineffectual and contemptible that the reader—the writer hoped—would enjoy the thought that at least he was better than *that*.

In the last few years, however, there has been a striking revival of heroic fantasy. This anthology, I hope, will be a worthy contribution to this revival. The Hero shall ride again!

L. SPRAGUE DE CAMP

SUNDERED from us by gulfs of time and stranger dimensions dreams the ancient world of Nehwon with its towers and jewels, its swords and sorceries. Nehwon's known realms crowd about the Inner Sea: northward the green-forested fierce Land of the Eight Cities, eastward the steppe-dwelling Mingol horsemen and the desert, where caravans creep from the rich Eastern Lands and the River Tilth. But southward, linked to the desert only by the Sinking Land and further warded by the Great Dyke and the Mountain of Hunger, are the rich grainfields and walled cities of Lankhmar, eldest and chiefest of Nehwon's lands. Dominating the Land of Lankhmar and crouching at the silty mouth of the River Hlal, in a secure corner between the grainfields, the Great Salt Marsh, and the Inner Sea, is the massive-walled mazy-alleyed metropolis of Lankhmar, thick with thieves and shaven priests, lean-framed magicians and fat-bellied merchants—Lankhmar the Imperishable, the City of the Black Toga.

In Lankhmar one market night, if we can believe the runic books of Sheelba of the Eyeless Face, there met for the first time those two dubious heroes and whimsical scoundrels, Fafhrd and the Gray Mouser. Fafhrd's origins were easy to perceive in his near seven-foot height and limber-looking ranginess, his hammered ornaments and huge longsword: he was clearly a barbarian from the Cold Waste north even of the Eight Cities and the Trollstep Mountains. The Mouser's antecedents were more cryptic and hardly to be deduced from his childlike stature, gray garb, mouse-skin hood shadowing flat swart face, and deceptively dainty rapier; but somewhere about him was the suggestion of cities and the South, the dark streets and also the sun-drenched spaces. As the twain eyed each other challengingly through the torchlit fog, they were already dimly aware that they were two long-sundered matching fragments of a greater hero and that each had found a comrade who would outlast a thousand quests and a lifetime of adventuring.

Thus Fafhrd (rhymes with "proffered") and Gray Mouser, invented by Fritz Leiber and his lifelong friend Harry Fischer in correspondence during the lean 1930s. After several abortive attempts, when Leiber was just beginning as a writer, he sold five novelettes about the formidable pair to the lamented mazazine Unknown Worlds (1939-43). After the Hitlerian War, he resumed work on the series and has published nine more Mouser stories in various magazines and a collection of the first seven such tales in book form (Two Sought Adventure, Gnome Press, 1957). Several of the stories have appeared in other anthologies and collections. More Mouser stories by Leiber and Fischer, working either together or independently, are promised.

BAZAAR
OF THE
BIZARRE

● FRITZ LEIBER

THE strange stars of the World of Nehwon glinted thickly above the black-roofed city of Lankhmar, where swords clink almost as often as coins. For once there was no fog.

In the Plaza of Dark Delights, which lies seven blocks south of the Marsh Gate and extends from the Fountain of Dark Abundance to the Shrine of the Black Virgin, the shop-lights glinted upward no more brightly than the stars glinted down. For there the vendors of drugs and the peddlers of curiosa and the hawkers of assignations light their stalls and crouching places with foxfire, glowworms, and firepots with tiny single windows, and they conduct their business almost as silently as the stars conduct theirs.

There are plenty of raucous spots a-glare with torches in nocturnal Lankhmar, but by immemorial tradition soft whispers and a pleasant dimness are the rule in the Plaza of Dark Delights. Philosophers often go there solely to meditate, students to dream, and fanatic-eyed theologians to spin like spiders abstruse new theories of the Devil and of the other dark forces ruling the universe. And if any of these find a little illicit fun by the way, their theories and dreams and theologies and demonologies are undoubtedly the better for it.

Tonight, however, there was a glaring exception to the

darkness rule. From a low doorway with a trefoil arch
new-struck through an ancient wall, light spilled into the
Plaza. Rising above the horizon of the pavement like some
monstrous moon a-shine with the ray of a murderous sun,
the new doorway dimmed almost to extinction the stars
of the other merchants of mystery.

Eerie and unearthly objects for sale spilled out of the
doorway a little way with the light, while beside the doorway crouched an avid-faced figure clad in garments never
before seen on land or sea . . . in the World of Nehwon.
He wore a hat like a small red pail, baggy trousers, and
outlandish red boots with upturned toes. His eyes were as
predatory as a hawk's, but his smile as cynically and
lasciviously cajoling as an ancient satyr's.

Now and again he sprang up and pranced about, sweeping and re-sweeping with a rough long broom the flagstones as if to clean a path for the entry of some fantastic
emperor, and he often paused in his dance to bow low
and loutingly, but always with upglancing eyes, to the
crowd gathering in the darkness across from the doorway
and to swing his hand from them toward the interior of the
new shop in a gesture of invitation at once servile and
sinister.

No one of the crowd had yet plucked up courage to step
forward into the glare and enter the shop, or even inspect
the rarities set out so carelessly yet temptingly before it.
But the number of fascinated peerers increased momently.
There were mutterings of censure at the dazzling new
method of merchandising—the infraction of the Plaza's
custom of darkness—but on the whole the complaints were
outweighed by the gasps and murmurings of wonder, admiration, and curiosity kindling ever hotter.

The Gray Mouser slipped into the Plaza at the Fountain
end as silently as if he had come to slit a throat or spy
on the spies of the Overlord. His rat-skin moccasins were
soundless. His sword Scalpel in its mouse-skin sheath did
not swish ever so faintly against either his tunic or cloak,
both of gray silk curiously coarse of weave, while the
glances he shot about him from under his gray silk hood
half thrown back were freighted with menace and a freez-
ing sense of superiority.

Inwardly the Mouser was feeling very much like a

schoolboy—a schoolboy in dread of rebuke and a crushing assignment of homework. For in the Mouser's pouch of rat-skin was a note scrawled in dark brown squid-ink on silvery fish-skin by Sheelba of the Eyeless Face, inviting the Mouser to be at this spot at this time.

Sheelba was the Mouser's supernatural tutor and—when the whim struck Sheelba—guardian, and it never did to ignore his invitations, for Sheelba had eyes to track down the unsociable though he did not carry them between his cheeks and forehead.

But the tasks Sheelba would set the Mouser at times like these were apt to be peculiarly onerous and even noisome —such as procuring nine white cats with never a black hair among them, or stealing five copies of the same book of magic runes from five widely separated sorcerous libraries, or obtaining specimens of the dung of four kings living or dead—so the Mouser had come early, to get the bad news as soon as possible, and he had come alone, for he certainly did not want his comrade Fafhrd to stand snickering by while Sheelba delivered his little wizardly homilies to a dutiful Mouser . . . and perchance thought of extra assignments.

Sheelba's note, invisibly graven somewhere inside the Mouser's skull, read merely, "When the star Akul bedizens the Spire of Rhan, be you by the Fountain of Dark Abundance," and the note was signed only with the little featureless oval which is Sheelba's sigil.

The Mouser glided now through the darkness to the Fountain, which was a squat black pillar from the rough rounded top of which a single black drop welled and dripped every twenty elephant's heartbeats.

The Mouser stood beside the Fountain and, extending a bent hand, measured the altitude of the green star Akul. It had still to drop down the sky seven finger-widths more before it would touch the needle-point of the slim star-silhouetted distant minaret of Rhan.

The Mouser crouched doubled-up by the black pillar and then vaulted lightly atop it to see if that would make any great difference in Akul's altitude. It did not.

He scanned the nearby darkness for motionless figures . . . especially that of one robed and cowled like a monk— cowled so deeply that one might wonder how he saw to walk. There were no figures at all.

The Mouser's mood changed. If Sheelba chose not to come courteously beforehand, why he could be boorish too! He strode off to investigate the new bright arch-doored shop, of whose infractious glow he had become inquisitively aware at least a block before he had entered the Plaza of Dark Delights.

Fafhrd the Northerner opened one wine-heavy eye and without moving his head scanned half the small firelit room in which he slept naked. He shut that eye, opened the other, and scanned the other half.

There was no sign of the Mouser anywhere. So far so good! If his luck held, he would be able to get through to-night's embarrassing business without being jeered at by the small gray rogue.

He drew from under his stubbly cheek a square of violet serpent-hide pocked with tiny pores so that when he held it between his eyes and the dancing fire it made stars. Studied for a time, these stars spelled out obscurely the message: "When Rhan-dagger stabs the darkness in Akul-heart, seek you the Source of the Black Drops."

Drawn boldly across the prickholes in an orange-brown like dried blood—in fact spanning the violet square—was a seven-armed swastika, which is one of the sigils of Ningauble of the Seven Eyes.

Fafhrd had no difficulty in interpreting the Source of the Black Drops as the Fountain of Dark Abundance. He had become wearily familiar with such cryptic poetic language during his boyhood as a scholar of the singing skalds.

Ningauble stood to Fafhrd very much as Sheelba stood to the Mouser except that the Seven-Eyed One was a somewhat more pretentious archimage, whose taste in the thaumaturgical tasks he set Fafhrd ran in larger directions such as the slaying of dragons, the sinking of four-masted magic ships, and the kidnapping of ogre-guarded enchanted queens.

Also, Ningauble was given to quiet realistic boasting, especially about the grandeur of his vast cavern-home, whose stony serpent-twisting back corridors led, he often averred, to all spots in space and time—provided Ningauble instructed one beforehand exactly how to step those rocky crook'd low-ceilinged passageways.

Fafhrd was driven by no great desire to learn Ningauble's formulas and enchantments, as the Mouser was driven to learn Sheelba's, but the Septinocular One had enough holds on the Northerner, based on the latter's weaknesses and past misdeeds, so that Fafhrd had always to listen patiently to Ningauble's wizardly admonishments and vaunting sorcerous chit-chat—but *not*, if humanly or inhumanly possible, while the Gray Mouser was present to snigger and grin.

Meanwhile, Fafhrd, standing before the fire, had been whipping, slapping, and belting various garments and weapons and ornaments onto his huge brawny body with its generous stretches of thick short curling red-gold hairs. When he opened the outer door and, also booted and helmeted now, glanced down the darkling alleyway preparatory to leaving and noted only the hunch-backed chestnut vendor asquat by his brazier at the next corner, one would have sworn that when he did stride forth toward the Plaza of Dark Delights it would be with the clankings and thunderous tread of a siege tower approaching a thick-walled city.

Instead the lynx-eared old chestnut vendor, who was also a spy of the Overlord, had to swallow down his heart when it came sliding crookedly up his throat as Fafhrd rushed past him, tall as a pine tree, swift as the wind, and silent as a ghost.

The Mouser elbowed aside two gawkers with shrewd taps on the floating rib and strode across the dark flagstones toward the garishly bright shop with its doorway like an up-ended heart. It occurred to him they must have had masons working like fiends to have cut and plastered that archway so swiftly. He had been past here this afternoon and noted nothing but blank wall.

The outlandish porter with the red cylinder hat and twisty red shoe-toes came frisking out to the Mouser with his broom and then went curtsying back as he re-swept a path for this first customer with many an obsequious bow and smirk.

But the Mouser's visage was set in an expression of grim and all-skeptical disdain. He paused at the heaping of objects in front of the door and scanned it with disapproval. He drew Scalpel from its thin gray sheath and with the top of the long blade flipped back the cover on the topmost of a pile of musty books. Without going any closer he briefly scanned the first page, shook his head, rapidly turned a half dozen more pages with Scalpel's tip, using the sword as if it were a teacher's wand to point out words here and there—because they were ill-chosen, to judge from his expression—and then abruptly closed the book with another sword-flip.

Next he used Scalpel's tip to lift a red cloth hanging from a table behind the books and peer under it suspiciously, to rap contemptuously a glass jar with a human head floating in it, to touch disparagingly several other objects, and to waggle reprovingly at a foot-chained owl which hooted at him solemnly from its high perch.

He sheathed Scalpel and turned toward the porter with a sour, lifted-eyebrow look which said—nay, shouted—plainly, "Is *this* all you have to offer? Is this garbage your excuse for defiling the Dark Plaza with glare?"

Actually the Mouser was mightily interested by every least item which he had glimpsed. The book, incidentally, had been in a script which he not only did not understand, but did not even recognize.

Three things were very clear to the Mouser: first, that this stuff offered here for sale did not come from anywhere in the World of Nehwon, no, not even from Nehwon's farthest outback; second, that all this stuff was, in some way which he could not yet define, extremely dangerous; third, that all this stuff was monstrously fascinating and that he, the Mouser, did not intend to stir from this place until he had personally scanned, studied, and if need be tested every last intriguing item and scrap.

At the Mouser's sour grimace, the Porter went into a convulsion of wheedling and fawning caperings, seemingly torn between a desire to kiss the Mouser's foot and to point out with flamboyant caressing gestures every object in his shop.

He ended by bowing so low that his chin brushed the pavement, sweeping an ape-long arm toward the interior of the shop, and gibbering in atrocious Lankhmarese, "Every object to pleasure the flesh and senses and imagination of man. Wonders undreamed. Very cheap, very cheap! Yours for a penny! The Bazaar of the Bizarre. Please to inspect, O King!"

The Mouser yawned a very long yawn with the back of his hand to his mouth; next he looked around him again with the weary patient worldly smile of a duke who knows he must put up with many boredoms to encourage business in his demesne; finally he shrugged faintly and entered the shop.

Behind him the Porter went into a jigging delirium of glee and began to re-sweep the flagstones like a man maddened with delight.

Inside, the first thing the Mouser saw was a stack of slim books bound in gold-lined fine-grained red and violet leather.

The second was a rack of gleaming lenses and slim brass tubes calling to be peered through.

The third was a slim dark-haired girl smiling at him mysteriously from a gold-barred cage that swung from the ceiling.

Beyond that cage hung others with bars of silver and strange green, ruby, orange, ultramarine, and purple metals.

Fafhrd saw the Mouser vanish into the shop just as his left hand touched the rough chill pate of the Fountain of Dark Abundance and as Akul poised precisely on Rhantop as if it were that needle-spire's green-lensed pinnacle-lantern.

He might have followed the Mouser, he might have done no such thing, he certainly would have pondered the briefly glimpsed event, but just then there came from behind him a long low "Hsssssst!"

Fafhrd turned like a giant dancer, and his longsword Graywand came out of its sheath swiftly and rather more silently than a snake emerges from its hole.

Ten arm-lengths behind him, in the mouth of an alleyway darker than the Dark Plaza would have been without its new commercial moon, Fafhrd dimly made out two robed and deeply cowled figures poised side by side.

One cowl held darkness absolute. Even the face of a Negro of Klesh might have been expected to shoot ghostly bronzy gleams. But here there were none.

In the other cowl there nested seven very faint pale greenish glows. They moved about restlessly, sometimes circling each other, swinging mazily. Sometimes one of the seven horizontally oval gleams would grow a little brighter, seemingly as it moved forward toward the mouth of the cowl—or a little darker, as it drew back.

Fafhrd sheathed Graywand and advanced toward the figures. Still facing him, they retreated slowly and silently down the alley.

Fafhrd followed as they receded. He felt a stirring of interest . . . and of other feelings. To meet his own supernatural mentor alone might be only a bore and a mild nervous strain; but it would be hard for anyone entirely to repress a shiver of awe at encountering at one and the same time both Ningauble of the Seven Eyes and Sheelba of the Eyeless Face.

Moreover, that those two bitter wizardly rivals should have joined forces, that they should apparently be operating together in amity. . . . Something of great note must be afoot! There was no doubting that.

The Mouser meantime was experiencing the snuggest, most mind-teasing, most exotic enjoyments imaginable. The sleekly leather-bound gold-stamped books turned out to contain scripts stranger far than that in the book whose pages he had flipped outside—scripts that looked like skeletal beasts, cloud swirls, and twisty-branched bushes and trees—but for a wonder he could read them all without the least difficulty.

The books dealt in the fullest detail with such matters as the private life of devils, the secret histories of murderous cults, and—these were illustrated—the proper dueling techniques to employ against sword-armed demons and the erotic tricks of lamias, succubi, bacchantes, and hamadryads.

The lenses and brass tubes, some of the latter of which were as fantastically crooked as if they were periscopes for seeing over the walls and through the barred windows of other universes, showed at first only delightful jeweled patterns, but after a bit the Mouser was able to see through them into all sorts of interesting places: the treasure-rooms of dead kings, the bedchambers of living queens, the council-crypts of rebel angels, and the closets in which the gods hid plans for worlds too frighteningly fantastic to risk creating.

As for the quaintly-clad slim girls in their playfully widely-barred cages, well, they were pleasant pillows on which to rest eyes momentarily fatigued by book-scanning and tube-peering.

Ever and anon one of the girls would whistle softly at the Mouser and then point cajolingly or imploringly or with languorous hintings at a jeweled crank set in the wall whereby her cage, suspended on a gleaming chain running through gleaming pulleys, could be lowered to the floor.

At these invitations the Mouser would smile with a bland amorousness and nod and softly wave a hand from the finger-hinge as if to whisper, "Later . . . later. Be patient."

After all, girls had a way of blotting out all lesser, but not thereby despicable, delights. Girls were for dessert.

Ningauble and Sheelba receded down the dark alleyway with Fafhrd following them until the latter lost patience and, somewhat conquering his unwilling awe, called out nervously, "Well, are you going to keep on fleeing me backwards until we all pitch into the Great Salt Marsh? What do you want of me? What's it all about?"

But the two cowled figures had already stopped, as he could perceive by the starlight and the glow of a few high windows, and now it seemed to Fafhrd that they had stopped a moment before he had called out. A typical sorcerers' trick for making one feel awkward! He gnawed his lip in the darkness. It was ever thus!

"O My Gentle Son. . . ." Ningauble began in his most sugary-priestly tones, the dim puffs of his seven eyes now hanging in his cowl as steadily and glowing as mildly as the Pleiades seen late on a summer night through a greenish mist rising from a lake freighted with blue vitriol and corrosive gas of salt.

"I asked what it's all about!" Fafhrd interrupted harshly. Already convicted of impatience, he might as well go the whole hog.

"Let me put it as a hypothetical case," Ningauble replied imperturbably. "Let us suppose, My Gentle Son, that there is a man in a universe and that a most evil force comes to this universe from another universe, or perhaps from a congeries of universes, and that this man is a brave man who wants to defend his universe and who counts his life as a trifle and that moreover he has to counsel him a very wise and prudent and public-spirited uncle who knows all about these matters which I have been hypothecating—"

"The Devourers menace Lankhmar!" Sheelba rapped out in a voice as harsh as a tree cracking and so suddenly that Fafhrd almost started—and for all we know, Ningauble too.

Fafhrd waited a moment to avoid giving false impressions and then switched his gaze to Sheelba. His eyes had been growing accustomed to the darkness and he saw much more now than he had seen at the alley's mouth, yet he still saw not one jot more than absolute blackness inside Sheelba's cowl.

"Who are the Devourers?" he asked.

It was Ningauble, however, who replied, "The Devourers are the most accomplished merchants in all the many universes—so accomplished, indeed, that they sell only trash. There is a deep necessity in this, for the Devourers must occupy all their cunning in perfecting their methods of selling and so have not an instant to spare in considering the worth of what they sell—indeed, they dare not concern themselves with such matters for a moment, for fear of losing their golden touch—and yet such are their skills that their wares are utterly irresistible, indeed the finest wares in all the many universes—if you follow me?"

Fafhrd looked hopefully toward Sheelba; but, since the latter did not this time interrupt with some pithy summation, he nodded to Ningauble.

Ningauble continued, his seven eyes beginning to weave a bit, judging from the movements of the seven green glows, "As you might readily deduce, the Devourers possess all the mightiest magics garnered from the many universes, whilst their assault groups are led by the most aggressive wizards imaginable, supremely skilled in all methods of battling, whether it be with the wits, or the feelings, or with the beweaponed body.

"The method of the Devourers is to set up shop in a new world and first entice the bravest and the most adventuresome and the supplest-minded of its people—who have so much imagination that with just a touch of suggestion they do most of the work of selling themselves.

"When these are safely ensnared, the Devourers proceed to deal with the remainder of the population: meaning simply that they sell and sell and sell!—sell trash and take good money and even finer things in exchange."

Ningauble sighed windily and a shade piously. "All this is very bad, My Gentle Son," he continued, his eye-glows weaving hypnotically in his cowl, "but natural enough in universes administered by such gods as we have—natural enough and perhaps endurable. However—" (He paused) "—there is worse to come! The Devourers want not only the patronage of all beings in all universes, but—doubtless because they are afraid someone will some day raise the ever-unpleasant question of the true worth of things—they want all their customers reduced to a state of slavish and submissive suggestibility, so that they are fit for nothing whatever but to gawk at and buy the trash the Devourers offer for sale. This means of course that eventually the Devourers' customers will have nothing wherewith to pay the Devourers for their trash, but the Devourers do not seem to be concerned with this eventuality. Perhaps they feel that there is always a new universe to exploit. And perhaps there is!"

"Monstrous!" Fafhrd commented. "But what do the Devourers gain from all these furious commercial sorties, all this mad merchandising? What do they really want?"

Ningauble replied, "The Devourers want only to amass cash and to raise little ones like themselves to amass more cash and they want to compete with each other at cash-amassing (Is that coincidentally a city, do you think, Fafhrd? Cashamash?) and the Devourers want to brood about their great service to the many universes—it is their claim that servile customers make the most obedient subjects for the gods—and to complain about how the work of amassing cash tortures their minds and upsets their digestions. Beyond this, each of the Devourers also secretly collects and hides away forever, to delight no eyes but his own, all the finest objects and thoughts created by true men and women (and true wizards and true demons) and bought by the Devourers at bankruptcy prices and paid for with trash or—this is their ultimate preference—with nothing at all."

"Monstrous indeed!" Fafhrd repeated. "Merchants are

ever an evil mystery and these sound the worst. But what
has all this to do with me?"

"O My Gentle Son," Ningauble responded, the piety in
his voice now tinged with a certain clement disappointment, "you force me once again to resort to hypothecating.
Let us return to the supposition of this brave man whose
whole universe is direly menaced and who counts his life
a trifle and to the related supposition of this brave man's
wise uncle, whose advice the brave man invariably fol-
lows—"

"The Devourers have set up shop in the Plaza of Dark
Delights!" Sheelba interjected so abruptly and in such
iron-harsh syllables that this time Fafhrd actually did
start. "You must obliterate this outpost tonight!"

Fafhrd considered that for a bit, then said, in a tentative
sort of voice, "You will both accompany me, I presume,
to aid me with your wizardly sendings and castings in what
I can see must be a most perilous operation, to serve me
as a sort of sorcerous artillery and archery corps while
I play assault battalion—"

"O My Gentle Son. . . ." Ningauble interrupted in tones
of deepest disappointment, shaking his head so that his
eye-glows jogged in his cowl.

"You must do it alone!" Sheelba rasped.

"Without any help at all?" Fafhrd demanded. "No! Get
someone else. Get this doltish brave man who always fol-
lows his scheming uncle's advice as slavishly as you tell
me the Devourers' customers respond to their merchandising. Get *him!* But as for me—No, I say!"

"Then leave us, coward!" Sheelba decreed dourly, but
Ningauble only sighed and said quite apologetically, "It
was intended that you have a comrade in this quest, a
fellow soldier against noisome evil—to wit, the Gray
Mouser. But unfortunately he came early to his appoint-
ment with my colleague here and was enticed into the shop
of the Devourers and is doubtless now deep in their snares,
if not already extinct. So you can see that we do take
thought for your welfare and have no wish to overburden
you with solo quests. However, My Gentle Son, if it still be
your firm resolve—"

Fafhrd let out a sigh more profound than Ningauble's.
"Very well," he said in gruff tones admitting defeat, "I'll
do it for you. Someone will have to pull that poor little

gray fool out of the pretty-pretty fire—or the twinkly-twinkly water!—that tempted him. But how do I go about it?" He shook a big finger at Ningauble. "And no more Gentle-Sonning!"

Ningauble paused. Then he said only, "Use your own judgment."

Sheelba said, "Beware the Black Wall!"

Ningauble said to Fafhrd, "Hold, I have a gift for you," and held out to him a ragged ribbon a yard long, pinched between the cloth of the wizard's long sleeve so that it was impossible to see the manner of hand that pinched. Fafhrd took the tatter with a snort, crumpled it into a ball, and thrust it into his pouch.

"Have a greater care with it," Ningauble warned. "It is the Cloak of Invisibility, somewhat worn by many magic usings. Do not put it on until you near the Bazaar of the Devourers. It has two minor weaknesses: it will not make you altogether invisible to a master sorcerer if he senses your presence and takes certain steps. Also, see to it that you do not bleed during this exploit, for the cloak will not hide blood."

"I've a gift too!" Sheelba said, drawing from out of his black cowl-hole—with sleeve-masked hand, as Ningauble had done—something that shimmered faintly in the dark like. . . .

Like a spiderweb.

Sheelba shook it, as if to dislodge a spider, or perhaps two.

"The Blindfold of True Seeing," he said as he reached it toward Fafhrd. "It shows all things as they really are! Do not lay it across your eyes until you enter the Bazaar. On no account, as you value your life or your sanity, wear it now!"

Fafhrd took it from him most gingerly, the flesh of his fingers crawling. He was inclined to obey the taciturn wizard's instructions. At this moment he truly did not much care to see the true visage of Sheelba of the Eyeless Face.

The Gray Mouser was reading the most interesting book of them all, a great compendium of secret knowledge written in a script of astrologic and geomantic signs, the meanings of which fairly leaped off the page into his mind.

To rest his eyes from that—or rather to keep from gob-bling the book too fast—he peered through a nine-elbowed brass tube at a scene that could only be the blue heaven-pinnacle of the universe where angels flew shimmeringly like dragonflies and where a few choice heroes rested from their great mountain-climb and spied down critically on the antlike labors of the gods many levels below.

To rest his eye from *that,* he looked up between the scar-let (bloodmetal?) bars of the inmost cage at the most winsome slim fair jet-eyed girl of them all. She knelt, sit-ting on her heels, with her upper body leaned back a little. She wore a red velvet tunic and had a mop of golden hair so thick and pliant that she could sweep it in a neat cur-tain over her upper face, down almost to her pouting lips. With the slim fingers of one hand she would slightly part these silky golden drapes to peer at the Mouser playfully, while with those of the other she rattled golden castanets in a most languorously slow rhythm, though with occasional swift staccato bursts.

The Mouser was considering whether it might not be as well to try a turn or two on the ruby-crusted golden crank next his elbow, when he spied for the first time the glim-mering wall at the back of the shop. What could its materi-al be?—he asked himself. Tiny diamonds countless as the sand set in smoky glass? Black opal? Black pearl? Black moonshine?

Whatever it was, it was wholly fascinating, for the Mouser quickly set down his book, using the nine-crooked spy-tube to mark his place—a most engrossing pair of pages on dueling where were revealed the Universal Parry and its five false variants and also the three true forms of the Secret Thrust—and with only a finger-wave to the ensorceling blonde in red velvet he walked quickly toward the back of the shop.

As he approached the Black Wall he thought for an instant that he glimpsed a silver wraith, or perhaps a sil-ver skeleton, walking toward him out of it, but then he saw that it was only his own darkly handsome reflec-tion, pleasantly flattered by the lustrous material. What had momentarily suggested silver ribs was the reflection of the silver lacings on his tunic.

He smirked at his image and reached out a finger to touch *its* lustrous finger when—Lo, a wonder!—his hand went into the wall with never a sensation at all save a faint tingling coolth promising comfort like the sheets of a fresh-made bed.

He looked at his hand inside the wall and—Lo, another wonder!—it was all a beautiful silver faintly patterned with tiny scales. And though his own hand indubitably, as he could tell by clenching it, it was scarless now and a mite slimmer and longer fingered—altogether a more handsome hand than it had been a moment ago.

He wriggled his fingers and it was like watching small silver fish dart about—fingerlings!

What a droll conceit, he thought, to have a dark fish-pond or rather swimming pool set on its side indoors, so that one could walk into the gracious erect fluid quietly and gracefully, instead of all the noisy, bouncingly athletic business of diving!

And how charming that the pool should be filled not with wet soppy cold water, but with a sort of moondark essence of sleep!—an essence with beautifying cosmetic properties too!—a sort of mudbath without the mud. The Mouser decided he must have a swim in this wonder pool at once, but just then his gaze lit on a long high black couch toward the other end of the dark liquid wall, and beyond the couch a small high table set with viands and a crystal pitcher and goblet.

He walked along the wall to inspect these, his handsome reflection taking step for step with him.

He trailed his hand in the wall for a space and then withdrew it, the scales instantly vanishing and the familiar old scars returning.

The couch turned out to be a narrow high-sided black coffin lined with quilted black satin and piled at one end with little black satin pillows. It looked most invitingly comfortable and restful—not quite as inviting as the Black Wall, but very attractive just the same: there was even a rack of tiny black books nested in the black satin for the occupant's diversion and also a black candle, unlit.

The collation on the little ebony table beyond the coffin consisted entirely of black foods. By sight and then by nibbling and sipping the Mouser discovered their nature: thin slices of a very dark rye bread crusted with poppy seeds and dripped with black butter; slivers of charcoal-seared steak; similarly broiled tiny thin slices of calf's liver sprinkled with dark spices and liberally pricked with capers; the darkest grape jellies; truffles cut paper thin and mushrooms fried black; pickled chestnuts; and of course ripe olives and black fish eggs—caviar. The black drink, which foamed when he poured it, turned out to be stout laced with the bubbly wine of Ilthmar.

He decided to refresh the inner Mouser—the Mouser who lived a sort of blind soft greedy undulating surface-life between his lips and his belly—before taking a dip in the Black Wall.

Fafhrd reëntered the Plaza of Dark Delights walking warily and with the long tatter that was the Cloak of Invisibility trailing from between left forefinger and thumb and with the glimmering cobweb that was the Blindfold of True Seeing pinched even more delicately by its edge between the same digits of his right hand. He was not yet altogether certain that the trailing gossamer hexagon was completely free of spiders.

Across the Plaza he spotted the bright-mouthed shop— the shop he had been told was an outpost of the deadly Devourers—through a ragged gather of folk moving about restlessly and commenting and speculating to one another in harsh excited undertones.

The only feature of the shop Fafhrd could make out at all clearly at this distance was the red-capped red-footed baggy-trousered Porter, not capering now but leaning on his long broom beside the trefoil-arched doorway.

With a looping swing of his left arm Fafhrd hung the Cloak of Invisibility around his neck. The ragged ribband hung to either side down his chest in its wolfskin jerkin only halfway to his wide belt which supported longsword and short-ax. It did not vanish his body to the slightest degree that he could see, and he doubted it worked at all— like many another thaumaturge, Ningauble never hesitated to give one useless charms, not for any treacherous reason, necessarily, but simply to improve one's morale. Fafhrd strode boldly toward the shop.

The Northerner was a tall broad-shouldered formidable-looking man—doubly formidable by his barbaric dress and weaponing in supercivilized Lankhmar—and so he took it for granted that the ordinary run of city folk stepped out of his way; indeed it had never occurred to him that they should not.

He got a shock. All the clerks, seedy bravos, scullery folk, students, slaves, second-rate merchants and second-class courtesans who would automatically have moved aside for him (though the last with a saucy swing of the hips) now came straight at him, so that he had to dodge and twist and stop and even sometimes dart back to avoid being toe-tramped and bumped. Indeed one fat pushy proud-stomached fellow almost carried away his cobweb, which he could see now by the light of the shop was free of spiders—or if there were any spiders still on it, they must be very small.

He had so much to do, dodging Fafhrd-blind Lankhmarians, that he could not spare one more glance for the shop until he was almost at the door. And then before he took his first close look, he found that he was tilting his head so that his left ear touched the shoulder below it and that he was laying Sheelba's spiderweb across his eyes.

The touch of it was simply like the touch of any cobweb when one runs face into it walking between close-set bushes at dawn. Everything shimmered a bit as if seen through a fine crystal grating. Then the least shimmering vanished, and with it the delicate clinging sensation, and Fafhrd's vision returned to normal—as far as he could tell.

It turned out that the doorway to the Devourers' shop was piled with garbage—garbage of a particularly offensive sort: old bones, dead fish, butcher's offal, moldering grace-cloths folded in uneven squares like badly bound uncut books, broken glass and potsherds, splintered boxes, large stinking dead leaves orange-spotted with blight, bloody rags, tattered discarded loincloths, large worms nosing about, centipedes a-scuttle, cockroaches a-stagger, maggots a-crawl —and less agreeable things.

Atop all perched a vulture which had lost most of its feathers and seemed to have expired of some avian eczema. At least Fafhrd took it for dead, but then it opened one white-filmed eye.

The only conceivably salable object outside the shop— but it was a most notable exception—was the tall black iron statue, somewhat larger than life size, of a lean swordsman of dire yet melancholy visage. Standing on its square pedestal beside the door, the statue leaned forward just a little on its long two-handed sword and regarded the Plaza dolefully.

The statue almost teased awake a recollection in Fafhrd's mind—a recent recollection, he fancied—but then there was a blank in his thoughts and he instantly dropped the puzzle. On raids like this one, relentlessly swift action was paramount. He loosened his ax in its loop, noiselessly whipped out Graywand and, shrinking away from the piled and crawling garbage just a little, entered the Bazaar of the Bizarre.

The Mouser, pleasantly replete with tasty black food and heady black drink, drifted to the Black Wall and thrust in his right arm to the shoulder. He waved it about, luxuriating in the softly flowing coolth and balm—and admiring its fine silver scales and more than human handsomeness. He did the same with his right leg, swinging it like a dancer exercising at the bar. Then he took a gently deep breath and drifted farther in.

Fafhrd on entering the Bazaar saw the same piles of gloriously bound books and racks of gleaming brass spytubes and crystal lenses as had the Mouser—a circumstance which seemed to overset Ningauble's theory that the Devourers sold only trash.

He also saw the eight beautiful cages of jewel-gleaming metals and the gleaming chains that hung them from the ceiling and went to the jeweled wall cranks.

Each cage held a gleaming, gloriously hued, black- or light-haired spider big as a rather small person and occasionally waving a long jointed claw-handed leg, or softly opening a little and then closing a pair of fanged downswinging mandibles, while staring steadily at Fafhrd with eight watchful eyes set in two jewel-like rows of four.

Set a spider to catch a spider, Fafhrd thought, thinking of his cobweb, and then wondered what the thought meant.

He quickly switched to more practical questions then, but he had barely asked himself whether before proceeding further he should kill the very expensive-looking spiders, fit to be the coursing beasts of some jungle empress!—another count against Ning's trash-theory!—when he heard a faint splashing from the back of the shop. It reminded

him of the Mouser taking a bath—the Mouser loved baths,
slow luxurious ones in hot soapy scented oil-dripped water,
the small gray sybarite!—and so Fafhrd hurried off in that
direction with many a swift upward overshoulder glance.

He was detouring the last cage, a scarlet-metaled one
holding the handsomest spider yet, when he noted a book
set down with a crooked spy-tube in it—exactly as the
Mouser would keep his place in a book by closing it on
a dagger.

Fafhrd paused to open the book. Its lustrous white pages
were blank. He put his impalpably cobwebbed eye to the
spy-tube. He glimpsed a scene that could only be the smoky
red hell-nadir of the universe, where dark devils scuttled
about like centipedes and where chained folk gazed yearn-
ingly upward at the damned, who writhed in the grip of
black serpents whose eyes shone and whose fangs dripped
and whose nostrils breathed fire.

As he dropped tube and book, he heard the faint sonorous quick dull report of bubbles being expelled from a
fluid at its surface. Staring instantly toward the dim back
of the shop, he saw at last the pearl-shimmering Black
Wall and a silver skeleton eyed with great diamonds reced-
ing into it. However, this costly bone-man—once more
Ning's trash-theory disproven!—still had one arm sticking
part way out of the wall, and this arm was not bone,
whether silver, white, brownish, or pink, but live-looking
flesh covered with proper skin.

As the arm sank into the wall, Fafhrd sprang forward as
fast as he ever had in his life and grabbed the hand just
before it vanished. He knew then he had hold of his friend,
for he would recognize anywhere the Mouser's grip, no
matter how enfeebled. He tugged, but it was as if the
Mouser were mired in black quicksand. He laid Graywand
down and grasped the Mouser by the wrist too and braced
his feet against the rough black flags and gave a tremendous heave.

The silver skeleton came out of the wall with a black
splash, metamorphosing as it did into a vacant-eyed Gray
Mouser, who without a look at his friend and rescuer went
staggering off in a curve and pitched head over heels into
the black coffin.

But before Fafhrd could hoist his comrade from this

new gloomy predicament, there was a swift clash of footsteps and there came racing into the shop, somewhat to
Fafhrd's surprise, the tall black iron statue. It had forgotten or simply stepped off its pedestal, but it had remembered its two-handed sword, which it brandished about most
fiercely while shooting searching black glances like iron
darts at every shadow and corner and nook.

The black gaze passed Fafhrd without pausing, but halted
at Graywand lying on the floor. At the sight of that longsword the statue started visibly, snarled its iron lips, its
black eyes narrowed, it shot glances more ironly stabbing
than before, and it began to move about the shop in sudden zigzag rushes, sweeping its darkly flashing sword in
low scythe-strokes.

At that moment the Mouser peeped moon-eyed over the
edge of the coffin, lifted a limp hand and waved it at the
statue, and in a soft sly foolish voice cried, "Yoo-hoo!"

The statue paused in its searchings and scythings to
glare at the Mouser in mixed contempt and puzzlement.

The Mouser rose to his feet in the black coffin, swaying
drunkenly, and dug in his pouch.

"Ho, slave!" he cried to the statue with maudlin gayety,
"your wares are passing passable. I'll take the girl in red
velvet." He pulled a coin from his pouch, goggled at it
closely, then pitched it at the statue. "That's one penny.
And the nine-crook'd spy-tube. That's another penny." He
pitched it. "And *Gron's Grand Compendium of Exotic Lore*—
another penny for you! Yes, and here's one more for supper
—very tasty, 'twas. Oh and I almost forgot—here's for
tonight's lodging!" He pitched a fifth large copper coin at
the demonic black statue and, smiling blissfully, flopped
back out of sight. The black quilted satin could be heard
to sigh as he sank in it.

Four-fifths of the way through the Mouser's penny-pitch-
ing, Fafhrd decided it was useless to try to unriddle his
comrade's nonsensical behavior and that it would be far
more to the point to make use of this diversion to snatch
up Graywand. He did so on the instant, but by that time
the black statue was fully alert again, if it had ever been
otherwise. Its gaze switched to Graywand the instant
Fafhrd touched the longsword and it stamped its foot,
which rang against the stone, and cried a harsh metallic "Ha!"

Apparently the sword became invisible as Fafhrd grasped it, for the black statue did not follow him with its iron eyes as he shifted position across the room. Instead it swiftly laid down its own mighty blade and caught up a long narrow silver trumpet and set it to its lips.

Fafhrd thought it wise to attack before the statue summoned reinforcements. He rushed straight at the thing, swinging back Graywand for a great stroke at the neck— and steeling himself for an arm-numbing impact.

The statue blew and, instead of the alarm blare Fafhrd had expected, there silently puffed out straight at him a great cloud of white powder that momentarily blotted out everything, as if it were the thickest of fogs from Hlal-river.

Fafhrd retreated, choking and coughing. The demon-blown fog cleared quickly, the white powder falling to the stony floor with unnatural swiftness, and he could see again to attack, but now the statue apparently could see him too, for it squinted straight at him and cried its metallic "Ha!" again and whirled its sword around its iron head preparatory to the charge—rather as if winding itself up.

Fafhrd saw that his own hands and arms were thickly filmed with the white powder, which apparently clung to him everywhere except his eyes, doubtless protected by Sheelba's cobweb.

The iron statue came thrusting and slashing in, Fafhrd took the great sword on his, chopped back, and was parried in return. And now the combat assumed the noisy deadly aspects of a conventional longsword duel, except that Graywand was notched whenever it caught the chief force of a stroke, while the statue's somewhat longer weapon remained unmarked. Also whenever Fafhrd got through the other's guard with a thrust—it was almost impossible to reach him with a slash—it turned out that the other had slipped his lean body or head aside with unbelievably swift and infallible anticipations.

It semed to Fafhrd—at least at the time—the most fell, frustrating, and certainly the most wearisome combat in which he had ever engaged, so he suffered some feelings of hurt and irritation when the Mouser reeled up in his coffin again and leaned an elbow on the black-satin-quilted side and rested chin on fist and grinned hugely at the battlers and from time to time laughed wildly and shouted such enraging nonsense as, "Use Secret Thrust Two-and-a-Half, Fafhrd—it's all in the book!" or "Jump in the oven! —there'd be a master stroke of strategy!" or—this to the statue—"Remember to sweep under his feet, you rogue!"

Backing away from one of Fafhrd's sudden attacks, the statue bumped the table holding the remains of the Mouser's repast—evidently its anticipatory abilities did not extend to its rear—and scraps of black food and white potsherds and jags of crystal scattered across the floor.

The Mouser leaned out of his coffin and waved a finger waggishly. "You'll have to sweep that up!" he cried and went off into a gale of laughter.

Backing away again, the statue bumped the black coffin. The Mouser only clapped the demonic figure comradely on the shoulder and called, "Set to it again, clown! Brush him down! Dust him off!"

But the worst was perhaps when, during a brief pause while the combatants gasped and eyed each other dizzily, the Mouser waved coyly to the nearest giant spider and called his inane "Yoo-hoo!" again, following it with, "I'll see you, dear, after the circus."

Fafhrd, parrying with weary desperation a fifteenth or a fiftieth cut at his head, thought bitterly, *This comes of trying to rescue small heartless madmen who would howl at their grandmothers hugged by bears. Sheelba's cobweb has shown me the Gray One in his true idiot nature.*

The Mouser had first been furious when the sword-skirling clashed him awake from his black satin dreams, but as soon as he saw what was going on he became enchanted at the wildly comic scene.

For, lacking Sheelba's cobweb, what the Mouser saw was only the zany red-capped porter prancing about in his ridiculous tip-curled red shoes and aiming with his broom great strokes at Fafhrd, who looked exactly as if he had climbed a moment ago out of a barrel of meal. The only part of the Northerner not whitely dusted was a shadowy dark mask-like stretch across his eyes.

What made the whole thing fantastically droll was that miller-white Fafhrd was going through all the motions— and emotions!—of a genuine combat with excruciating precision, parrying the broom as if it were some great jolting scimitar or two-handed broadsword even. The broom would go sweeping up and Fafhrd would gawk at it, giving a marvellous interpretation of apprehensive goggling despite his strangely shadowed eyes. Then the broom would come sweeping down and Fafhrd would brace himself and seem to catch it on his sword only with the most prodigious effort—and then pretend to be jolted back by it!

The Mouser had never suspected Fafhrd had such a perfected theatric talent, even if it was acting of a rather mechanical sort, lacking the broad sweeps of true dramatic genius, and he whooped with laughter.

Then the broom brushed Fafhrd's shoulder and blood sprang out.

Fafhrd, wounded at last and thereby knowing himself unlikely to outendure the black statue—although the latter's iron chest was working now like a bellows—decided on swifter measures. He loosened his hand-ax again in its loop and at the next pause in the fight, both battlers having outguessed each other by retreating simultaneously, whipped it up and hurled it at his adversary's face.

Instead of seeking to dodge or ward off the missile, the black statue lowered its sword and merely wove its head in a tiny circle.

The ax closely circled the lean black head, like a silver wood-tailed comet whipping around a black sun, and came back straight at Fafhrd like a boomerang—and rather more swiftly than Fafhrd had sent it.

But time slowed for Fafhrd then and he half ducked and caught it left-handed as it went whizzing past his cheek.

His thoughts too went for a moment as fast as his actions. He thought of how his adversary, able to dodge every frontal attack, had not avoided the table or the coffin behind him. He thought of how the Mouser had not laughed now for a dozen clashes and he looked at him and saw him, though still dazed-seeming, strangely pale and sober-faced, appearing to stare with horror at the blood running down Fafhrd's arm.

So crying as heartily and merrily as he could, "Amuse yourself! Join in the fun, clown!—here's your slap-stick," Fafhrd tossed the ax toward the Mouser.

Without waiting to see the result of that toss—perhaps

not daring to—he summoned up his last reserves of speed and rushed at the black statue in a circling advance that drove it back toward the coffin.

Without shifting his stupid horrified gaze, the Mouser stuck out a hand at the last possible moment and caught the ax by the handle as it spun lazily down.

As the black statue retreated near the coffin and poised for what promised to be a stupendous counterattack, the Mouser leaned out and, now grinning foolishly again, sharply rapped its black pate with the ax.

The iron head split like a coconut but did not come apart. Fafhrd's hand-ax, wedged in it deeply, seemed to turn all at once to iron like the statue, and its black haft was wrenched out of the Mouser's hand as the statue stiffened up straight and tall.

The Mouser stared at the split head woefully, like a child who hadn't known knives cut.

The statue brought its great sword flat against its chest, like a staff on which it might lean but did not, and it fell rigidly forward and hit the floor with a ponderous clank.

At that stony-metallic thundering, white wildfire ran across the Black Wall, lightening the whole shop like a distant levin-bolt, and the iron-basalt thundering echoed from deep within it.

Fafhrd sheathed Graywand, dragged the Mouser out of the black coffin—the fight hadn't left him the strength to lift even his small friend—and shouted in his ear, "Come on! Run!"

The Mouser ran for the Black Wall.

Fafhrd snagged his wrist as he went by and plunged toward the arched door, dragging the Mouser after him.

The thunder faded out and there came a low whistle, cajolingly sweet.

Wildfire raced again across the Black Wall behind them —much more brightly this time, as if a lightning storm were racing toward them.

The white glare striking ahead imprinted one vision indelibly on Fafhrd's brain: the giant spider in the inmost cage pressed against the blood-red bars to gaze down at them. It had pale legs and a velvet red body and a mask of sleek thick golden hair from which eight jet eyes peered, while its fanged jaws hanging down in the manner of the wide blades of a pair of golden scissors rattled together in a wild staccato rhythm like castanets.

That moment the cajoling whistle was repeated. It too seemed to be coming from the red and golden spider.

But strangest of all to Fafhrd was to hear the Mouser, dragged unwillingly along behind him, cry out in answer to the whistling, "Yes, darling, I'm coming. Let me go, Fafhrd! Let me climb to her! Just one kiss! Sweetheart!"

"Stop it, Mouser," Fafhrd growled, his flesh crawling in mid-plunge. "It's a giant spider!"

"Wipe the cobwebs out of your eyes, Fafhrd," the Mouser retorted pleadingly and most unwittingly to the point. "It's a gorgeous girl! I'll never see her ticklesome like—and I've paid for her! *Sweetheart!*"

Then the booming thunder drowned his voice and any more whistling there might have been, and the wildfire came again, brighter than day, and another great thunderclap right on its heels, and the floor shuddered and the whole shop shook, and Fafhrd dragged the Mouser through the trefoil-arched doorway, and there was another great flash and clap.

The flash showed a semicircle of Lankhmarians peering ashen-faced overshoulder as they retreated across the Plaza of Dark Delights from the remarkable indoor thunderstorm that threatened to come out after them.

Fafhrd spun around. The archway had turned to blank wall.

The Bazaar of the Bizarre was gone from the World of Nehwon.

The Mouser, sitting on the dank flags where Fafhrd had dragged him, babbled wailfully, "The secrets of time and space! The lore of the gods! The mysteries of Hell! Black nirvana! Red and gold Heaven! Five pennies gone forever!"

Fafhrd set his teeth. A mighty resolve, rising from his many recent angers and bewilderments, crystallized in him.

Thus far he had used Sheelba's cobweb—and Ningauble's tatter too—only to serve others. Now he would use them for himself! He would peer at the Mouser more closely and at every person he knew. He would study even his own reflection! But most of all he would stare Sheelba and Ning to their wizardly cores!

There came from overhead a low "Hssst!"

As he glanced up he felt something snatched from around his neck and, with the faintest tingling sensation, from off his eyes.

For a moment there was a shimmer traveling upward and through it he seemed to glimpse distortedly, as through thick glass, a black face with a cobwebby skin that entirely covered mouth and nostrils and eyes.

Then that dubious flash was gone, and there were only two cowled heads peering down at him from over the wall top. There was chuckling laughter.

Then both cowled heads drew back out of sight, and there was only the edge of the roof and the sky and the stars and the blank wall.

THE SUN has dimmed. From the world-ocean, which reflects its bloody beams, rises a single vast continent, Zothique—a land of walled cities and boundless deserts, of degenerate kings and bloodless hermits. Islands, some fair and some frightful, dot the seas about Zothique. South across the amaranth-colored Indaskian Sea lies Cyntrom. To the west are Naat, the Isle of the Necromancers; and the Isle of the Crabs. Eastward one comes to Uccastrog, the Isle of the Torturers; Sotar, the realm of King Adompha of the abominable garden; Tosk, the Isle of the Ape-Men; the cannibal isle of Yumatot; the dread archipelagoes of the Ilozian Sea, haunted by griffins and vampires; Ornava, the Isle of Birds; and farthest of all, the unnamed isle of the gazolba bird. Among men, the age of material science has been forgotten for eons. In its place, the old gods, demons, and magics have returned, in more evil and more frightful guises than ever.

On this sinister stage the late Clark Ashton Smith—a retiring, artistic, poetic, self-educated Californian and a member of the Lovecraft-Weird Tales circle—laid fifteen of his ninety-odd stories of fantasy and science fiction. Of Smith's total production, over half appeared in the years 1931-34 and over half were published in Weird Tales. In his later years, Smith wrote stories only at long intervals. The reason for this decline in output is that he had no strong desire to write prose at all, since he deemed himself primarily a poet. He wrote stories only when he needed money, and he needed it most urgently in the early 30s to support his aged parents. Arkham House has published four collections of Smith's stories and two of his verse. Two or three more volumes of stories are planned.

Whether or not Smith appreciated his own gifts as a writer of fantastic fiction, most of his Zothique stories are masterpieces of macabre horror, relieved by flashes of ironic humor and bejeweled with rare words. The present story is, to my way of thinking, one of the most horrible. It is not for the squeamish. So do not complain that you have not been warned!

THE DARK EIDOLON

• CLARK ASHTON SMITH

Thasaidon, lord of seven hells
Wherein the single Serpent dwells,
With volumes drawn from pit to pit
Through fire and darkness infinite—
Thasaidon, sun of nether skies,
Thine ancient evil never dies,
For aye thy somber fulgors flame
On sunken worlds that have no name,
Man's heart enthrones thee, still supreme,
Though the false sorcerers blaspheme.
                              —The Song of Xeethra.

ON Zothique, the last continent of Earth, the sun no longer shone with the whiteness of its prime, but was dim and tarnished as if with a vapor of blood. New stars without number had declared themselves in the heavens, and the shadows of the infinite had fallen closer. And out of the shadows, the older gods had returned to man: the gods forgotten since Hyperborea, since Mu and Poseidonis, bearing other names but the same attributes. And the elder demons had also returned, battening on the fumes of evil sacrifice, and fostering again the primordial sorceries.

Many were the necromancers and magicians of Zothique, and the infamy and marvel of their doings were legended everywhere in the latter days. But among them all there was none greater than Namirrha, who imposed his black yoke on the cities of Xylac, and later, in a proud delirium, deemed himself the veritable peer of Thasaidon, lord of Evil.

Namirrha had built his abode in Ummaos, the chief town of Xylac, to which he came from the desert realm of Tasuun with the dark renown of his thaumaturgies like a cloud of desert storm behind him. And no man knew that in coming to Ummaos he returned to the city of his birth; for all deemed him a native of Tasuun. Indeed, none could have dreamt that the great sorcerer was one with the beggar-boy, Narthos, an orphan of questionable parentage, who had begged his daily bread in the streets and bazaars of Ummaos. Wretchedly had he lived, alone and despised; and a hatred of the cruel, opulent city grew in his heart like a smothered flame that feeds in secret, biding the time when it shall become a conflagration consuming all things.

Bitterer always, through his boyhood and early youth, was the spleen and rancor of Narthos toward men. And one day the prince Zotulla, a boy but little older than he, riding a restive palfrey, came upon him in the square before the imperial palace; and Narthos implored an alms. But Zotulla, scorning his plea, rode arrogantly forward, spurring the palfrey; and Narthos was ridden down and trampled under its hooves. And afterward, nigh to death from the trampling, he lay senseless for many hours, while the people passed him by unheeding. And at last, regaining his senses, he dragged himself to his hovel; but he limped a little thereafter all his days, and the mark of one hoof remained like a brand on his body, fading never. Later, he left Ummaos and was forgotten quickly by its people. Going southward into Tasuun, he lost his way in the great desert, and was near to perishing. But finally he came to a small oasis, where dwelt the wizard Ouphaloc, a hermit who preferred the company of honest jackals and hyenas to that of men. And Ouphaloc, seeing the great craft and evil in the starveling boy, gave succor to Narthos and sheltered him. He dwelt for years with Ouphaloc, becoming the wizard's pupil and the heir of his demon-wrested lore. Strange things he learned in that hermitage, being fed on fruits and grain that had sprung not from the watered earth, and wine that was not the juice of terrene grapes. And like Ouphaloc, he became a master in devildom and drove his own bond with the archfiend Thasaidon. When Ouphaloc died, he took the name of

Namirrha, and went forth as a mighty sorcerer among the wandering peoples and the deep-buried mummies of Tasuun. But never could he forget the miseries of his boyhood in Ummaos and the wrong he had endured from Zotulla; and year by year he spun over in his thoughts the black web of revenge. And his fame grew ever darker and vaster, and men feared him in remote lands beyond Tasuun. With bated whispers they spoke of his deeds in the cities of Yoros, and in Zul-Bha-Sair, the abode of the ghoulish deity Mordiggian. And long before the coming of Namirrha himself, the people of Ummaos knew him as a fabled scourge that was direr than simoom or pestilence.

Now, in the years that followed the going-forth of the boy Narthos from Ummaos, Pithaim, the father of Prince Zotulla, was slain by the sting of a small adder that had crept into his bed for warmth on an autumn night. Some said that the adder had been purveyed by Zotulla, but this was a thing that no man could verily affirm. After the death of Pithaim, Zotulla, being his only son, was emperor of Xylac, and ruled evilly from his throne in Ummaos. Indolent he was, and tyrannic, and full of strange luxuries and cruelties; but the people, who were also evil, acclaimed him in his turpitude. So he prospered, and the lords of Hell and Heaven smote him not. And the red suns and ashen moons went westward over Xylac, falling into that seldom-voyaged sea, which, if the mariners' tales were true, poured evermore like a swiftening river past the infamous isle of Naat, and fell in a worldwide cataract upon nether space from the far, sheer edge of Earth.

Grosser still he grew, and his sins were as overswollen fruits that ripen above a deep abyss. But the winds of time blew softly; and the fruits fell not. And Zotulla laughed amid his fools and his eunuchs and his lemans; and the tale of his luxuries was borne afar, and was told by dim outland peoples, as a twin marvel with the bruited necromancies of Namirrha.

It came to pass, in the year of the Hyena and the month of the star Canicule, that a great feast was given by Zotulla to the inhabitants of Ummaos. Meats that had been cooked in exotic spices from Sotar, isle of the east, were spread everywhere; and the ardent wines of Yoros and Xylac, filled as with subterranean fires, were poured inexhaustibly from huge urns for all. The wines awoke a furious mirth and a royal madness; and afterward they brought a slumber no less profound than the Lethe of the tomb. And one by one, as they drank, the revellers fell down in the streets, the houses and gardens, as if a plague had struck them; and Zotulla slept in his banquet-hall of gold and ebony, with his odalisques and chamberlains about him. So, in all Ummaos, there was no man or woman wakeful at the hour when Sirius began to fall toward the west.

Thus it was that none saw or heard the coming of Namir-rha. But awakening heavily in the latter forenoon, the emperor Zotulla heard a confused babble, a troublous clamor of voices from such of his eunuchs and women as had awakened before him. Inquiring the cause, he was told that a strange prodigy had occurred during the night; but, being still bemused with wine and slumber, he comprehended little enough of its nature, till his favorite concubine, Obexah, led him to the eastern portico of the palace, from which he could behold the marvel with his own eyes.

Now the palace stood alone at the center of Ummaos, and to north, west and south, for wide intervals of distance, there stretched the imperial gardens, full of superbly arching palms and loftily spiring fountains. But to eastward was a broad open area, used as a sort of common, between the palace and the mansions of high optimates. And in this space, which had lain wholly vacant at eve, a building towered colossal and lordly beneath the full-risen sun, with domes like monstrous fungi of stone that had come up in the night. And the domes, rearing level with those of Zotulla, were builded of death-white marble; and the huge façade, with multi-columned porticoes and deep balconies, was wrought in alternate zones of night-black onyx and porphyry hued as with dragons' blood. And Zotulla swore lewdly, calling with hoarse blasphemies on the gods and devils of Xylac; and great was his dumfoundment, deeming the marvel a work of wizardry. The women gathered about him, crying out with shrill cries of awe and terror; and more and more of his courtiers, awakening, came to swell the hub-bub; and the fat castradoes diddered in their cloth-of-gold like immense black jellies in golden basins. But Zotulla, mindful of his dominion as emperor of all Xylac, sought to conceal his own trepidation, saying:

"Now who is this that has presumed to enter Ummaos

like a jackal in the dark, and has made his impious den in proximity and counterview with my palace? Go forth, and inquire the miscreant's name; but, ere you go, instruct the headsman to make sharp his double-handed sword."

Then, fearing the emperor's wrath if they tarried, certain of the chamberlains went forth unwillingly and approached the portals of the strange edifice. It seemed that the portals were deserted till they drew near, and then, on the threshold, there appeared a titanic skeleton, taller than any man of earth; and it strode forward to meet them with ell-long strides. The skeleton was swathed in a loin-cloth of scarlet silk with a buckle of jet, and it wore a black turban, starred with diamonds, whose topmost foldings nearly touched the high lintel. Eyes like flickering marsh-fires burned in its deep eye-sockets; and a blackened tongue like that of a long-dead man protruded between its teeth; but otherwise it was clean of flesh, and the bones glittered whitely in the sun as it came onward.

The chamberlains were mute before it, and there was no sound except the golden creaking of their girdles, the shrill rustling of their silks, as they shook and trembled. And the foot-bones of the skeleton clicked sharply on the pavement of black onyx as it paused; and the putrefying tongue began to quiver between its teeth; and it uttered these words in an unctuous, nauseous voice:

"Return, and tell the emperor Zotulla that Namirrha, seer and magician, has come to dwell beside him."

Hearing the skeleton speak as if it had been a living man, and hearing the dread name of Namirrha as men hear the tocsin of doom in some fallen city, the chamberlains could stand before it no longer, and they fled with ungainly swiftness and bore the message to Zotulla.

Now, learning who it was that had come to neighbor with him in Ummaos, the emperor's wrath died out like a feeble and blustering flame on which the wind of darkness has blown; and the vinous purple of his cheeks was mottled with a strange pallor; and he said nothing, but his lips mumbled loosely as if in prayer or malediction. And the news of Namirrha's coming passed like the flight of evil night-birds through all the palace and throughout the city, leaving a noisome terror that abode in Ummaos thereafter till the end. For Namirrha, through the black renown of his thaumaturgies and the frightful entities who served him, had become a power that no secular sovereign dared dispute; and men feared him everywhere, even as they feared the gigantic, shadowy lords of Hell and of outer space. And in Ummaos, people said that he had come on the desert wind from Tasuun with his underlings, even as the pestilence comes, and had reared his house in an hour with the aid of devils beside Zotulla's palace. And they said that the foundations of the house were laid on the adamantine cope of Hell; and in its floors were pits at whose bottom burned the nether fires, or stars could be seen as they passed under in lowermost night. And the followers of Namirrha were the dead of strange kingdoms, the demons of sky and earth and the abyss, and mad, impious, hybrid things that the sorcerer himself had created from forbidden unions.

Men shunned the neighborhood of his lordly house; and in the palace of Zotulla few cared to approach the windows and balconies that gave thereon; and the emperor himself spoke not of Namirrha, pretending to ignore the intruder; and the women of the harem babbled evermore with an evil gossip concerning Namirrha and his concubines. But the sorcerer himself was not beheld by the people of the city, though some believed that he walked forth at will, clad with invisibility. His servitors likewise were not seen; but a howling as of the damned was sometimes heard to issue from his portals; and sometimes there came a stony cachinnation, as if some adamantine image had laughed aloud; and sometimes there was a chuckling like the sound of shattered ice in a frozen hell. Dim shadows moved in the porticoes when there was neither sunlight nor lamp to cast them; and red, eery lights appeared and vanished in the windows at eve, like a blinking of demoniac eyes. And slowly the ember-colored suns went over Xylac, and were quenched in far seas; and the ashy moons were blackened as they fell nightly toward the hidden gulf. Then, seeing that the wizard had wrought no open evil, and that none had endured palpable harm from his presence, the people took heart; and Zotulla drank deeply, and feasted in oblivious luxury as before; and dark Thasaidon, prince of all turpitudes, was the true but never-acknowledged lord of Xylac. And in time the men of Ummaos bragged a little of Namirrha and his dread thaumaturgies, even as they had boasted of the purple sins of Zotulla.

But Namirrha, still unbeheld by living men and living

women, sat in the inner halls of that house which his devils had reared for him, and spun over and over in his thoughts the black web of revenge. And in all Ummaos there was none, even among his fellow-beggars, who recalled the beggar-boy Narthos. And the wrong done by Zotulla to Narthos in old time was the least of those cruelties which the emperor had forgotten.

Now, when the fears of Zotulla were somewhat lulled, and his women gossiped less often of the neighboring wizard, there occurred a new wonder and a fresh terror. For, sitting one eve at his banquet-table with his courtiers about him, the emperor heard a noise as of myriad iron-shod hooves that came trampling through the palace gardens. And the courtiers also heard the sound, and were startled amid their mounting drunkenness; and the emperor was angered, and he sent certain of his guards to examine into the cause of the trampling. But peering forth upon the moon-bright lawns and parterres, the guards beheld no visible shape, though the loud sounds of trampling still went to and fro. It seemed as if a rout of wild stallions passed and re-passed before the façade of the palace with tumultuous gallopings and capricoles. And a fear came upon the guards as they looked and listened; and they dared not venture forth, but returned to Zotulla. And the emperor himself grew sober when he heard their tale; and he went forth with high blusterings to view the prodigy. And all night the unseen hooves rang out sonorously on the pavements of onyx, and ran with deep thuddings over the grasses and flowers. The palm-fronds waved on the windless air as if parted by racing steeds; and visibly the tall-stemmed lilies and broad-petaled exotic blossoms were trodden under. And rage and terror nested together in Zotulla's heart as he stood in a balcony above the garden, hearing the spectral tumult, and beholding the harm done to his rarest flower-beds. The women, the courtiers and eunuchs cowered behind him, and there was no slumber for any occupant of the palace; but toward dawn the clamor of hooves departed, going toward Namirrha's house.

When the dawn was full-grown above Ummaos, the emperor walked forth with his guards about him, and saw that the crushed grasses and broken-down stems were blackened as if by fire where the hooves had fallen. Plainly were the marks imprinted, like the tracks of a great company of horses, in all the lawns and parterres; but they ceased at the verge of the gardens. And though everyone believed that the visitation had come from Namirrha, there was no proof of this in the grounds that fronted the sorcerer's abode; for here the turf was untrodden.

"A pox upon Namirrha, if he has done this!" cried Zotulla. "For what harm have I ever done to him? Verily, I shall set my heel on the dog's neck; and the torture-wheel shall serve him even as these horses from Hell have served my blood-red lilies of Sotar and my vein-colored irises of Naat and my orchids from Uccastrog which were purple as the bruises of love. Yea, though he stand the viceroy of Thasaidon above Earth, and overlord of ten thousand devils, my wheel shall break him, and fires shall heat the wheel white-hot in its turning, till he withers black as the seared blossoms." Thus did Zotulla make his brag; but he issued no orders for the execution of the threat; and no man stirred from the palace toward Namirrha's house. And from the portals of the wizard none came forth; or if any came, there was no visible sign or sound.

So the day went over, and the night rose, bringing later a moon that was slightly darkened at the rim. And the night was silent; and Zotulla, sitting long at the banquet-table, drained his wine-cup often and wrathfully, muttering new threats against Namirrha. And the night wore on, and it seemed that the visitation would not be repeated. But at midnight, lying in his chamber with Obexah, and fathom-deep in slumber from his wine, Zotulla was awakened by a monstrous clangor of hooves that raced and capered in the palace porticoes and in the long balconies. All night the hooves thundered back and forth, echoing awfully in the vaulted stone, while Zotulla and Obexah, listening, huddled close amid their cushions and coverlets; and all the occupants of the palace, wakeful and fearful, heard the noise but stirred not from their chambers. A little before dawn the hooves departed suddenly; and afterward, by day, their marks were found on the marble flags of the porches and balconies; and the marks were countless, deep-graven, and black as if branded there by flame.

Like mottled marble were the emperor's cheeks when he saw the hoof-printed floors; and terror stayed with him henceforward, following him to the depths of his inebriety, since he knew not where the haunting would cease. His women murmured and some wished to flee from Ummaos, and it seemed that the revels of the day and evening were shadowed by ill wings that left their umbrage in the yellow wine and bedimmed the aureate lamps. And again, toward midnight, the slumber of Zotulla was broken by the hooves, which came galloping and pacing on the palace-roof and through all the corridors and halls. Thereafter, till dawn, the hooves filled the palace with their iron clatterings, and they rang hollowly on the topmost domes, as if the coursers of gods had trodden there, passing from heaven to heaven in tumultuous cavalcade.

Zotulla and Obexah, lying together while the terrible hooves went to and fro in the hall outside their chamber, had no heart or thought for sin, nor could they find any comfort in their nearness. In the gray hour before dawn they heard a great thundering high on the barred brazen door of the room, as if some mighty stallion, rearing, had drummed there with his forefeet. And soon after this, the hooves went away, leaving a silence like an interlude in some gathering storm of doom. Later, the marks of the hooves were found everywhere in the halls, marring the bright mosaics. Black holes were burnt in the golden-threaded rugs and the rugs of silver and scarlet; and the high white domes were pitted pox-wise with the marks; and far up on the brazen door of Zotulla's chamber the prints of a horse's forefeet were incised deeply.

Now, in Ummaos, and throughout Xylac, the tale of this haunting became known, and the thing was deemed an ominous prodigy, though people differed in their interpretations. Some held that the sending came from Namirrha, and was meant as a token of his supremacy above all kings and emperors; and some thought that it came from a new wizard who had risen in Tinarath, far to the east, and who wished to supplant Namirrha. And the priests of the gods of Xylac held that their various deities had dispatched the haunting, as a sign that more sacrifices were required in the temples.

Then, in his hall of audience, whose floor of sard and jasper had been grievously pocked by the unseen hooves, Zotulla called together many priests and magicians and soothsayers, and asked them to declare the cause of the sending and devise a mode of exorcism. But, seeing that there was no agreement among them, Zotulla provided the several priestly sects with the wherewithal of sacrifice to their sundry gods, and sent them away; and the wizards and prophets, under threat of decapitation if they refused, were enjoined to visit Namirrha in his mansion of sorcery and learn his will, if haply the sending were his and not the work of another.

Loth were the wizards and the soothsayers, fearing Namirrha, and caring not to intrude upon the frightful mysteries of his obscure mansion. But the swordsmen of the emperor drove them forth, lifting great crescent blades against them when they tarried; so one by one, in a straggling order, the delegation went toward Namirrha's portals and vanished into the devil-builded house.

Pale, muttering and distraught, like men who have looked upon hell and have seen their doom, they returned before sunset to the emperor. And they said that Namirrha had received them courteously and had sent them back with this message:

"Be it known to Zotulla that the haunting is a sign of that which he has long forgotten; and the reason of the haunting will be revealed to him at the hour prepared and set apart by destiny. And the hour draws near: for Namirrha bids the emperor and all his court to a great feast on the afternoon of the morrow."

Having delivered this message, to the wonder and consternation of Zotulla, the delegation begged his leave to depart. And though the emperor questioned them minutely, they seemed unwilling to relate the circumstances of their visit to Namirrha; nor would they describe the sorcerer's fabled house, except in a vague manner, each contradicting the other as to what he had seen. So, after a little, Zotulla bade them go, and when they had gone he sat musing for a long while on the invitation of Namirrha, which was a thing that he cared not to accept but feared to decline. That evening he drank even more liberally than was his wont; and he slept a Lethean slumber, nor was there any noise of trampling hooves about the palace to awaken him. And silently, during the night, the prophets and the magicians passed like furtive shadows from Ummaos; and no man saw them depart; and at morning they were gone from Xylac into other lands, never to return. . . .

Now, on that same evening, in the great hall of his house, Namirrha sat alone, having dismissed the familiars who attended him ordinarily. Before him, on an altar of jet, was the dark, gigantic statue of Thasaidon which a devil-begotten sculptor had wrought in ancient days for an evil king of Tasuun, called Pharnoc. The archdemon was depicted in the guise of a full-armored warrior, lifting a spiky mace as if in heroic battle. Long had the statue lain in the desert-sunken palace of Pharnoc, whose very site was disputed by the nomads; and Namirrha, by his divination, had found it and had reared up the infernal image to abide with him always thereafter. And often, through the mouth of the statue, Thasaidon would utter oracles to Namirrha, or would answer interrogations.

Before the black-armored image there hung seven silver lamps, wrought in the form of horses' skulls, with flames issuing changeably in blue and purple and crimson from their eye-sockets. Wild and lurid was their light, and the face of the demon, peering from under his crested helmet, was filled with malign, equivocal shadows that shifted and changed eternally. And sitting in his serpent-carven chair, Namirrha regarded the statue grimly, with a deep-furrowed frown between his eyes: for he had asked a certain thing of Thasaidon, and the fiend, replying through the statue, had refused him. And rebellion was in the heart of Namirrha, grown mad with pride, and deeming himself the lord of all sorcerers and a ruler by his own right among the princes of devildom. So, after long pondering, he repeated his request in a bold and haughty voice, like one who addresses an equal rather than the all-formidable suzerain to whom he has sworn a fatal fealty.

"I have helped you heretofore in all things," said the image, with stony and sonorous accents that were echoed metallically in the seven silver lamps. "Yea, the undying worms of fire and darkness have come forth like an army at your summons, and the wings of nether genii have risen to occlude the sun when you called them. But, verily, I will not aid you in this vengeance you have planned: for the emperor Zotulla has done me no wrong and has served me well though unwittingly; and the people of Xylac, by reason of their turpitudes, are not the least of my terrestrial worshippers. Therefore, Namirrha, it were well for you to live in peace with Zotulla, and well to forget this olden wrong that was done to the beggar-boy Narthos. For the ways of destiny are strange, and the workings of its laws are sometimes hidden; and truly, if the hooves of Zotulla's palfrey had not spurned you and trodden you under, your life had been otherwise, and the name and renown of Namirrha had still slept in oblivion as a dream undreamed. Yea, you would tarry still as a beggar in Ummaos, content with a beggar's guerdon, and would never have fared forth to become the pupil of the wise and learned Ouphaloc; and I, Thasaidon, would have lost the lordliest of all necromancers who have accepted my service and my bond. Think well, Namirrha, and ponder these matters: for both of us, it would seem, are indebted to Zotulla in all gratitude for the trampling that he gave you."

"Yea, there is a debt," Namirrha growled implacably. "And truly, I will pay the debt tomorrow, even as I have planned. . . . There are Those who will aid me, Those who will answer my summoning in your despite."

"It is an ill thing to affront me," said the image, after an interval. "And also, it is not well to call upon Those that you designate. However, I perceive clearly that such is your intent. You are proud and stubborn and revengeful. Do, then, as you will, but blame me not for the outcome."

So, after this, there was silence in the hall where Namirrha sate before the eidolon; and the flames burned darkly, with changeable colors, in the skull-shapen lamps; and the shadows fled and returned, unresting, on the face of the statue and the face of Namirrha. Then, toward midnight, the necromancer rose and went upward by many spiral stairs to a high dome of his house in which was a single small round window that looked forth on the constellations. The window was set in the top of the dome; but Namirrha had contrived, by means of his magic, that one entering by the last spiral of the stairs would suddenly seem to descend rather than climb, and, reaching the final step, would peer *downward* through the window while stars passed under him in a giddying gulf. There, kneeling, Namirrha touched a secret spring in the marble, and the circular pane slid back without sound. Then, lying prone on the curved interior of the dome, with his face over the abyss, and his long beard trailing stiffly into space, he whispered a prehuman rune, and held speech with certain entities who belonged neither to Hell nor the mundane elements, and were more fearsome to invoke than the infernal genii or the devils of earth, air, water, and flame. With them he made his compact, defying Thasaidon's will, while the air curdled about him with their voices, and rime gathered palely on his sable beard from the cold that was wrought by their breathing as they leaned earthward.

Laggard and loth was the awakening of Zotulla from his wine; and quickly, ere he opened his eyes, the daylight was poisoned for him by the thought of that invitation which he feared to accept or decline. But he spoke to Obexah, saying:

"Who, after all, is this wizardly dog, that I should obey his summons like a beggar called in from the street by some haughty lord?"

Obexah, a golden-skinned and oblique-eyed girl from Uccastrog, Isle of the Torturers, eyed the emperor subtly, and said:

"O Zotulla, it is yours to accept or refuse, as you deem fitting. And truly, it is a small matter for the lord of Ummaos and all Xylac, whether to go or stay, since naught can impugn your sovereignty. Therefore, were it not as well to go?" For Obexah, though fearful of the wizard, was curious regarding that devil-builded house of which so little was known; and likewise, in the manner of women, she wished to behold the famed Namirrha, whose mien and appearance were still but a far-brought legend in Ummaos.

"There is something in what you say," admitted Zotulla. "But an emperor, in his conduct, must always consider the public good; and there are matters of state involved, which a woman can scarcely be expected to understand."

So, later in the forenoon, after an ample and well-irrigated breakfast, he called his chamberlains and courtiers about him and took counsel with them. And some advised him to ignore the invitation of Namirrha; and others held that the invitation should be accepted, lest a graver evil than the trampling of ghostly hooves should be sent upon the palace and the city.

Then Zotulla called the many priesthoods before him in a body, and sought to resummon those wizards and soothsayers who had fled privily in the night. Among all the latter, there was none who answered the crying of his name through Ummaos; and this aroused a certain wonder. But the priests came in greater number than before, and thronged the hall of audience so that the paunches of the foremost were straitened against the imperial dais and the buttocks of the hindmost were flattened on the rear walls and pillars. And Zotulla debated with them the matter of acceptance or refusal. And the priests argued, as before, that Namirrha was nowise concerned with the sending; and his invitation, they said, portended no harm nor bale to the emperor; and it was plain, from the terms of the message, that an oracle would be imparted to Zotulla by the wizard; and this oracle, if Namirrha were a true arch-image, would confirm their own holy wisdom and reëstablish the divine source of the sending; and the gods of Xylac would again be glorified.

Then, having heard the pronouncement of the priests, the emperor instructed his treasurers to load them down with new offerings; and, calling unctuously upon Zotulla and all his household the vicarious blessings of their several gods, the priests departed. And the day wore on, and the sun passed its meridian, falling slowly beyond Ummaos through the spaces of afternoon that were floored with sea-ending deserts. And still Zotulla was irresolute; and he called his wine-bearers, bidding them pour for him the strongest and most magistral of their vintages; but in the wine he found neither certitude nor decision.

Sitting still on his throne in the hall of audience, he heard, toward middle afternoon, a mighty and clamorous outcry that arose at the palace portals. There were deep wailings of men and the shrillings of eunuchs and women, as if terror passed from tongue to tongue, invading the halls and apartments. And the fearful clamor spread throughout all the palace, and Zotulla, rousing from the lethargy of wine, was about to send his attendants to inquire the cause.

Then, into the hall, there filed an array of tall mummies, clad in royal cerements of purple and scarlet, and wearing gold crowns on their withered craniums. And after them, like servitors, came gigantic skeletons who wore loin-cloths of nacarat orange and about whose upper skulls, from brow to crown, live serpents of banded saffron and ebon had wrapped themselves for head-dresses. And the mummies bowed before Zotulla, saying with thin, sere voices:

"We, who were kings of the wide realm of Tasuun aforetime, have been sent as a guard of honor for the emperor Zotulla, to attend him as is befitting when he goes forth to the feast prepared by Namirrha."

Then with dry clickings of their teeth, and whistlings as of air through screens of fretted ivory, the skeletons spoke:

"We, who were giant warriors of a race forgotten, have also been sent by Namirrha, so that the emperor's household, following him to the feast, should be guarded from all peril and should fare forth in such pageantry as is meet and proper."

Witnessing these prodigies, the wine-bearers and other attendants cowered about the imperial dais or hid behind the pillars, while Zotulla, with pupils swimming starkly in a bloodshot white, with face bloated and ghastly pale, sat frozen on his throne and could utter no word in reply to the ministers of Namirrha.

Then, coming forward, the mummies said in dusty accents: "All is made ready, and the feast awaits the arrival of Zotulla." And the cerements of the mummies stirred and fell open at the bosom, and small rodent monsters, brown as bitumen, eyed as with accursed rubies, reared forth from the eaten hearts of the mummies like rats from their holes and chittered shrilly in human speech, repeating the words. The skeletons in turn took up the solemn sentence; and the black and saffron serpents hissed it from their skulls; and the words were repeated lastly in baleful rumblings by certain furry creatures of dubious form, hitherto unseen by Zotulla, who sat behind the ribs of the skeletons as if in cages of white wicker.

Like a dreamer who obeys the doom of dreams, the emperor rose from his throne and went forward, and the mummies surrounded him like an escort. And each of the skeletons drew from the reddish-yellow folds of his loincloth a curiously pierced archaic flute of silver; and all began a sweet and evil and deathly fluting as the emperor went out through the halls of the palace. A fatal spell was in the music: for the chamberlains, the women, the guards, the eunuchs, and all members of Zotulla's household even to the cooks and scullions, were drawn like a procession of night-walkers from the rooms and alcoves in which they had vainly hidden themselves; and, marshaled by the flutists, they followed after Zotulla. A strange thing it was to behold this mighty company of people, going forth in the slanted sunlight toward Namirrha's house, with a cortège of dead kings about them, and the blown breath of skeletons thrilling eldritchly in the silver flutes. And little was Zotulla comforted when he found the girl Obexah at his side, moving, as he, in a thralldom of involitient horror, with the rest of his women close behind.

Coming to the open portals of Namirrha's house, the emperor saw that they were guarded by great crimson-wattled things, half dragon, half man, who bowed before him, sweeping their wattles like bloody besoms on the flags of dark onyx. And the emperor passed with Obexah between the louting monsters, with the mummies, the skeletons and his own people behind him in strange pageant, and entered a vast and multicolumned hall, where the daylight, following timidly, was drowned by the baleful arrogant blaze of a thousand lamps.

Even amid his horror, Zotulla marvelled at the vastness of the chamber, which he could hardly reconcile with the mansion's outer length and height and breadth, though these indeed were of most palatial amplitude. For it seemed that he gazed down great avenues of topless pillars, and vistas of tables laden with piled-up viands and thronged urns of wine, that stretched away before him into luminous distance and gloom as of starless night.

In the wide intervals between the tables, the familiars of Namirrha and his other servants went to and fro incessantly, as if a fantasmagoria of ill dreams were embodied before the emperor. Kingly cadavers in robes of time-rotten brocade, with worms seething in their eye-pits, poured a blood-like wine into cups of the opalescent horn of unicorns. Lamias, trident-tailed, and four-breasted chimeras, came in with fuming platters lifted high by their brazen claws. Dog-headed devils, tongued with lolling flames, ran forward to offer themselves as ushers for the company. And before Zotulla and Obexah, there appeared a curious being with the full-fleshed lower limbs and hips of a great black woman and the clean-picked bones of some titanic ape from thereupward. And this monster signified by certain indescribable becks of its finger-bones that the emperor and his odalisque were to follow it.

Verily, it seemed to Zotulla that they had gone a long way

into some malignly litten cavern of Hell, when they came
to the end of that perspective of tables and columns down
which the monster had led them. Here, at the room's end,
apart from the rest, was a table at which Namirrha sat
alone, with the flames of the seven horse-skull lamps burning restlessly behind him, and the mailed black image of
Thasaidon towering from the altar of jet at his right hand.
And a little aside from the altar, a diamond mirror was
upborne by the claws of iron basilisks.

Namirrha rose to greet them, observing a solemn and
funereal courtesy. His eyes were bleak and cold as distant
stars in the hollows wrought by strange fearful vigils. His
lips were like a pale-red seal on a shut parchment of doom.
His beard flowed stiffly in black-anointed banded locks
across the bosom of his vermilion robe, like a mass of
straight black serpents. Zotulla felt the blood pause and
thicken about his heart, as if congealing into ice. And
Obexah, peering beneath lowered lids, was abashed and
frightened by the visible horror that invested this man and
hung upon him even as royalty upon a king. But amid
her fear, she found room to wonder what manner of man
he was in his intercourse with women.

"I bid you welcome, O Zotulla, to such hospitality as is
mine to offer," said Namirrha, with the iron ringing of
some hidden funereal bell deep down in his hollow voice.
"Prithee, be seated at my table."

Zotulla saw that a chair of ebony had been placed for
him opposite Namirrha; and another chair, less stately and
imperial, had been placed at the left hand for Obexah. And
the twain seated themselves; and Zotulla saw that his people were sitting likewise at other tables throughout the
huge hall, with the frightful servitors of Namirrha waiting
upon them busily, like devils attending the damned.

Then Zotulla perceived that a dark and corpse-like hand
was pouring wine for him in a crystal cup; and upon the
hand was the signet-ring of the emperors of Xylac, set with
a monstrous fire-opal in the mouth of a golden bat: even
such a ring as Zotulla himself wore perpetually on his in-
dex-finger. And, turning, he beheld at his right hand a figure
that bore the likeness of his father, Pithaim, after the
poison of the adder, spreading through all his limbs, had
left behind it the purple bloating of death. And Zotulla,
who had caused the adder to be placed in the bed of

Pithaim, cowered in his seat and trembled with a guilty fear. And the thing that wore the similitude of Pithaim, whether corpse or ghost or an image wrought by Namirrha's enchantment, came and went at Zotulla's elbow, waiting upon him with stark, black, swollen fingers that never fumbled. Horribly he was aware of its bulging, unregarding eyes, and its livid purple mouth that was locked in a rigor of mortal silence, and the spotted adder that peered at intervals with chill orbs from its heavy-folded sleeve as it leaned beside him to replenish his cup or to serve him with meat. And dimly, through the icy mist of his terror, the emperor beheld the shadowy-armored shape, like a moving replica of the still, grim statue of Thasaidon, which Namirrha had reared up in his blasphemy to perform the same office for himself. And vaguely, without comprehension, he saw the dreadful ministrant that hovered beside Obexah: a flayed and eyeless corpse in the image of her first lover, a boy from Cyntrom who had been cast ashore in shipwreck on the Isle of the Torturers. There Obexah had found him, lying beyond the ebbing wave; and reviving the boy, she had hidden him awhile in a secret cave for her own pleasure, and had brought him food and drink. Later, wearying, she had betrayed him to the Torturers, and had taken a new delight in the various pangs and ordeals inflicted upon him before death by that cruel, pernicious people.

"Drink," said Namirrha, quaffing a strange wine that was red and dark as if with disastrous sunsets of lost years. And Zotulla and Obexah drank the wine, feeling no warmth in their veins thereafter, but a chill as of hemlock mounting slowly toward the heart.

"Verily, 'tis a good wine," said Namirrha, "and a proper one in which to toast the furthering of our acquaintance: for it was buried long ago with the royal dead, in amphorae of somber jasper shapen like funeral urns; and my ghouls found it, whenas they came to dig in Tasuun."

Now it seemed that the tongue of Zotulla froze in his mouth, as a mandrake freezes in the rime-bound soil of winter; and he found no reply to Namirrha's courtesy.

"Prithee, make trial of this meat," quoth Namirrha, "for it is very choice, being the flesh of that boar which the Torturers of Uccastrog are wont to pasture on the well-minced leavings of their wheels and racks; and, moreover, my cooks have spiced it with the powerful balsams of the tomb, and have farced it with the hearts of adders and the tongues of black cobras."

Naught could the emperor say; and even Obexah was silent, being sorely troubled in her turpitude by the presence of that flayed and piteous thing which had the likeness of her lover from Cyntrom. And her dread of the necromancer grew prodigiously; for his knowledge of this old, forgotten crime, and the raising of the fantasm, appeared to her a more baleful magic than all else.

"Now, I fear," said Namirrha, "that you find the meat devoid of savor, and the wine without fire. So, to enliven our feasting, I shall call forth my singers and my musicians."

He spoke a word unknown to Zotulla or Obexah, which sounded throughout the mighty hall as if a thousand voices in turn had taken it up and prolonged it. Anon there appeared the singers, who were she-ghouls with shaven bodies and hairy shanks, and long yellow tushes full of shredded carrion curving across their chaps from mouths that fawned hyena-wise on the company. Behind them entered the musicians, some of whom were male devils pacing erect on the hind-quarters of sable stallions and plucking with the fingers of white apes at lyres of the bone and sinew of cannibals from Naat; and others were pied satyrs puffing their goatish cheeks at hautboys made from the femora of young witches, or bagpipes formed from the bosom-skin of Negro queens and the horn of rhinoceri.

They bowed before Namirrha with grotesque ceremony. Then, without delay, the she-ghouls began a most dolorous and execrable howling, as of jackals that have sniffed their carrion; and the satyrs and devils played a lament that was like the moaning of desert-born winds through forsaken palace harems. And Zotulla shivered, for the singing filled his marrow with ice, and the music left in his heart a desolation as of empires fallen and trod under by the iron-shod hooves of time. Ever, amid that evil music, he seemed to hear the sifting of sand across withered gardens, and the windy rustling of rotted silks upon couches of bygone luxury, and the hissing of coiled serpents from the low fusts of shattered columns. And the glory that had been Ummaos seemed to pass away like the blown pillars of the simoom.

"Now that was a brave tune," said Namirrha when the music ceased and the she-ghouls no longer howled. "But verily I fear that you find my entertainment somewhat dull. Therefore, my dancers shall dance for you."

He turned toward the great hall, and described in the air an enigmatic sign with the fingers of his right hand. In answer to the sign, a hueless mist came down from the high roof and hid the room like a fallen curtain for a brief interim. There was a babel of sounds, confused and muffled, beyond the curtain, and a crying of voices faint as if with distance.

Then, dreadfully, the vapor rolled away, and Zotulla saw that the laden tables were gone. In the wide interspaces of the columns, his palace-inmates, the chamberlains, the eunuchs, the courtiers and odalisques and all the others, lay trussed with thongs on the floor, like so many fowls of gorgeous plumage. Above them, in time to a music made by the lyrists and flutists of the necromancer, a troupe of skeletons pirouetted with light clickings of their toe-bones; and a rout of mummies bounded stiffly; and others of Namirrha's creatures moved with monstrous caperings. To and fro they leapt on the bodies of the emperor's people, in the paces of an evil saraband. At every step they grew taller and heavier, till the saltant mummies were as the mummies of Anakim, and the skeletons were boned like colossi; and louder the music rose, drowning the faint cries of Zotulla's people. And huger still became the dancers, towering far into vaulted shadow among the vast columns, with thudding feet that wrought thunder in the room; and those whereon they danced were as grapes trampled for a vintage in autumn; and the floor ran deep with a sanguine must.

As a man drowning in a noisome, night-bound fen, the emperor heard the voice of Namirrha:

"It would seem that my dancers please you not. So now I shall present you a most royal spectacle. Arise and follow me, for the spectacle is one that requires an empire for its stage."

Zotulla and Obexah rose from their chairs in the fashion of night-walkers. Giving no backward glance at their ministering phantoms, or the hall where the dancers bounded, they followed Namirrha to an alcove beyond the altar of Thasaidon. Thence, by the upward-coiling stairways, they came at length to a broad high balcony that faced Zotulla's palace and looked forth above the city roofs toward the bourn of sunset.

It seemed that several hours had gone by in that hellish feasting and entertainment; for the day was near to its close, and the sun, which had fallen from sight behind the imperial palace, was barring the vast heavens with bloody rays.

"Behold," said Namirrha, adding a strange vocable to which the stone of the edifice resounded like a beaten gong.

The balcony pitched a little, and Zotulla, looking over the balustrade, beheld the roofs of Ummaos lessen and sink beneath him. It seemed that the balcony flew skyward to a prodigious height, and he peered down across the domes of his own palace, upon the houses, the tilled fields and the desert beyond, and the huge sun brought low on the desert's verge. And Zotulla grew giddy; and the chill airs of the upper heavens blew upon him. But Namirrha spoke another word, and the balcony ceased to ascend.

"Look well," said the necromancer, "on the empire that was yours, but shall be yours no longer." Then, with arms outstretched toward the sunset, and the gulfs beyond the sunset, he called aloud the twelve names that were perdition to utter, and after them the tremendous invocation: *Gna padambis devompra thungis furidor avoragomon.*

Instantly, it seemed that great ebon clouds of thunder beetled against the sun. Lining the horizon, the clouds took the form of colossal monsters with heads and members somewhat resembling those of stallions. Rearing terribly, they trod down the sun like an extinguished ember; and racing as in some hippodrome of Titans, they rose higher and vaster, coming toward Ummaos. Deep, calamitous rumblings preceded them, and the earth shook visibly, till Zotulla saw that these were not immaterial clouds, but actual living forms that had come forth to tread the world in macrocosmic vastness. Throwing their shadows for many leagues before them, the coursers charged as if devil-ridden into Xylac, and their feet descended like falling mountain crags upon far oases and towns of the outer waste.

Like a many-turreted storm they came, and it seemed that the world sank gulfward, tilting beneath the weight.

Still as a man enchanted into marble, Zotulla stood and beheld the ruining that was wrought on his empire. And closer drew the gigantic stallions, racing with inconceivable speed, and louder was the thundering of their footfalls, that now began to blot the green fields and fruited orchards lying for many miles to the west of Ummaos. And the shadow of the stallions climbed like an evil gloom of eclipse, till it covered Ummaos; and looking up, the emperor saw their eyes halfway between earth and zenith, like baleful suns that glare down from soaring cumuli.

Then, in the thickening gloom, above that insupportable thunder, he heard the voice of Namirrha, crying in mad triumph:

"Know, Zotulla, that I have called up the coursers of Thamogorgos, lord of the abyss. And the coursers will tread your empire down, even as your palfrey trod and trampled in former time a beggar-boy named Narthos. And learn also that I, Namirrha, was that boy." And the eyes of Namirrha, filled with a vainglory of madness and bale, burned like malign, disastrous stars at the hour of their culmination.

To Zotulla, wholly mazed with the horror and tumult, the necromancer's words were no more than shrill, shrieked overtones of the tempest of doom; and he understood them not. Tremendously, with a rending of staunch-built roofs, and an instant cleavage and crumbling down of mighty masonries, the hooves descended upon Ummaos. Fair temple-domes were pashed like shells of the haliotis, and haughty mansions were broken and stamped into the ground even as gourds; and house by house the city was trampled flat with a crashing as of worlds beaten into chaos. Far below, in the darkened streets, men and camels fled like scurrying emmets but could not escape. And implacably the hooves rose and fell, till ruin was upon half the city, and night was over all. The palace of Zotulla was trodden under, and now the forelegs of the coursers loomed level with Namirrha's balcony, and their heads towered awfully above. It seemed that they would rear and trample down the necromancer's house; but at that moment they parted to left and right, and a dolorous glimmering came from the low sunset; and the coursers went on, treading under them that portion of Ummaos which lay to the eastward. And Zotulla and Obexah and Namirrha looked down on the city's fragments as on a shard-strewn midden, and heard the cataclysmic clamor of the hooves departing toward eastern Xylac.

"Now that was a goodly spectacle," quoth Namirrha. Then, turning to the emperor, he added malignly: "Think not that I have done with thee, however, or that doom is yet consummate."

It seemed that the balcony had fallen to its former elevation, which was still a lofty vantage above the sharded ruins. And Namirrha plucked the emperor by the arm and led him from the balcony to an inner chamber, while Obexah followed mutely. The emperor's heart was crushed within him by the trampling of such calamities, and despair weighed upon him like a foul incubus on the shoulders of a man lost in some land of accursed night. And he knew not that he had been parted from Obexah on the threshold of the chamber, and that certain of Namirrha's creatures, appearing like shadows, had compelled the girl to go downward with them by the stairs, and had stifled her outcries with their rotten cerements as they went.

The chamber was one that Namirrha used for his most unhallowed rites and alchemies. The rays of the lamps that illumed it were saffron-red like the spilt ichor of devils, and they flowed on aludels and crucibles and black athanors and alembics whereof the purpose was hardly to be named by mortal man. The sorcerer heated in one of the alembics a dark liquid full of star-cold lights, while Zotulla looked on unheeding. And when the liquid bubbled and sent forth a spiral vapor, Namirrha distilled it into goblets of gold-rimmed iron, and gave one of the goblets to Zotulla and retained the other himself. And he said to Zotulla with a stern imperative voice: "I bid thee quaff this liquor."

Zotulla, fearing that the draft was poison, hesitated. And the necromancer regarded him with a lethal gaze, and cried loudly: "Fearest thou to do as I?" and therewith he set the goblet to his lips.

So the emperor drank the draft, constrained as if by the bidding of some angel of death, and a darkness fell upon his senses. But, ere the darkness grew complete, he saw that Namirrha had drained his own goblet. Then, with unspeakable agonies, it seemed that the emperor died; and his soul floated free; and again he saw the chamber, though with bodiless eyes. And discarnate he stood in the saffron-crimson light, with his body lying as if dead on the floor beside him, and near it the prone body of Namirrha and the two fallen goblets.

Standing thus, he beheld a strange thing: for anon his own body stirred and arose, while that of the necromancer remained still as death. And Zotulla looked on his own lineaments and his figure in its short cloak of azure samite sewn with black pearls and balas-rubies; and the body lived before him, though with eyes that held a darker fire and a deeper evil than was their wont. Then, without corporeal ears, Zotulla heard the figure speak, and the voice was the strong, arrogant voice of Namirrha, saying:

"Follow me, O houseless phantom, and do in all things as I enjoin thee."

Like an unseen shadow, Zotulla followed the wizard, and the twain went downward by the stairs to the great banquet hall. They came to the altar of Thasaidon and the mailed image, with the seven horse-skull lamps burning before it as formerly. Upon the altar, Zotulla's beloved leman Obexah, who alone of women had power to stir his sated heart, was lying bound with thongs at Thasaidon's feet. But the hall beyond was deserted, and nothing remained of that Saturnalia of doom except the fruit of the treading, which had flowed together in dark pools among the columns.

Namirrha, using the emperor's body in all ways for his own, paused before the dark eidolon; and he said to the spirit of Zotulla: "Be imprisoned in this image, without power to free thyself or to stir in any wise."

Being wholly obedient to the will of the necromancer, the soul of Zotulla was embodied in the statue, and he felt its cold, gigantic armor about him like a strait sarcophagus, and he peered forth immovably from the bleak eyes that were overhung by its carven helmet.

Gazing thus, he beheld the change that had come on his own body through the sorcerous possession of Namirrha: for below the short azure cloak, the legs had turned suddenly to the hind legs of a black stallion, with hooves that glowed redly as if heated by infernal fires. And even as Zotulla watched this prodigy, the hooves glowed white and incandescent, and fumes mounted from the floor beneath them.

Then, on the black altar, the hybrid abomination came pacing haughtily toward Obexah, and smoking hoofprints appeared behind it as it came. Pausing beside the girl, who lay supine and helpless regarding it with eyes that were pools of frozen horror, it raised one glowing hoof and set the hoof on her naked bosom between the small breast-cups of golden filigree begemmed with rubies. And the girl screamed beneath that atrocious treading as the soul of one newly damned might scream in hell; and the hoof glared with intolerable brilliance, as if freshly plucked from a furnace wherein the weapons of demons were forged.

At that moment, in the cowed and crushed and sodden shade of the emperor Zotulla, close-locked within the adamantine image, there awoke the manhood that had slumbered unaroused before the ruining of his empire and the trampling under of his retinue. Immediately a great abhorrence and a high wrath were alive in his soul, and mightily he longed for his own right arm to serve him, and a sword in his right hand.

Then it seemed that a voice spoke within him, chill and bleak and awful, and as if uttered inwardly by the statue itself. And the voice said: "I am Thasaidon, lord of the seven hells beneath the earth, and the hells of man's heart above the earth, which are seven times seven. For the moment, O Zotulla, my power is become thine for the sake of a mutual vengeance. Be one in all ways with the statue that has my likeness, even as the soul is one with the flesh. Behold! there is a mace of adamant in thy right hand. Lift up the mace, and smite."

Zotulla was aware of a great power within him, and giant thews about him that thrilled with the power and responded agilely to his will. He felt in his mailed right hand the haft of the huge spiky-headed mace; and though the mace was beyond the lifting of any man in mortal flesh, it seemed no more than a goodly weight to Zotulla. Then, rearing the mace like a warrior in battle, he struck down with one crashing blow the impious thing that wore his own rightful flesh united with the legs and hooves of a demon courser. And the thing crumpled swiftly down and lay with the brain spreading pulpily from its shattered skull on the shining jet. And the legs twitched a little and then grew still; and the hooves glowed from a fiery, blinding white to the redness of red-hot iron, cooling slowly.

For a space there was no sound, other than the shrill screaming of the girl Obexah, mad with pain and the terror of those prodigies which she had beheld. Then, in the soul of Zotulla, grown sick with that screaming, the chill, awful voice of Thasaidon spoke again:

"Go free, for there is nothing more for thee to do." So the spirit of Zotulla passed from the image of Thasaidon and found in the wide air the freedom of nothingness and oblivion.

But the end was not yet for Namirrha, whose mad, arrogant soul had been loosened from Zotulla's body by the blow, and had returned darkly, not in the manner planned by the magician, to its own body lying in the room of accursed rites and forbidden transmigrations. There Namirrha woke anon, with a dire confusion in his mind, and a partial forgetfulness: for the curse of Thasaidon was upon him now because of his blasphemies.

Nothing was clear in his thought except a malign, exorbitant longing for revenge; but the reason thereof, and the object, were as doubtful shadows. And still prompted by that obscure animus, he arose; and girding to his side an enchanted sword with runic sapphires and opals in its hilt, he descended the stairs and came again to the altar of Thasaidon, where the mailed statue stood impassive as before, with the poised mace in its immovable right hand, and below it, on the altar, the double sacrifice.

A veil of weird darkness was upon the senses of Namirrha, and he saw not the stallion-legged horror that lay dead with slowly blackening hooves; and he heard not the moaning of the girl Obexah, who still lived beside it. But his eyes were drawn by the diamond mirror that was upheld in the claws of black iron basilisks beyond the altar; and going to the mirror, he saw therein a face that he knew no longer for his own. And because his eyes were shadowed and his brain filled with shifting webs of delusion, he took the face for that of the emperor Zotulla. Insatiable as Hell's own flame, his old hatred rose within him; and he drew the enchanted sword and began to hew therewith at the reflection. Sometimes, because of the curse laid upon him, and the impious transmigration which he had performed, he thought himself Zotulla warring with the necromancer;

and again, in the shiftings of his madness, he was Namirrha smiting at the emperor; and then, without name, he fought a nameless foe. And soon the sorcerous blade, though tempered with formidable spells, was broken close to the hilt, and Namirrha beheld the image still unharmed. Then, howling aloud the half-forgotten runes of a most tremendous curse, made invalid through his forgettings, he hammered still with the heavy sword-hilt on the mirror, till the runic sapphires and opals cracked in the hilt and fell away at his feet in little fragments.

Obexah, dying on the altar, saw Namirrha battling with his image, and the spectacle moved her to mad laughter like the pealing of bells of ruined crystal. And above her laughter, and above the cursings of Namirrha, there came anon like a rumbling of swift-risen storm the thunder made by the macrocosmic stallions of Thamogorgos, returning gulfward through Xylac over Ummaos, to trample down the one house that they had spared aforetime.

AT THE EDGE of the World, where the River Ocean flows,
and where Fairyland sometimes moors itself to the world
we know, lurk many strange and perilous things. Some of
these are the Golden Box, and the Gladsome Beast, and the
City of Never, and the Bird of the Difficult Eye. Strangest
and most perilous of all is the Tower of the Gibbelins,
joined to our world by a bridge and moored by golden

chains, lest it drift back to the moon whence it came. This is one of the many conceits of the late Lord Dunsany, who early in this century adapted the heroic-fantasy genre, pioneered by William Morris, to the short-story form.

Dunsany was a man of towering physical stature, fiery temperament, and poetical sensitivity. He was a writer, soldier, poet, and sportsman all rolled into one. There was a conflict between his background and upbringing — that of a conventional hunting-shooting-fishing-and-soldiering Anglo-Irish peer — and his personal literary interests and tastes. In view of this contradiction, and his wide range of interests, and the fact that he wrote all his long life with a quill pen, his production of sixty-odd books of fiction, verse, essays, autobiography, and drama is nothing less than phenomenal.

Dunsany was a writer's writer. That is to say, he was a careful craftsman with strong opinions on the fine points of writing, who never attained great mass popularity but who, nevertheless, much influenced many later writers. Nearly all later authors of fantasy, for example, owe something to him. Some of them have plainly gone through a "Dunsany period" in their own writings, just as many main-stream writers have gone through a "Hemingway period" before they found their own proper style and métier. Dunsany's series of fantastic yarns told by Jorkens, the cadging old clubman, inspired such series as Arthur Clarke's Tales of the White Hart and the Gavagan's Bar stories of de Camp and Pratt — not that the latter were direct imitations, but that these later writers were all carrying Jorkens around in their subconscious when they in their turn were groping for subjects to write about. Here is one of Dunsany's polished gems of fantastic fiction.

THE HOARD
OF THE
GIBBELINS

• LORD DUNSANY

THE Gibbelins eat, as is well known, nothing less good than man. Their evil tower is joined to Terra Cognita, to the lands we know, by a bridge. Their hoard is beyond reason; avarice has no use for it; they have a separate cellar for emeralds and a separate cellar for sapphires; they have filled a hole with gold and dig it up when they need it. And the only use that is known for their ridiculous wealth is to attract to their larder a continual supply of food. In times of famine they have even been known to scatter rubies abroad, a little trail of them to some city of Man, and sure enough their larders would soon be full again.

Their tower stands on the other side of that river known to Homer—*ho rhoos Okeanoio*, as he called it—which surrounds the world. And where the river is narrow and fordable the tower was built by the Gibbelins' gluttonous sires, for they liked to see burglars rowing easily to their steps. Some nourishment that common soil has not the huge trees drained there with their colossal roots from both banks of the river.

There the Gibbelins lived and discreditably fed.

Alderic, Knight of the Order of the City and the Assault, hereditary Guardian of the King's Peace of Mind,

71

a man not unremembered among the makers of myth, pondered so long upon the Gibbelins' hoard that by now he deemed it his. Alas that I should say of so perilous a venture, undertaken at dead of night by a valorous man, that its motive was sheer avarice! Yet upon avarice only the Gibbelins relied to keep their larders full, and once in every hundred years sent spies into the cities of men to see how avarice did, and always the spies returned again to the tower saying that all was well.

It may be thought that, as the years went on and men came by fearful ends on that tower's wall, fewer and fewer would come to the Gibbelins' table: but the Gibbelins found otherwise.

Not in the folly and frivolity of his youth did Alderic come to the tower, but he studied carefully for several years the manner in which burglars met their doom when they went in search of the treasure that he considered his. In every case they had entered by the door.

He consulted those who gave advice on this quest; he noted every detail and cheerfully paid their fees, and determined to do nothing that they advised, for what were their clients now? No more than examples of the savoury art, mere half-forgotten memories of a meal; and many, perhaps, no longer even that.

These were the requisites for the quest that these men used to advise: a horse, a boat, mail armour, and at least three men-at-arms. Some said, "Blow the horn at the tower door"; others said, "Do not touch it."

Alderic thus decided: he would take no horse down to the river's edge, he would not row along it in a boat, and he would go alone and by way of the Forest Unpassable.

How pass, you may say, by the unpassable? This was his plan: there was a dragon he knew of who if peasants' prayers are heeded deserved to die, not alone because of the number of maidens he cruelly slew, but because he was bad for the crops; he ravaged the very land and was the bane of a dukedom.

Now Alderic determined to go up against him. So he took horse and spear and pricked till he met the dragon, and the dragon came out against him breathing bitter smoke. And to him Alderic shouted, "Hath foul dragon ever slain true knight?" And well the dragon knew that this had never been, and he hung his head and was silent, for he was glutted with blood. "Then," said the knight, "if thou would'st ever taste maiden's blood again thou shalt be my trusty steed, and if not, by this spear there shall befall thee all that the troubadours tell of the dooms of thy breed."

And the dragon did not open his ravening mouth, nor rush upon the knight, breathing out fire; for well he knew the fate of those that did these things, but he consented to the terms imposed, and swore to the knight to become his trusty steed.

It was on a saddle upon this dragon's back that Alderic afterwards sailed above the unpassable forest, even above the tops of those measureless trees, children of wonder. But first he pondered that subtle plan of his which was more profound than merely to avoid all that had been done before; and he commanded a blacksmith, and the blacksmith made him a pickaxe.

Now there was great rejoicing at the rumour of Alderic's quest, for all folk knew that he was a cautious man, and they deemed that he would succeed and enrich the world, and they rubbed their hands in the cities at the thought of largesse; and there was joy among all men in Alderic's country, except perchance among the lenders of money, who feared they would soon be paid. And there was rejoicing also because men hoped that when the Gibbelins were robbed of their hoard, they would shatter their high-built bridge and break the golden chains that bound them to the world, and drift back, they and their tower, to the moon, from which they had come and to which they rightly belonged. There was little love for the Gibbelins, though all men envied their hoard.

So they all cheered, that day when he mounted his dragon, as though he was already a conqueror, and what pleased them more than the good that they hoped he would do to the world was that he scattered gold as he rode away; for he would not need it, he said, if he found the Gibbelins' hoard, and he would not need it more if he smoked on the Gibbelins' table.

When they heard that he had rejected the advice of those that gave it, some said that the knight was mad, and others said he was greater than those that gave the advice, but none appreciated the worth of his plan.

He reasoned thus: for centuries men had been well advised and had gone by the cleverest way, while the Gibbelins came to expect them to come by boat and to look for them at the door whenever their larder was empty, even as a man looketh for a snipe in the marsh; but how, said Alderic, if a snipe should sit in the top of a tree, and would men find him there? Assuredly never! So Alderic decided to swim the river and not to go by the door, but to pick his way into the tower through the stone. Moreover, it was in his mind to work below the level of the ocean, the river (as Homer knew) that girdles the world, so that as soon as he made a hole in the wall the water should pour in, confounding the Gibbelins, and flooding the cellars rumoured to be twenty feet in depth, and therein he would dive for emeralds as a diver dives for pearls.

And on the day that I tell of he galloped away from his home scattering largesse of gold, as I have said, and passed through many kingdoms, the dragon snapping at maidens as he went, but being unable to eat them because of the bit in his mouth, and earning no gentler reward than a spurthrust where he was softest. And so they came to the swart arboreal precipice of the unpassable forest. The dragon rose at it with a rattle of wings. Many a farmer near the edge of the world saw him up there where yet the twilight lingered, a faint, black, wavering line; and mistaking him for a row of geese going inland from the ocean, went into their houses cheerily rubbing their hands and saying that winter was coming, and that we should soon have snow. Soon even there the twilight faded away, and when they descended at the edge of the world it was night and the moon was shining. Ocean, the ancient river, narrow and shallow there, flowed by and made no murmur. Whether the Gibbelins banqueted or whether they watched by the door, they also made no murmur. And Alderic dismounted and took his armour off, and saying one prayer to his lady, swam with his pickaxe. He did not part from his sword, for fear that he meet with a Gibbelin. Landed the other side, he began to work at once, and all went well with him. Nothing put out its head from any window, and all were lighted so that nothing within could see him in the dark. The blows of his pickaxe were dulled in the deep walls. All night he worked, no sound came to molest him, and at dawn the last rock swerved and tumbled inwards, and the river poured in after. Then Alderic took a stone, and went to the bottom step, and hurled the stone at the door; he heard the echoes roll into the tower, then he ran back and dived through the hole in the wall.

He was in the emerald-cellar. There was no light in the lofty vault above him, but, diving through twenty feet of water, he felt the floor all rough with emeralds, and open coffers full of them. By a faint ray of the moon he saw that the water was green with them, and, easily filling a satchel, he rose again to the surface; and there were the Gibbelins waist-deep in the water, with torches in their hands! And, without saying a word, *or even smiling*, they neatly hanged him on the outer wall—and the tale is one of those that have not a happy ending.

BEFORE THE dawn of recorded history, at the western extremity of the Continent (for Europe, Asia, and Africa then were one) the mighty Tartessian Empire spread its bulk across the Euskerian lands. Its gleaming capital, Torrutseish, was the many-times-removed progenitor of historical Tartessos, near modern Cádiz. In those days, however, the sea, which now washes Cádiz, lay many leagues to westward.

South of the Euskerian lands rose the mountain range of Atlantis, where fierce blond barbarians dwelt. Northward stretched the silver strands of Aremoria, home of inspired bards and bloodthirsty feuds. Westward across the Sirenian Sea lay the golden isles of the Hesperides, and beyond these the sinking subcontinent of Pusâd or Poseidonis, confused by later story-tellers with Atlantis. On Poseidonis, the strongest power was that of windswept Lorsk.

In this dawn world, magic was rife and effective; for not yet had iron, which dissolves all spells and banishes all spirits, come into common use. And to Torrutseish came the youth Gezun: hulking, jovial, amorous, rash, imprudent and impudent, quick of wit, and convinced that here at last he should make his fortune.

When this volume's predecessor, Swords and Sorcery, appeared, some reviewers asked why I had not included any of my own stories. One answer was that I more admired the stories I did include. Another was that putting one's own pieces in an anthology that one edits seems somehow unsporting, like shooting fish in a bathtub.

However, I have written stories of heroic fantasy: one novel, The Tritonian Ring, and five short stories, of which this is one. All have been published before. All are laid in the same setting, the novel a few centuries earlier than the shorts. So it is not, I hope, unfair to the reader to let him judge for himself as to whether my works in this genre deserve to be ranked with those of my colleagues. For obvious reasons, I am not in a position to make this judgment myself.

THE HUNGRY
HERCYNIAN

• L. SPRAGUE DE CAMP

KURTEVAN'S Tower stood in one of the oldest sections of Torrutseish, capital of the mighty Tartessian Empire. The tapering cylinder of dark-red stone arose from inside a walled inclosure. As Lord Noish approached it, it looked black against the fading purple of the Euskerian spring sunset.

Parting the curtains of his litter to peer out at the Tower of Kurtevan, Lord Noish did not like its looks. He knew that the edifice was called Kurtevan's Tower after an eminent wizard who had lived and died before Noish's time. The gutted and fire-blackened shell had stood for generations, none daring to demolish or restore it for fear of the baleful influences that might linger on the spot, until a new tenant had quietly moved in and set about refurbishing the ruin.

Nobody seemed to know about this newcomer, but one morning the inclosure rang with the sound of hammer and adze as carpenters trimmed new boards and beams. Noish had looked in at the office of the Registrar of Records and learned that the lot had been bought by one Zyc the Hercynian.

That was curious. Hercynians, Noish understood, were a cannibal race living far to the east, beyond the wild Galatha. If the Galatha were barbarians, the Hercynians were true savages. Noish had seen a couple brought to Torrutseish as slaves, but so wild, frightened, and stupid were

79

they that they proved unsalable and were killed to save the cost of feeding them.

It was odd, then, that one of that race should gather enough trade metal to buy a house and lot in teeming Torrutseish. The average Galathan, for instance, could not understand buying and selling and got insulted if one tried to bargain with him. Everything had to be an exchange of gifts. Hercynians probably understood nothing beyond taking whatever they had power to seize.

Yet here was Noish, the richest lord of Torrutseish's second caste, jogging in his litter up to the gate in the brick wall surrounding this painted primitive's tower. Voices murmured in the dark, and Bokarri the wizard thrust his narrow, sallow face in at the curtains.

"Good my lord!" said Bokarri. "They'll not admit us."

"What? Not admit *me*?"

"The ostiary says you may enter—but alone and on foot only."

Lord Noish heaved his bulk out of the litter. A big, fat, jolly-looking man, he waddled up to the gate.

Instead of the usual single peephole with a copper plate hung on a pin inside for a shutter, this gate had two, one at normal eye-level and one a couple of feet higher. The upper one was now open, as though the gatekeeper were standing on a box inside.

Noish stared up at the aperture, though the light was now too dim, even with the help of the lanthorns carried by his whifflers, to see anything of the face on the other side. He called:

"Varlet, know you who I am?"

"You are Lord Noish, are you not?" rumbled a strongly accented voice of startling depth.

"And you say you'll admit me only alone and on foot?"

"That is right."

Noish ran a hand over his bald pate. If this had been just an ordinary citizen, a member of the fifth or sixth castes, Noish could have returned home, armed a few score servants and retainers, and come back to take the place by storm.

But this was different. Although, as a foreigner, this Zyc would have only the most fragile legal rights, and although Noish could probably override these by his wealth, power, and caste status, he very much wanted a favor from Zyc, who would not help Noish if the latter invaded his precincts by force.

Noish had summoned Bokarri, his regular magician, with a request for a spell to get rid of Noish's great rival for the favor of King Ikusiven of Tartessia, the chief minister Haldu. Bokarri had failed Noish, saying that such an operation was beyond a mere general practitioner like himself, and he must call in a specialist. Zyc was the specialist.

Noish's head bearer started to protest at his master's rashness, but Noish waved him to silence and walked in as the gate swung. Then he flinched as the light of the lanthorns fell upon the gatekeeper. This was a Laistrugonian eight feet tall, with long black hair falling over his massive shoulders. In his hand he bore a club that could have squashed Lord Noish like a bug. The Laistrugon slammed the gate behind Noish and shot home the huge bolt.

"This way, sir," he said.

The giant led the way to the base of the tower, opened the door, and let Noish in ahead of him.

The ground floor of the Tower of Kurtevan was lit by a single lamp in a wall bracket. Its flame fluttered in the draft caused by the closing of the door. The ground floor, a single big circular room, seemed empty save for a few chests and pieces of furniture against the walls. The Laistrugonian led Noish across the great room to the circular stairway that spiraled up to the floor above.

On the second storey, Noish entered a room lit by several lamps. Here he found Zyc the Hercynian sitting naked amid a heap of cushions on the floor. Zyc was a dark, stocky man with flattish features and wide cheek bones, which gave him a dish-faced look. His skin seemed to be a yellowish brown. That, however, was hard to tell, because his face was covered with paint, the right half red and the left half white. His body was also covered with painted designs. Where paint was lacking, the shaman's hide was coated with dirt. He had had all the hair shaved from his head, and a glossy-black stubble was just growing back in. Around his neck hung a necklace of human remains: finger bones, teeth, dried ears, and other parts symmetrically arranged.

Zyc was gnawing the meat from a bone—a joint of

beef, Noish was relieved to see. Other bones, picked more
or less clean, lay about him on the floor. His movements
were quick and sure as if he were bursting with animal
vigor.

Noish approached, wrinkling his nose against the
stench.

"You are Zyc?"

The shaman grunted an affirmative, then spoke with
his mouth full. "What you want?"

Noish drew a long breath to get his self-control. An
ordinary Tartessian who used him with such insolence
would soon have regretted it. He replied:

"Magic. I would destroy a man."

"How? What man?" said Zyc between chews.

Noish forced a grim smile. "You might offer me a seat,
my good fellow."

Zyc said to the Laistrugon: "Kumo, give this man a
cushion and go."

Noish took the cushion, plunked his massive rump upon
it, and continued: "Bokarri assures me your discretion is to
be trusted. Is that true?"

"Of course. What you think I am?"

Noish deemed it wiser not to say. He replied: "It had
better be, my friend. If you know about me, you know that
I can pay back any betrayal."

Noish explained about the minister Haldu. One by one,
the men who had stood between Noish and the highest post
open to a second-caste Tartessian had been removed: one
poisoned, another stabbed, a third sent abroad on a dangerous mission, a fourth frightened into retirement.

But Lord Haldu, the shrewd and energetic chief minister, still sat in his seat of honor. He showed no sign of
losing his grip with age, of perishing from a pox, or of
falling out with King Ikusiven. The time had come, therefore, to remove him, but in such a manner that Lord
Noish should not be suspected.

"I could not," said Noish, "simply invite him to dinner
and poison him. For one thing, he brings his own taster;
for another, I should too patently gain by being next in
line for the ministry."

Zyc tossed his bone aside, wiped his mouth on the back
of his hand, and spat on the floor. "What sort of man, this
king?" he asked.

Noish shrugged. "A man like other men, for all the supposed divinity of the first caste. He tries to live up to his proper rôle without the intelligence needed to do so."

Zyc thoughtfully sucked the meat juice off his fingers. "Very dignified man? Particular about—you know—what you call—formalities?"

"Oh, very. 'Tis as much as your life is worth to take any liberties with him."

"What happen if Lord Haldu went to king and told him plain truth about himself?"

Noish chuckled. "I see whither blows the breeze. That would be the end of Lord Haldu—at least of his ministry, and probably of him as well. But how would you force Haldu into so rash a course? Any public man knows that, as says the philosopher Goishek, truth is too precious a thing to be cast abroad."

Zyc belched. "We see. Can you get Haldu and king to your house and drug Haldu's wine?"

"Aye, that I can. I'll give a feast. While the king's caste rules forbid his eating with us of the second caste, there's nought to stop him from coming to enjoy the entertainment afterwards. Then I suppose Haldu, full of your truth drug, will tell the king what a sorry witling the fellow is. But stay: the same physic would have affected Haldu's taster, thereby betraying our part in the plot."

"Not so. Taster simple slave. Nobody notice whether he tell the truth or not."

"Excellent, my good savage; most sapiently thought out. But ere we plunge further into this plotsome thicket, what will be your scot?"

"Ha ha!" Zyc gave a barking laugh, showing all his teeth, and spat again. "Plenty."

"I can pay any reasonable weight of trade metal."

"Don't want trade metal," snarled the Hercynian. "Have enough."

"What then?"

"Want young girl, not over eighteen, and plump."

"Oh, you mean a slave?" Noish paused in wary puzzlement. "Why can't you take the trade metal and buy your own?"

"I no buy slave. You buy, bring secretly to me. If I buy, people see me, know I buy. Slave disappear, constables come looking."

"Oh." A horrid suspicion formed in Noish's mind. "You, then wish this maid not for the usual purposes, but to. . . ."

"Aye, ha ha! You Tartessians funny people. Let master kill slave, but don't let him do what he like with body."

"We regard cannibalism as immoral," said Noish, drawing his black Euskerian cloak virtuously about him. "Though, to speak the truth, the more important reason in the minds of my countrymen is a superstitious fear of the ghosts of persons not properly buried. But look here, my man, even with my power I cannot afford to be involved in such an outrage—"

"No girl, no truth drug," said Zyc. "Me and Kumo haven't had *good* meal since we came to Torrutseish. You fetch girl; you protect me afterwards if anybody ask questions. I give you magical truth drug; you get to be minister. You say nothing; I say nothing."

Again Noish made his decision, though not without some small shudder. "Very well. Give me the drug, and when I'm minister you shall have the wench."

"Ha! Me stupid? Girl first, then drug."

There ensued a long argument. Finally they agreed that Noish should buy the girl at once but hold her for delivery until after the drug had done its work. He added:

"Do you care whether she's a virgin?"

Zyc flashed his teeth. "Nay. Virgins, not-virgins, all taste same."

Gezun of Gadaira (as he now called himself) jogged on his mule Dostaen up the road along the south shore of the broad Baitis. As he made a turn, he came in sight of Torrutseish on the island made by the forking and rejoining of the river. The world's largest city was surrounded by a great circular wall of red, white, and black stone, arranged in a brilliant mosaic pattern. Behind the wall rose tall towers of similar construction. The bright Euskerian spring sun blazed on the gilding of spires and tourelles and on the streaming flags bearing the owl of Tartessia.

Gezun was a native of the sinking continent of Pusâd or Poseidonis across the Sirenian Sea, who at the age of twelve had been kidnapped by slavers and sold in Gadaira. His master, the wizard Sancheth Sar, had died the previous year, freeing Gezun and leaving him half his collection of magical books and paraphernalia. But the heir to the other half, a nephew of Sancheth, swindled Gezun out of all the more important items.

The rest had gone in the course of Gezun's naïve attempt to set himself up as a master magician in Gadaira. Some had been stolen, some destroyed, and some lost in a game with his chief rival, the wizard Nikurteu.

Gezun's only remaining magical property was a ring of star metal, which warded the wearer against charms. Sancheth had told him that there were less than a score of these in existence, mostly in the hands of kings and leading magicians.

Then Gezun learned that he had gotten the daughter of his neighbor, the merchant Berota, with child. Gezun and Jarra had been carrying on for some time and Gezun would gladly have wedded her. Berota, however, had different plans for his daughter, which did not include marriage to an unsuccessful and debt-ridden young magician and a foreign-born freedman at that.

Learning that Berota had hired the town's leading bullies to kill him, Gezun had thrown his remaining possessions into a pair of saddle bags, turned loose his collection of pets, and ridden off into the night. Having jogged a hundred and sixty miles up the Baitis, he now neared the imperial capital.

Like most Pusadians he was big—at seventeen he towered over the Euskerians—with a swarthy skin and thick curly black hair. While Sancheth was alive, Gezun had dreamed of riding up to Torrutseish and winning the daughter of the king in some heroic contest. Now he knew that, while King Ikusiven did indeed have a daughter, the daughter had three lovers and a mustache. Moreover, in the rigid Tartessian caste system his chances of meeting this dubious prize were nil.

Passage by ferry-raft across the south arm of the Baitis cost Gezun one of his few remaining pieces of trade metal, a miniature copper axhead bearing the cartouche of King Ikusiven.

Downstream from where the rope that guided the ferry was belayed to a big old cork oak near the water's edge, the shoreline had been revetted into a series of docks and quays. In some of these, ships were drawn up. One of these ships had just pulled in: a long low galley with the orca symbol of the far-northern isle of Foworia upon its sail. A load of slaves had been herded off and were now being marched up towards the city by a gang of beetle-browed sea rovers.

The head of the procession reached the south gate before Gezun, who had to sit slouched on Dostaen, watching the captives shamble past with downcast eyes and blank faces. One in particular caught his eye: a young woman in the remains of a Hesperian dress; young, dark, and with beautifully molded contours and a proud carriage. She cast him a noncommittal glance and passed on, but Gezun tingled.

Gezun felt in his wallet and gave up any thought of buying the girl. Still, curious about her fate, he followed the sad procession into the city. At least, he might learn what happened to her. Then, when he had established himself, who knew?

The slave procession marched a few hundred paces and debouched into a great agora, which included the slave mart. The Foworians kicked and beat their way through the swarm of beggars, hucksters, pimps, and plain citizens to a cleared inclosure. This open space contained the slave block, the officials who conducted the business, and a couple of King Ikusiven's slingers strolling about to see that unauthorized persons stayed out of the area.

Lolling on his mule, Gezun could easily see over the heads of the crowd into the inclosure. At the moment, a pair of tall reddish-blond Atlanteans were up for sale. They did not bring much, for the Torrutseishans too well knew the intractable nature of these fierce mountaineers. The pair were finally knocked down to a contractor for the royal silver mines in the country of the Turdetanians. The Atlanteans, having donned their buckskin kilts and vermilion-dyed goatskin mantles, were led off to the short and brutish lives remaining to them.

Then came a batch of naked Gamphasants from Lake Kokutos, south of the mountains of Atlantis: tall thin dark-brown folk with curly black hair, offered by a group of Kerneans in fluttery robes and kaffias, with rings in their ears. The Gamphasants were snapped up quickly, being known for their fatalistic docility and for the ease with which they could be trained into good gardeners and stable boys.

At last came the Foworians' captives, a motley group from the western islands. Most were Hesperians, considered clever and courteous, but tricky and given to running away. They went, one by one, until the girl who had attracted Gezun's attention stood naked on the block.

She looked even better than with her clothes on. Gezun's blood pulsed as he looked; but, of course. . . .

The bidding became brisker and more determined. It settled down into a contest between two men who leaned against the rope, glaring as each capped the other's bid. One was a big, stout, bald man in the ornate garb of a Tartessian noble. Gezun could see his gilded litter lying on the fringe of the crowd, and the bearers leaning against it.

The other was also fat, but smaller, with a halo of silky-white hair and a long white beard, which contrasted with the youthfulness of his smooth pink skin. His cloak was neither the somber black of Euskeria, nor the blue-and-white favored in the Hesperides, but bore the tartan pattern of Poseidonis.

"Twenty nasses," said the bald man.

"Twenty-two," said the white-haired bidder, in a Lorskan accent.

"Twenty-five," said the bald one, and took a threatening step towards his rival. "Mark ye, churl! Know you not against whom you're bidding these unwonted sums?"

"I neither know nor care," said the beard. "Twenty-seven."

"For the last time, insolent knave, I warn you—"

"Sirs!" interjected the auctioneer. "For one bidder to threaten another is quite out of order, even for you, my lord Noish. I'll appeal to the minister—"

"The minister can go puke," said Noish. "I'll say what I please, and I warn this foreign filth—"

"Ha!" shouted the beard. "That for you!"

Gezun was too far to see clearly what happened. However, he had an impression that the bearded one tossed a spurt of white powder at Lord Noish. The latter recoiled and began to cough. He coughed and coughed and coughed until he turned purple and tears ran down his cheeks. Every time he got his coughing under control, he turned to the auctioneer to try to bid and went off into another spasm. At last he staggered to his litter, heaved himself in, and was borne off to the laughter of the throng.

"Now," said the bearded one, "I believe that my bid of twenty-seven nasses is the highest hitherto. Unless you hear another, I shall take possession of my merchandise."

The bearded man waddled off with his new slave. Gezun kicked Dostaen into motion and trotted after until he caught up with the man. He leaned over and said in Lorskan:

"Good-day, Grandfather. Come you from my parts?"

"I take it you're Lorskan, lad?" said the beard.

"Aye. My name was Döpueng Shysh. Here I go by Gezun of Gadaira."

"Say you so?" replied the oldster amiably. "I've known several of your clan. Are you the son of that cousin of Squire Tr'nu, that was stolen by Aremorian pirates a few years back?"

"The same. And you, sir?"

"I am Derezong Tâsh, sometime court wizard to King Vuar, until in one of his fits of caprice he decided that my head would look better without a body attached."

"You're a great man, sir."

"Oh, not at all," said Derezong, grinning smugly nevertheless. "Merely a poor refugee like yourself. Are you a free man at present?"

"Yes," said Gezun, conscious of the slave brand on his hand. "My master freed me in his will."

"Then why not return to Lorsk and your family?"

"I'd liefer return with fortune in hand, and meseems the Tartessian Empire offers wider opportunity. If you need an apprentice, I served the late Sancheth Sar, and so. . . ."

"Thank you, but I have an apprentice already and cannot afford another," said Derezong. "Howsomever, if you've but now arrived in Torrutseish and have not yet found lodging, you may use my poor place until you do."

Gezun poured out thanks, for this was just what he had been angling for. All this time, the Hesperian girl had trudged after Derezong without saying a word. Derezong turned to her and said in Lorskan:

"Now, my dear, tell us who *you* are."

She looked blank, as also when he repeated the question in Euskerian. When he finally asked it in bad Hesperian, she brightened and said that she was Yorida, the daughter of a baker of Sederado.

Derezong said to Gezun in Lorskan: "She'll make a fine concubine. In Mneset I had a most admirable harem of fourteen lovely concubines as well as numerous children and grandchildren. But alas, I had to quit the palace by lowering myself down the outer wall by a rope, wherefore my poor family had perforce to be abandoned. I only hope Vuar didn't slay the lot in pure spitefulness. Now that I begin to prosper once more, I've bought Yorida as the first step in collecting a new family. A wise proceeding, think you not?"

Gezun agreed with a forced smile. They reached Derezong's house, a small crumbly affair wedged between two much larger ones.

"A hovel, I grant," said Derezong, "but another year will see us in a better, I hope. Enter."

The door was opened by another Lorskan, a hard-faced fellow of about thirty and bigger than Gezun.

"My apprentice, Zhamel Se," said Derezong and introduced Gezun. Zhamel gave Gezun a scowl. Derezong asked Zhamel: "And what have you purchased for our dinner today?"

Gezun slipped out to find a stable where he could keep his mule. When he returned, he found Derezong's front room empty except for Zhamel, who was setting out drinking vessels and a jug of wine. Zhamel set down the jug, looked at Gezun, pulled out a knife big enough to split kindling, and began trimming his fingernails with it.

"A fine bit of bronze," he said. "I keep it sharp in case some young springald should try to worm himself into my place with Derezong."

"I understand," said Gezun, wondering if there were not some way by which he could safely murder Zhamel.

Then Derezong came out, leading Yorida in a servant's dress. The wizard dropped into the armchair and motioned for wine. When Zhamel had poured, Derezong raised his mug.

"To the windy plains of bison-swarming Lorsk!" he said. "Yorida looks more civilized now, does she not? Zhamel and I scrubbed her from top to toe. She bore such an accumulation of soil that you could almost have plowed it and raised a crop of barley thereon. Give the maid a drink too, Zhamel. You'll excuse this sour slop, Master Gezun, but I cannot yet afford the green wine of Zhysk. . . ."

The oldster babbled on, and drank, and babbled some more. Gezun, trying to keep up with him, soon found his head spinning. Several winecups later, Zhamel and Yorida disappeared into the back room to cook dinner.

"These Euskerians eat at uncanny hours," said Derezong. "Dinner in the dark of evening just before they go to bed. But my Lorskan stomach still insists upon its main meal by daylight. I wonder what detains those twain. Let's hope Zhamel casts not covetous eyes. . . ."

Derezong heaved himself out of the armchair and toddled back out of sight. There were voices, and then Yorida appeared to pick up the empty mugs.

Gezun got up from his stool. He had drunk enough to bring out his natural recklessness, albeit not enough to make him visibly unsteady.

"Yorida!" he said.

"Sir?"

"Harken, you don't wish to bed with old whitebeard, do you?" he said in Hesperian. "And scrub his floors and wash his shirts and haul water from the city wells?"

"Well, but what—"

"Come with me instead! I'm madly in love with you! I've burned for you ever since I saw you. We'll flee to the mountains and live as free lovers among the trees and flowers." He grabbed her wrist.

"But Master Gezun, I belong to him! I cannot—"

"Rubbish! The philosopher Goishek proves that every man's his own property. I'll show you life and love as they ought to be lived. Come on!"

Without waiting for further argument, Gezun caught up his saddle bags and dragged Yorida out Derezong's front door, then pell-mell along the street leading to the stable where Dostaen boarded.

"But my dinner!" wailed Yorida.

"What's food?" said Gezun. "I love you; what more do you want?"

Shortly afterward, Gezun's mule, restive under the double load, trotted across the wooden bridge that spanned the shallow northern arm of the Baitis. Gezun turned northeast toward the range of mountains that rose against the sky in olive-brown waves, sharply shadowed by the setting sun.

It was ten or twelve days later—Gezun was not sure which—when he went out to forage. He had learned in the course of his holiday that Euskeria harbored few edible wild plants. The only kind that he had found so far were chestnut trees, and they did not bear this early in the season. The sheep he had stolen had enough meat on it still for a couple more meals, but it was getting decidedly high. He did not dare to steal another lest the local shepherds get suspicious and hunt him down.

Furthermore, Yorida's complaints about the discomfort of the cave and the uncertainty of the food supply had become steadily more strident. The meadows might be carpeted with gorgeous wildflowers glistening with the morning dew, but the sight no longer sent Gezun off into poetical raptures. In fact, he looked upon them with dour resentment because he could not eat them.

He had, however, achieved one triumph, in making a workable bow. This had proved a long and complicated process, requiring most of his time for several days. He had to find a yew tree for the bowstave, and a lime tree whose bark could be twisted into string, and a dead crow for feathering, and so on.

As it was, he had no proper arrowheads. He would have to rely on blunt-headed stunning arrows, effective against birds and rabbits only, until he could grind down the bones of the sheep into piercing arrowheads.

He did not know if he could work up enough power to bring down a buck, or even a young aurochs. Still, it might be worth trying, provided that he were near enough to a tree to climb if an aurochs charged. He did not care to try to dodge, as Euskerian bullfighters dodged bulls in the arena.

After half a day's stalking, he brought down one rabbit. Coming back to his love nest, it occurred to him to sneak up on the cave from above, spy on Yorida, and then jump out and surprise her.

He made a long detour to keep out of her sight. He got lost and had to climb a hill to find himself again. At last he approached the cave from above. As he came out of a grove of pine that crested the hill, he heard voices and looked down the slope to see a group of men leading off Yorida.

"*Hé!*" he shouted and ran down the hill, leaping from rock to rock.

The men looked around. There was a flash of bronze as weapons came out.

"Let her go!" yelled Gezun, stopping to string his bow and nock an arrow.

One man held a big shield of hide up in front of him while the others crowded behind him. Gezun let fly. The arrow wobbled in flight, hit the shield, and bounced off.

The men laughed as they saw what sort of arrow it was. Somebody called a command. Leaving one man to hold Yorida, the others—four of them—started for Gezun at a trot. Two had swords and one a hunting spear. Gezun could not see how the fourth man was armed. He shot another arrow, hoping to hit one in the face, but the shot went wild and the men kept on.

Gezun, looking from one to the other, began backing up. As they neared, bronze rapiers ready, he turned and fled.

At least he could outrun them, being younger and longer of leg. He was speeding away from his pursuers when a distant cry from Yorida made him glance back:

"Gezun! Beware!"

The fourth man was whirling a sling. As Gezun looked, the slinger let fly. Gezun dropped flat, and the stone whizzed over him. He sprang up and ran on.

Before the slinger could wind up another missile, Gezun was out of his range, running swiftly towards the place where he had staked out his mule. As he ran he wept, partly from bereavement and partly from the rage of humiliation.

Lord Noish looked out over his company, surveying the scene as if he were a general overlooking a battlefield and hiding his thoughts behind a bland smile. The lords sat in a horseshoe, each on his silver-inlaid stool with the little table of mammoth ivory and ebony in front of him. The servants had cleared away the viands and set out wine cups, into which they were pouring the green wine of Zhysk. As Girios, Noish's head butler, approached the place at which sat Haldu the chief minister, he exchanged a quick look with his master.

Noish's smile broadened by the thickness of a hair, and he nodded ever so slightly. Girios poured wine into a new empty cup, although another cup, still half full, sat on the table before Lord Haldu. At Haldu's motion, the taster who crouched on the floor beside him took the newly-poured cup and drank a sip of it, then replaced it beside the old. By the time Haldu had drained the first cup the effect of the draft from the second, if any, would have manifested itself upon the taster.

A trumpet winded. A footman in the doorway cried: "The king!"

The Tartessian lords rose from their stools. As King Ikusiven appeared, everybody dropped to hands and knees and touched his forehead to the ground—even Lord Seindan, who had just finished vomiting into the vase that Noish had caused to be set out for those who drank too much.

"Rise, gentlemen," said the king, coming forward.

His armed guards crowded into the doorway, the lamplight gleaming softly on the gilded bronzen scales of their harness. Despite his padded robe and the extra soles on his shoes, it was plain that Ikusiven was a small man of spindly build. Lord Noish waved the king to the chair of pretence at the head of the horseshoe, which he himself had just vacated, and took another stool that Girios had ready.

"You may sit," said King Ikusiven. "We have been having fine weather, have we not?" His own slave poured his own wine into his own jeweled golden winecup and handed it to him.

"Excellent weather, sire," said Noish. "Although perhaps not so good as the year before last."

"As you say," said Ikusiven, scratching a flea bite. "We shall, however, need more rain for a good crop."

"Exactly, sire; we shall need more rain. Perhaps we should all pray to Roi?"

"A meritorious idea; I shall order special sacrifices to the heaven god. At least, this year is not so dry as last."

While this was going on, Lord Haldu turned to his taster, asking: "Any cramps?"

"No sir; it's good wine. My lone objection," continued

the taster, "is that you never let me drink a whole mug of this good stuff, but only a sip."

As he spoke, the taster's face took on a strained, unhappy look, as if he were trying not to speak but could not help himself. Haldu looked astonished, then laughed. He said:

"Here, you must have forgotten 'tis not the feast of fools. Girios, bring an extra winecup and fill it for my taster. He's but now rebelled against my inhuman treatment."

Lord Haldu then drank from the cup that the taster had just tested. King Ikusiven was saying:

"The worst weather in the memory of man was when I was a boy of ten."

"There is no possible doubt of that, sire," said Noish.

"It rained all spring, ruined the crops by flooding, and drowned many of the peasants' beasts. Which reminds me: I shall soon order a lion hunt in the valley of Jumbiar. The beasts have become very bold and destructive there."

"We shall all look forward to it most keenly," said Noish.

"No doubt. This time I will confine myself to the slaying of a single lion. As it is already established that I am the mightiest lion hunter in Tartessia, I feel I should allow the rest of you a chance at glory also."

"Of course, King Ikusiven," said Noish. "You are without doubt the greatest lion hunter of not only this but also of all ages. Is't not so, Haldu?"

Lord Haldu raised his head from his winecup. "That's what we say, although we know he is but a cowardly weakling who has never faced a live lion in his life."

Jaws dropped around the tables. Silence fell. King Ikusiven carefully set down his jeweled cup, leaned forward, and said:

"What said you, my lord? If that be a jest, I find it in most execrable taste."

Haldu's face now bore the same flushed, unhappy look that had overspread that of the taster. "No jest, sire. I did but speak what we all know: That your lion slaying has always been a fraud, since you have neither thews nor courage for such a feat."

Ikusiven's face now flushed, too, but with fury. He flung

down his personal winecup with such force that one of
the uncut jewels leaped from its socket and bounced
across the floor. Then he jumped to his feet and clapped
his hands. Everybody else perforce rose also.

The guards hastened into the room. Pointing at Haldu,
the king said:

"Take him! My minister, it seems, has gone mad, for
he has just vilely slandered and insulted me in the face
of all. It is the end of your favor, dog—"

The guards leaped upon Lord Haldu, who made no resistance but stammered: "S-sire! I meant no disrespect.
It's just that I cannot help speaking sooth—"

"Head him!" screamed the king.

The guards forced Haldu to his knees. A guard stepped
up, swung a great bronze blade, and cut off Haldu's head,
which rolled trickling across the floor while the spouting
body collapsed.

The guards carried out the remains—three carrying the
body and one the head—while the slaves mopped up
the blood. Ikusiven's servant had thoughtfully picked up the
king's winecup and refilled it. Ikusiven, pale and trembling, sank back into the armchair and took a big gulp
of wine. When he raised his eyes from his cup he said:

"Whether I have the courage to face a lion, I have it to
punish insolence and sedition, which is more to the point."

"As you say, sire," said Noish. He beckoned the musicians, who filed in and took their places, and signalled to
the keeper of the dancing bear to be ready to begin his
act.

"Noish," said the king, "Are you fain to succeed this
unfortunate madman as chief minister?"

Noish dropped to his knees, protesting his unworthiness
—but not protesting too hard.

Two days later, when Lord Noish was securely installed
in his new office, one of his servants announced a visitor:
Bokarri the wizard.

"Well?" said Noish, looking not at all jolly.

"Good morning, good my lord," said the small sorcerer.
"I see our plans have come to a most admirable fruition."

"Come to the point, my man. The business of the entire
empire waits upon my word, and I have no time to waste."

"Very well, great and good sir. I do but ask the fee due

me for my help in attaining your present celestial emi-
nence."

"How much?"

"A mere trifle for a god-on-earth like yourself. A thousand nasses of gold."

"Are you mad, fellow? All you did was refer me to that
savage. He's the one who merits the reward, not you."

"But sir, 'tis a well-established usage that the general
practitioner splits the fee evenly with the specialist."

"Then ask Zyc for your share of his fee. Now begone!"

Bokarri's voice rose. "Lord Noish! I demand justice! I'll
not quietly be bilked of my just due, though you be the
highest dignitary in Tartessia—"

"Porkedio!" shouted Noish. "Give this rogue a good drub-
bing and cast him forth. Slay him if he attempts to approach me again."

Gezun sat in the audience chamber of Bokarri the wizard, narrating his adventures: ". . . . so I came back to
search for her, for I cannot live without her. I have a post
as assistant beastkeeper in the royal gardens and, when
not bearing the animals' food in and ordure out, I inquire
after Yorida, but to no avail."

Gezun wiped away a tear. He had not told Bokarri how
he had stolen Yorida from Derezong in the first place.

Bokarri stroked his vulpine face—a face now surrounded
by bandages and discolored by bruises. "If I help you to
find this wench, what can you pay me? It's likely to be
a costly enterprise, and you strike me not as a youth of
caste or affluence."

Gezun slipped off his ring. "Here's a ring of star metal,
forged from the original Tahakh by the great wizard-smith,
Fekata of Gbu, which came down to my late master Sancheth Sar and was given by him to me. Examine it."

Bokarri scrutinized the dull-gray iron with glittering
eyes.

"Help me recover my sweetheart and you shall have it,"
said Gezun. "There's no room for haggling, because I know
its price full well, while on the other hand 'tis the only
thing of value I possess."

Bokarri turned the ring over a few times, then said:
"Done, if you'll leave the ring with me as surety. First

I must go into a trance and send my soul forth to seek Yorida."

The wizard lighted a little brazier in front of him, inhaled the smoke, and leaned back with his eyes closed. Gezun waited patiently and long. At last Bokarri roused himself, saying:

"She was taken by men of the household of Lord Noish, the new chief minister. Furthermore, it has come to me that tomorrow night this Noish means to deliver Yorida to Zyc the Hercynian for his own uses."

"Lyr's barnacles!" cried Gezun. "A Hercynian? He might even *eat* her!"

The fact was that Bokarri's trance was a fake. He already knew all about the bringing back to Torrutseish of Yorida by a squad of Noish's henchmen, and about Noish's plan to deliver her to Zyc. He knew, because Noish had besought him to find out where Yorida was, so that he could send his posse after her.

Bokarri was not a very competent magician, relying on spying and intrigue to make up for his lack of professional skill. But, in this case, his meager skill at divination had proved enough, and the flying squad had been sent right to the spot.

That, however, had been before Noish became chief minister. Now Bokarri bore a mortal grudge against Lord Noish because of the latter's refusal to pay his fee and the beating that he had received. Thus he was more than willing to help Gezun to snatch Yorida back. Still, however, he saw no reason for not squeezing the biggest possible fee from Gezun.

"That may be," he said calmly. "Now leave me whilst I consult the ghosts of my ancestors and the spirits of the elements. Return tomorrow at the hour of sunset, already fed; for we shall have a busy evening."

Gezun went. He hoped he was not being foolish in paying the wizard in advance, but the fellow would not work on any other terms. Gezun would have done the same if approached by an unknown like himself.

Bokarri, however, did not consult the ghosts of his ancestors or the spirits of the elements. Although he did control a small stable of spirits and demons, these were of almost no use to him. He had, by mistakes in ritual, allowed all the cleverer ones to escape from his control. The

feeble-minded collection remaining could seldom do anything for him that he could not do better himself.

Instead, he went to bed. Early next morning he called
upon Derezong, of whom he had heard as a rising new
wizard in Torrutseish. Since neither Gezun nor Noish had
mentioned Derezong to him, he did not know that Derezong was already involved in the fate of Yorida of Sederado. After the usual exchange of compliments, Bokarri
said:

"Good sir, I've come to you because your fame as a master illusionist fills Torrutseish, and the task I've undertaken calls for a skill along those lines exceeding my poor
own."

"You flatter me," said Derezong. "But what is your pro-
posal?"

"Well, there's a girl named Yorida. . . ." and Bokarri
went on to repeat what he knew of the young woman's past
and her precarious future. Although Derezong eyed him
sharply, Bokarri thought nothing of this.

"So," he concluded, "I must needs thwart this delivery
of Yorida to the bestial shaman tonight, and for this I need
your invincible help."

"Hm," said Derezong. "What's in this for me?"

"I'll pay a hundred nasses of pure gold." This, Bokarri
knew, was but a fraction of the value of Gezun's ring.

"How much is this Gezun paying you?"

"My most abject apologies, esteemed sir, but that I
can't tell you."

"Oh, well," said Derezong with a cherubic smile, "Your
tale has so touched my sympathies that I'll take your offer
without further chaffering."

So quick an acceptance startled Bokarri, who had expected a long and wearisome haggle. In fact, he wondered
uneasily whether there might not be more to Derezong's
interest in the case than met the eye. He could not, however, very well back out now.

That night, Gezun appeared as directed at Bokarri's
house. Bokarri told him:

"I'm sure that, within the next hour or two, Noish will
go from his house to the Tower of Kurtevan. I think he
and Yorida will each be carried in a separate litter, with

the usual escort of whifflers, probably passing along Turnip Street. I shall place you in a litter I've rented.

"When the leader of the gang of bearers sees my signal, he'll lead your litter down the Street of Silversmiths to the crossing of Turnip Street in time to foul Noish's procession. There'll be a fight, in which you shall take part. But, being outnumbered, you and the bearers will be driven off. Meanwhile, I'll snatch Yorida from her chair with the help of my magic."

Gezun said: "When Noish finds her gone, he'll have the city searched. Where will she be then?"

"On her way with you, I suppose."

"Whither shall I go?"

"Well, the Phaiaxians are said to be a civilized and hospitable people. Perhaps you could make a living among them."

Bokarri furnished Gezun with a stout cudgel and led him outside, where the bearers and the litter were waiting.

"Get in," said Bokarri. "Dzerhas knows where to go."

"But you?" said Gezun.

"I follow by another route. Obey my commands and all shall be well."

Doubtfully, Gezun climbed into the litter. He hit his head on the top, because the sedan chair had not been designed for Pusadian stature.

The prospect of starting out for unknown Phaiaxia, practically destitute and burdened by a girl, frightened him a little. Passionately as he yearned for Yorida, he was not sure that this would work. Having gone thus far, however, he did not feel like retreating.

The bearers hoisted the litter to their shoulders and jogged tirelessly through the darkness. They wound around corners and finally stopped. They stood in the dark, slapping mosquitoes, until Gezun climbed out to stretch his cramped limbs. One of their number, Gezun saw, had run ahead to a crossing. Gezun, however, was not familiar enough with the city to know where he was.

The bearers talked in low voices. Gezun learned that Dzerhas was a broken-down bullfighter with endless stories of his feats in the arena.

After a wearisome wait, the man who had gone ahead came running back. "The signal!" he said. "They come!"

"Which way?" asked Dzerhas.

"Down Turnip Street, as the wizard said."

Dzerhas turned to Gezun. "Get back in, sir, and quickly. We move."

Gezun climbed into the litter and was borne off, bouncing and swaying. Soon he heard voices ahead. They grew quickly louder, and the litter stopped. Lanthorn gleams came through the curtains. Dzerhas was shouting. The litter was set down with a bump.

Gripping his cudgel, Gezun squirmed out of the equipage to find himself in a street fight. His litter had been put down with the front shafts touching those of another and much more splendid litter approaching the same crossing from the left.

A big, fat man thrust a jowly, bald head out of this other sedan chair and shouted orders to his bearers, who seemed much more numerous than Gezun's group of five. Gezun soon saw the reason: that a second litter had been set down behind the first, and its bearers had run forward to reinforce their comrades.

There were also several tough-looking parties bearing clubs and wearing helmets and swords. A couple carried lanthorns on poles. By the feeble light of these, Gezun could see that all the fat man's retinue were dressed in tunics and kilts of the same pattern, black with red piping.

Fists and feet had begun to fly; blows and curses sounded. Gezun saw one of the black-and-red clad men knocked down by Dzerhas's staff. Bokarri's bearers, although fewer, had all come equipped with stout cudgels.

Gezun whooped and plunged into the fray, lashing about mightily with his stick. One of the helmeted men smashed at him with a cudgel. Gezun caught the blow on his own, and his return slash knocked the stick out of the smaller man's hand. The whiffler went for his sword. Before he could get it out, Gezun hit him on the head, knocking his helmet down over his eyes.

Before Gezun could finish his foe, a club struck his own head, filling the night with a blaze of stars. He staggered and struck blindly. His club thumped against something, and he stepped back to take his bearings.

Faces had begun to appear at doors and windows. Local people called back and forth to one another. One of the lanthorns was down and out. A man was down—

Gezun could not tell from which side—and another was crawling away on hands and knees.

Gezun struck a foe who came at him low with a knife, spinning the man half around into a huddle in the dirt. He rammed his stick into the belly of another and doubled the fellow up, took a nasty knock on his left arm, and realized that he was fighting almost alone. A glance showed that his men were falling back. Gezun, with swords coming at him, backed up, too, and ran with the rest.

Anon, Gezun and the bearers went back to the crossing. The place was now deserted but for one of their own crew, who lay there badly hurt. They placed the injured man in the abandoned litter and picked it up. Later, Gezun and his retinue arrived at the house of Bokarri.

Gezun knocked and identified himself. When he heard the bolt drawn back, he stepped in, followed by Dzerhas.

In the front room were Bokarri, Yorida, Zhamel, and Derezong. The last had just weighed out a hundred nasses of gold, in rings and ingots. These he was now dropping with musical tinkling sounds into a small buckskin bag. Bokarri said to Dzerhas:

"I'll weigh out the trade metal for you and your crew."

"Yorida!" exclaimed the confused Gezun. "And what do you here, Derezong?"

The Lorskan wizard smiled pinkly. "Recovering a piece of—ah—strayed property."

"But—but—how did you. . . ."

"Shortly after you and she eloped," said Derezong, "Noish's bully-boys invaded my house seeking her. Since she was not there to be found by the diligent search, I got rid of them by soft answers. So I bear you no ill-will; for, as things turned out, you saved her for me after all. Now, since it is late, Yorida and I will be getting home."

"What's this?" cried Gezun. "How got you Yorida from Lord Noish? I was too busy trading knocks to see."

"As to that," said Derezong, "whilst the attention of the minister and his rogues was directed upon you, Master Bokarri and I hauled the wench from the second litter. Then, lest our abduction be discovered inopportunely, I performed the incantation of Ansuan and cast a pinch of syr-powder, which formed a simulacrum of Yorida in the litter. We cut the cords that bound the authentic maid and hustled her away. I suppose that Noish has conveyed her double on to Kurtevan's Tower to present to Zyc. If so, there'll be more surprises this night. Come, child."

"Come nothing!" said Gezun. "She's mine!"

"By what right?" asked Derezong mildly, while Zhamel laid a hand upon his knife-hilt.

"By right of conquest. She loves me, and I'll fight to the death any wight who'd snatch her from me!"

"Be that true, my dear?" said Derezong to Yorida.

"It is not!" said Yorida.

"What?" shrieked Gezun.

"I said, it is not," repeated the girl. "You tore me away from Derezong's nice, comfortable house with its good food and soft cushions and carried me into the wild mountains, to live in a smelly old cave and sleep in the dirt, with nothing to eat but a stale loaf of barley bread and that tough old ram you killed. And all you did was talk about yourself, and make love to me three or four times a day until I was sore, and all the time I was too frightened to say anything for fear you'd slay me in a rage. Derezong is a nice, kind master who'll feed me well and won't want me oftener than once a week, and I'm glad to get back to him. So there."

"That," said Derezong, "would appear to be that. Good night, dear friends."

"Good night, noble sirs," said Dzerhas, following Derezong, Zhamel, and Yorida out.

Bokarri said: "You'd better get along, stripling, ere Lord Noish learns how he's been tricked."

"How will he know? It's Derezong has the wench, not I."

"But you were in the forefront of the battle, smiting down his minions scarce farther from him than I am from you. Think not that Noish, no fool, failed to mark your features."

Gezun said: "Hear: I gave you that ring in return for recovering Yorida. Now she hasn't been recovered, and I want it back."

"That her proper owner appeared to claim her is unfortunate for you, but affects our contract not. I found her as promised."

"Curse you! You know what I mean. You called Derezong into this enterprise; otherwise he need never have known."

"How was I to know he owned the girl? You told me nought. Anyway, she likes you not, from what little I could understand of her Hesperian gabble. Now pray excuse me, as I'm for bed."

"Give me that ring!"

"You shan't have it. Begone with you, boy!"

"Give it to me!"

"Out, knave, ere I cast a spell upon you! One—two—"

Gezun leaped forward and planted a large fist on Bokarri's jaw. The little wizard spun and staggered. Gezun followed him, punching and kicking. Bokarri cried out as Gezun slammed him into the wall. A woman's voice called from the back of the house.

Bokarri lay senseless against the wall, a trickle of blood running from his nose. Gezun tugged the ring of star metal off his finger, then glanced around. The wizard's strong box stood still on the floor, the key in the lock. Gezun opened the chest, swept up a handful of gold and silver and copper—rings, torcs, and little wedges shaped like axheads—and dropped the trade metal into his wallet. Footsteps sounded from the rear of the house.

Gezun hastened out the door, closed it softly behind him, and ran towards the stable in which his mule was kept.

Lord Noish's litter came up again to Zyc's gate. Again the upper shutter opened. The rumbling voice commanded:

"Lord Noish shall lead the maiden in; no others may enter."

Noish led the strangely silent Yorida in through the gate. To Noish's surprise, the girl did not even flinch as they passed the eight-foot Laistrugonian. Noish thought that she must be in some sort of a daze or trance.

Kumo conducted the pair in the door of the tower, and closed and bolted it behind them. Then he led them up the spiral stair to the second storey.

Zyc squatted nude among his cushions as before. This time he was not eating. The litter of gnawed bones had been cleaned up since Noish's previous visit. Zyc glared at Yorida with terrible eagerness, the whites of his eyes showing in a feverish gleam. His lips worked. Saliva drooled from his mouth.

"Ah," he said. "Lord Noish pay his debts, yes?"

"Aye," said Noish. "Here she is."

"Good. You go now."

"Now that I'm minister," said Noish, "perhaps we shall have further profitable dealings. I have an audacious plan—"

"Yes, yes; but you go now, quick." With an animal snarl, a half-roar, Zyc leaped up and hurled himself across the room upon Yorida, his teeth gleaming whitely.

As his clutching hands closed, however, the double of Yorida dissolved into a cloud of whitish powder, which drifted away and disappeared.

"*Arrr!*" roared Zyc. "Stop him, Kumo!"

The Laistrugonian already stood between Noish and the head of the stair towards which the nobleman was walking. At Zyc's shout, Noish turned around.

"*Hé!*" he cried. "What happened? She was real enough when we set out from my house. . . ."

"You fool Zyc, eh?" screamed the foaming shaman. "You no bring girl, you take place of her!"

Zyc started for Noish, who felt inside his tunic and drew a bronze dagger. As he raised his arm, however, his wrist was seized from behind by the Laistrugonian's huge hairy hand. Kumo easily twisted the wrist down, around, and up behind Noish's back until the dagger fell to the floor. Then he twisted farther until a joint gave with a snap.

Noish screamed with pain and horror. Kumo bit off Noish's right hand and began to chew it. Noish continued to scream as the staring eyes in his fat face saw Zyc approach him with gaping jaws.

Zyc tilted his head to one side, lunged, and snapped. Noish's shrieks were cut off as the Hercynian's teeth sank into his throat and met.

The sun was up when Gezun cleared the city of Tor-rutseish and trotted Dostaen out along the river road. He had lost much time in starting. First he had gone astray in the dark and had taken hours to find the stable. Then he had to rouse a grumbling stable master from bed to let his mule out. Then he had to find his way across the unfamiliar city to the east gate and wait for the gate to open for morning traffic.

Gezun had fretted sorely until he realized that Bokarri

could hardly have the law after him, because that would
mean appealing to the minister from whom he had just
helped to steal Yorida. Still and all, Noish himself might
have his agents out after him, so Gezun was glad to be
on his way.

Yorida? Pouf! What did he want with a girl who plainly
did not appreciate his virtues? Let her stay safe and
snug with Derezong; there were plenty more girls.

According to what Gezun had been told, if he kept on
up the Baitis to its headwaters, a bridle trail wound over
the mountains to the headwaters of the Anthemius. Thence
a road led down that stream to the land of Phaiaxia. Between his hard-won experience and the stake in trade metal
that he had taken from Bokarri, he should be able to
show the cultivated Phaiaxians a thing or two.

He burst into song as he rode.

FOR TEN thousand years did the Bright Empire of Melniboné flourish, ruling the world. Ten thousand years before history was recorded—or ten thousand years after history had ceased to be chronicled. For that span of time, reckon it how you will, the Bright Empire had thrived. Ravaged, at last, by the formless terror called Time, Melniboné fell, and newer nations succeeded her: Ilmiora, Sheegoth, Maidahk, S'aaleem. Then history began: India, China, Egypt, Assyria, Persia, Greece, and Rome—all these came after Melniboné. But none lasted ten thousand years.

And none dealt in the terrible mysteries, the secret sorceries of old Melniboné. None used such power or knew how. Only Melniboné ruled the earth for a hundred centuries—and then even she, shaken by the casting of frightful runes, attacked by powers greater than men—powers who decided that Melniboné's span of ruling had been overlong—crumbled, and her sons were scattered. They became wanderers across an earth that hated and feared them, siring few offspring, slowly dying, slowly forgetting the secrets of their mighty ancestors. Such a one was the cynical laughing Elric, a man of bitter brooding and gusty humor, proud prince of ruins, lord of a lost and humbled people; last son of Melniboné's sundered line of kings.

Elric, the moody-eyed wanderer—a lonely man who fought a world, living by his wits and his runesword Stormbringer. Elric, last lord of Melniboné, last worshiper of its grotesque and beautiful gods—reckless reaver and cynical slayer—torn by great griefs and with a knowledge locked in his skull that would turn lesser men into babbling idiots. Elric, moulder of madnesses, dabbler in wild delights, man of many contradictions: a frail albino given superhuman strength by his evil, sentient runesword; a man who willy-nilly becomes the focal point of the titanic struggle between the forces of Law and of Chaos to rule the world.

Michael Moorcock is a young Briton who has been a writer and an editor ever since his teens. The nine Elric novelettes, of which this is the fourth, appeared in the British magazine Science Fantasy and have been reprinted in two books published in Great Britain: The Stealer of Souls and Stormbringer. The second volume brings the story down to the final cosmic tragedy of Elric. Moorcock was not a little dismayed when a number of readers (including myself) insisted that of the nine stories they liked "Kings in Darkness" best, since it was the very story that the author himself liked least. All of which shows how much an author can depend upon his own judgment of his own works.

KINGS IN DARKNESS

● MICHAEL MOORCOCK

Three Kings in Darkness lie,
Gutheran of Org, and I,
Under a bleak and sunless sky—
The third beneath the Hill.
                    —Song of Veerkad

1.

IT was Elric, Lord of the lost and sundered Empire of Melniboné, who rode like a fanged wolf from a trap—all slavering madness and mirth. He rode from Nadsokor, City of Beggars, and there was hate in his wake. The citizens had judged him rightly for what he was—a nigromancer of superlative powers. Now they hounded him and also the grotesque little man who rode laughing at Elric's side; Moonglum the Outlander, from Elwher and the un-mapped East.

The flames of brands devoured the velvet of the night as the yelling, ragged throng pushed their bony nags in pursuit of the pair.

Starvelings and tattered jackals that they were, there was strength in their gaudy numbers, and long knives and bone bows glinted in the brandlight. They were too strong for a couple of men to fight, too few to represent serious danger in a hunt, so Elric and Moonglum had chosen to leave the city without dispute and now sped towards the full and rising moon, which stabbed its sickly beams through the darkness to show them the disturbing waters of the Varkalk River and a chance of escape from the incensed mob.

They had half a mind to stand and face the mob, since the Varkalk was their only alternative. But they knew well what the beggars would do to them, whereas they were uncertain what would become of them once they had entered the river. The horses reached the sloping banks of the Varkalk and reared, with hooves lashing.

Cursing, the two men spurred the steeds and forced them down towards the water. Into the river the horses plunged, snorting and spluttering. Into the river, which led a roaring course towards the hell-spawned Forest of Troos, which lay within the borders of Org, country of necromancy and rotting, ancient evil.

Elric blew water away from his mouth and coughed. "They'll not follow us to Troos, I think," he shouted at his companion.

Moonglum said nothing. He only grinned, showing his white teeth and the unhidden fear in his eyes. The horses swam strongly with the current, and behind them the ragged mob shrieked in frustrated blood-lust, while some of their number laughed and jeered.

"Let the forest do our work for us!"

Elric laughed back at them, wildly, as the horses swam on down the dark, straight river, wide and deep, towards a sun-starved morning, cold and spiky with ice. Scattered, slim-peaked crags loomed on either side of the flat plain, through which the river ran swiftly. Green-tinted masses of jutting blacks and browns spread colour through the rocks, and the grass was waving on the plain as if for some purpose. Through the dawnlight, the beggar crew chased along the banks, but eventually gave up their quarry to return, shuddering, to Nadsokor.

When they had gone, Elric and Moonglum made their mounts swim towards the banks and climb them, stumbling, to the top where rocks and grass had already given way to sparse forest land, which rose starkly on all sides, staining the earth with sombre shades. The foliage waved jerkily, as if alive—sentient.

It was a forest of malignantly erupting blooms, blood-coloured and sickly-mottled. A forest of bending, sinuously smooth trunks, black and shiny; a forest of spiked leaves of murky purples and gleaming greens—certainly an unhealthy place if judged only by the odour of rotting vegetation, which was almost unbearable, impinging as it did upon the fastidious nostrils of Elric and Moonglum.

Moonglum wrinkled his nose and jerked his head in the direction they had come. "Back now?" he enquired. "We can avoid Troos and cut swiftly across a corner of Org to be in Bakshaan in just over a day. What say you, Elric?"

Elric frowned. "I don't doubt they'd welcome us in Bakshaan with the same warmth we received in Nadsokor. They'll not have forgotten the destruction we wrought there—and the wealth we acquired from their merchants. No, I have a fancy to explore the forest a little. I have heard tales of Org and its unnatural forest and should like to investigate the truth of them. My blade and sorcery will protect us, if necessary."

Moonglum sighed. "Elric—this once, let us not court the danger."

Elric smiled icily. His scarlet eyes blazed out of his dead-white skin with peculiar intensity. "Danger? It can bring only death."

"Death is not to my liking, just yet," Moonglum said. "The fleshpots of Bakshaan, or if you prefer—Jadmar—on the other hand. . . ."

But Elric was already urging his horse onward, heading for the forest. Moonglum sighed and followed.

Soon dark blossoms hid most of the sky, which was dark enough, and they could see only a little way in all directions. The rest of the forest seemed vast and sprawling; they could sense this, though sight of most of it was lost in the depressing gloom.

Moonglum recognised the forest from descriptions he had heard from mad-eyed travellers who drank purposefully in the shadows of Nadsokor's taverns.

"This is the Forest of Troos, sure enough," he said to Elric. "It's told of how the Doomed Folk released tremendous forces upon the earth and caused terrible changes among men, beasts, and vegetation. This forest is the last they created, and the last to perish. They must have resented the planet giving them birth."

"A child will always hate its parents at certain times," Elric said impassively.

"Children of whom to be extremely wary, I should think," Moonglum retorted. "Some say that when they were at the peak of their power, they had no gods to frighten them."

"A daring people, indeed," Elric replied, with a faint smile. "They have my respect. But their lack of gods and fear was probably our downfall, if not theirs. Now fear and the gods are back, and that, at least, is comforting."

Moonglum puzzled over this for a short time, and then, eventually, said nothing.

He was beginning to feel uneasy.

The place was full of malicious rustlings and whispers, though no living animal inhabited it, as far as they could tell. There was a discomforting absence of birds, rodents, or insects; and, though they normally had no love for such creatures, they would have appreciated their company in the disconcerting forest.

In a quavering voice, Moonglum began to sing a song in the hope that it would keep his spirits up and his thoughts off the lurking forest.

"A grin and a word is my trade;
  From these, my profit is made.
  Though my body's not tall and my courage is small,
  My fame will take longer to fade."

So singing, with his natural amiability returning, Moonglum rode after the man he regarded as a friend—a friend who possessed something akin to mastery over the little man, though neither admitted it.

Elric smiled at Moonglum's song. "To sing of one's own lack of size and absence of courage is not an action designed to ward off one's enemies, Moonglum."

"But this way I offer no provocation," Moonglum replied glibly. "If I sing of my shortcomings, I am safe. If I were to boast of my talents, then someone might consider this to be a challenge and decide to teach me a lesson."

"True," Elric assented gravely, "and well-spoken."

He began pointing at certain blossoms and leaves, remarking upon their alien tint and texture, referring to them in words which Moonglum could not understand, though he knew the words to be part of a sorcerer's vocabulary. The albino seemed to be untroubled by the fears which beset the Eastlander; but often, Moonglum knew, appearances with Elric could hide the opposite of what they indicated.

They stopped for a short break while Elric sifted through some of the samples he had torn from trees and plants. He carefully placed his prizes in his belt-pouch but would say nothing of why he did so to Moonglum.

"Come," he said. "Troos's mysteries await us."

But then a new voice, a woman's, said softly from the gloom: "Save the excursion for another day, strangers."

Elric reined his horse, one hand at *Stormbringer's* hilt. The voice had had an unusual effect upon him. It had been low, deep and had, for a moment, sent the pulse in his throat throbbing. Incredibly, he sensed that he was suddenly standing on one of Fate's roads, but where the road would take him, he did not know. Quickly, he controlled his mind and then his body and looked towards the shadows from where the voice had come.

"You are very kind to offer us advice, madame," he said sternly. "Come, show yourself and give explanation. . . ."

She rode out then, very slowly, on a black-coated gelding that pranced with a power she could barely restrain. Moonglum drew an appreciative breath; for, although heavy-featured, she was incredibly beautiful. Her face and bearing were patrician, her eyes were grey-green, combining enigma and innocence. She was very young. For all her obvious womanhood and beauty, Moonglum aged her at seventeen or little more.

Elric frowned: "Do you ride alone?"

"I do now," she replied, trying to hide her obvious astonishment at the albino's weird lack of colouring. "I need aid—protection. Men who will escort me safely to Karlaak. There, they will be paid."

"Karlaak, by the Weeping Waste? It lies the other side of Ilmiora, a hundred leagues away and a week's travelling at speed." Elric did not wait for her to reply to this statement. "We are not hirelings, madame. We are noblemen in our own lands."

"Then you are bound by the vows of chivalry, sir, and cannot refuse my request."

Elric laughed shortly. "Chivalry, madame? We come not from the upstart nations of the South with their strange codes and rules of behaviour. We are nobles of older stock, whose actions are governed by our own desires. You would not ask what you do, if you knew our names."

She wetted her full lips with her tongue and said almost timidly: "You are . . . ?"

"Elric of Melniboné, madame, called Elric Womanslayer in the West, and this is Moonglum of Elwher; he has no conscience."

She gasped. "I have heard of you. There are stories—legends—the white-faced reaver, the hell-driven sorcerer with a blade that drinks the souls of men. . . ."

"Aye, that's true. And however magnified they are with the retelling, they cannot hint, those tales, at the darker truths which lie in their origin. Now, madame, do you still seek our aid?" Elric's voice was gentle, without menace, as he saw that she was very much afraid, although she had managed to control the signs of fear and her lips were tight with determination.

"I have no choice. I am at your mercy. My father, the Senior Senator of Karlaak, is very rich. Karlaak is called the City of the Jade Towers, as you will know, and such rare jades and ambers we have. Many could be yours."

"Be careful, madame, lest you anger me," warned Elric, although Moonglum's bright eyes lighted with avarice. "We are not nags to be hired or goods to be bought. Besides which," he smiled disdainfully, "I am from crumbling Imrryr, the Dreaming City, from the Isle of the Dragon, hub of Ancient Melniboné, and I know what beauty really is. Your baubles cannot tempt one who has looked upon the milky Heart of Arioch, upon the blinding iridescence that throbs from the Ruby Throne, upon the languorous and unnameable colours in the Actorios stone of the Ring of Kings. These are more than jewels, madame—they contain the life-stuff of the universe."

"I apologise, Lord Elric, and to you, Sir Moonglum."

Elric laughed, almost with affection. "We are grim clowns, lady; but the Gods of Luck aided our escape from Nadsokor, and we owe them a debt. We'll escort you to

Karlaak, City of the Jade Towers, and explore the Forest of Troos another time."

Her thanks was tempered with a wary look in her eyes.

"And now we have made introductions," said Elric, "perhaps you would be good enough to give your name and tell us your story."

"I am Zarozinia from Karlaak, a daughter of the Voashoon, the most powerful clan in Southeastern Ilmiora. We have kinsmen in the trading cities on the coasts of Pikarayd, and I went with two cousins and my uncle to visit them."

"A perilous journey, Lady Zarozinia."

"Aye, and there are not only natural dangers, sir. Two weeks ago we made our goodbyes and began the journey home. Safely we crossed the Straits of Vilmir and there employed men-at-arms, forming a strong caravan to journey through Vilmir and so to Ilmiora. We skirted Nadsokor, since we had heard that the City of Beggars is inhospitable to honest travellers. . . ."

Here, Elric smiled: "And sometimes to dishonest travellers, as we can appreciate."

Again the expression on her face showed that she had some difficulty in equating his obvious good humour with his evil reputation. "Having skirted Nadsokor," she continued, "we came this way and reached the borders of Org wherein, of course, Troos lies. Very warily we travelled, knowing dark Org's reputation, along the fringes of the forest. And then we were ambushed and our hired men-at-arms deserted us."

"Ambushed, eh?" broke in Moonglum. "By whom, madame, did you know?"

"By their unsavoury looks and squat shapes they seemed native Orgians. They fell upon the caravan, and my uncle and cousins fought bravely but were slain. One of my cousins slapped the rump of my gelding and sent it galloping so that I could not control it. I heard—terrible screams—mad, giggling shouts—and, when I at last brought my horse to a halt, I was lost. Later I heard you approach and waited in fear for you to pass, thinking you also were Orgians; but, when I heard your accents and some of your speech, I thought that you might help me."

"And help you we shall, madame," said Moonglum bowing gallantly from the saddle. "And I am indebted to you for convincing Lord Elric here of your need. But for you, we should be deep in this awful forest by now and experiencing strange terrors, no doubt. I offer my sorrow for your dead kinfolk and assure you that you will be protected from now onwards by more than words and brave hearts, for sorcery can be called up if needs be."

"Let's hope there'll be no need," frowned Elric. "You talk blithely of sorcery, friend Moonglum—you who hate me to use the art."

Moonglum grinned. "I was consoling the young lady, Elric. And I've had occasion to be grateful for your horrid powers, I'll admit. Now I suggest that we make camp for the night and so refreshed be on our way at dawn."

"I'll agree to that," said Elric, glancing almost with embarrassment at the girl. Again he felt the pulse in his throat begin to throb, and this time he had more difficulty in controlling it.

The girl also seemed fascinated by the albino. There was an attraction between them which might be strong enough to throw both their destinies along wildly different paths than any they had guessed.

Night came again quickly, for the days were short in those parts. While Moonglum tended the fire, nervously peering around him, Zarozinia, her richly embroidered cloth-of-gold gown shimmering in the firelight, walked gracefully to where Elric sat sorting the herbs he had collected. She glanced at him cautiously and then, seeing that he was absorbed, stared at him with open curiosity.

He looked up and smiled faintly, his eyes for once unprotected, his strange face frank and pleasant. "Some of these are healing herbs," he said, "and others are used in summoning spirits. Yet others give unnatural strength to the imbiber and some turn men mad. They will be useful to me."

She sat down beside him, her thick-fingered hands pushing her black hair back. Her full breasts lifted and fell rapidly.

"Are you really the terrible evil-bringer of the legends, Lord Elric? I find it hard to credit."

"I have brought evil to many places," he said, "but usually there has already been evil to match mine. I seek no excuses, for I know what I am and I know what I have done. I have slain malignant sorcerers and destroyed oppressors, but I have also been responsible for slaying fine men, and a woman, my cousin, whom I loved, I killed—or my sword did."

"And you are master of your sword?"

"Yes—perhaps. I often wonder. Without it, I am helpless." He put his hand around *Stormbringer's* hilt. "I should be grateful to it." Once again his red eyes seemed to become deeper, protecting some bitter emotion which was rooted at the core of his soul.

"I'm sorry if I revived unpleasant recollection. . . ."

"Do not feel sorry, Lady Zarozinia. The pain is within me—you did not put it there. In fact, I'd say you relieve it greatly by your presence."

Half-startled, she glanced at him and smiled. "I am no wanton, sir," she said, "but. . . ."

He got up quickly.

"Moonglum, is the fire going well?"

"Aye, Elric. She'll stay in for the night." Moonglum cocked his head on one side. It was unlike Elric to make such empty queries, but Elric said nothing further; so the Eastlander shrugged, turned away to check his gear.

Since he could think of little else to say, Elric turned and said quietly, urgently: "I'm a killer and a thief, not fit to. . . ."

"Lord Elric, I am. . . ."

"You are infatuated by a legend, that is all."

"No! If you feel what I feel, then you'll know it's more."

"You are young."

"Old enough."

"Beware. I must fulfill my destiny."

"Your destiny?"

"It is no destiny at all, but an awful thing called doom. And I have no pity at all except when I see something in my own soul. Then I have pity—and I pity. But I hate to look, and this is part of the doom which drives me. Not Fate, nor the Stars, nor Men, nor Demons, nor Gods. Look at me, Zarozinia—it is Elric, poor white chosen plaything of the Gods of Time—Elric of Melniboné who causes his own gradual and terrible destruction."

"It is suicide!"

"Aye. Suicide of a dreadful sinning kind, for I drive

myself to slow death. And those who go with me suffer also."

"You speak falsely, Lord Elric—from guilt-madness."

"Because I am guilty, Lady."

"And does Sir Moonglum go to doom with you?"

"He is unlike others—he is indestructible in his own self-assurance."

"I am confident, also, Lord Elric."

"But your confidence is that of youth; it is different."

"Need I lose it with my youth?"

"You have strength. You are as strong as we are. I'll grant you that."

She opened her arms, rising. "Then be reconciled, Elric of Melniboné."

And he was. He seized her greedily, kissed her with a deeper need than that of passion. For the first time, Cymoril of Imrryr was forgotten as they dropped to the soft turf, oblivious of Moonglum who polished away at his curved sword with wry jealousy.

They all slept and the fire waned.

Elric, in his joy, had forgotten, or not heeded, that he had a watch to take, and Moonglum, who had no source of strength but himself, stayed awake for as long as he could, but sleep overcame him.

In the shadows of the awful trees, figures moved with shambling caution.

The misshapen men of Org began to creep inwards towards the sleepers.

Then Elric opened his eyes, aroused by instinct, stared at Zarozinia's peaceful face beside him, moved his eyes without turning his head, and saw the danger. He rolled over, grasped *Stormbringer*, and tugged the runeblade from its sheath. The sword hummed, as if in anger at being awakened.

"Moonglum! Danger!" Elric bellowed in fear, for he had more to protect than his own life. The little man's head jerked up. His curved sabre was already across his knees, and he jumped to his feet, ran towards Elric as the Orgians closed in.

"I apologise," he said.

"My fault, I. . . ."

And then the Orgians were at them. Elric and Moonglum

stood over the girl as she came awake, saw the situation, and did not scream. Instead she looked around for a weapon but found none. She remained still, where she was —the only thing to do.

Smelling like offal, the gibbering Orgians, some of them, slashed at Elric and Moonglum with heavy blades like cleavers, long and dangerous.

Stormbringer whined and smote through a cleaver, cut into an Orgian's neck and beheaded him. Blood gurgled from the corpse as it slumped back across the fire. Moonglum ducked beneath a howling cleaver, lost his balance, fell, slashed at his opponent's legs, and hamstrung him so that he collapsed shrieking. Moonglum stayed on the ground and lunged upwards, taking another in the heart. Then he sprang to his feet and stood shoulder to shoulder with Elric while Zarozinia got up behind them.

"The horses," grunted Elric. "If it's safe, try to get them."

There were still seven Orgians standing, and Moonglum groaned as a cleaver sliced flesh from his left arm, retaliated, pierced the man's throat, turned slightly, and sheared off another's face. They pressed forward, taking the attack to the incensed Orgians. His left hand covered with his own blood, Moonglum painfully pulled his long poignard from its sheath and held it with his thumb along the handle, blocked an opponent's swing, closed in, and killed him with a ripping upward thrust of the dagger, the action of which caused his wound to pound with agony.

Elric held his great runesword in both hands and swung it in a semi-circle, hacking down the howling misshapen things. Zarozinia darted towards the horses, leaped onto her own, and led the other two towards the fighting men. Elric smote at another and got into his saddle, thanking his own forethought to leave the equipment on the horses in case of danger. Moonglum quickly joined him, and they thundered out of the clearing.

"The saddle-bags," Moonglum called in greater agony than that created by his wound. "We've left the saddle-bags!"

"What of it? Don't press your luck, my friend."

"But all our treasure's in them!"

Elric laughed, partly in relief, partly from real humour. "We'll retrieve them, friend, never fear."

"I know you, Elric. You've no value for the realities."

But even Moonglum was laughing as they left the enraged Orgians behind them and slowed to a canter.

Elric reached and hugged Zarozinia. "You have the courage of your noble clan in your veins," he said.

"Thank you," she replied, pleased with the compliment, "but we cannot match such swordsmanship as that displayed by you and Moonglum. It was fantastic."

"Thank the blade," he said shortly.

"No. I will thank you. I think you place too much reliance upon that hell weapon, however powerful it is."

"I need it."

"For what?"

"For my own strength and, now, to give strength to you."

"I'm no vampire," she smiled, "and need no such fearful strength as that supplies."

"Then be assured that I do," he told her gravely. "You would not love me if the blade did not give me what I need. I am like a spineless sea-thing without it."

"I do not believe that, but will not dispute with you now."

They rode for a while without speaking.

Later, they stopped, dismounted, and Zarozinia put herbs that Elric had given her upon Moonglum's wounded arm and began to bind it.

Elric was thinking deeply. The forest rustled with macabre, sensuous sounds. "We're in the heart of Troos," he said, "and our intention to skirt the forest has been forestalled. I have it in mind to call on the King of Org and so round off our visit."

Moonglum laughed. "Shall we send our swords along first? And bind our own hands?" His pain was already eased by the herbs, which were having quick effect.

"I mean it. We owe, all of us, much to the Orgians. They slew Zarozinia's uncle and cousins, they wounded you, and they now have our treasure. We have many reasons for asking the King for recompense. Also, they seem stupid and should be easy to trick."

"Aye. The king will pay us back for our lack of common-sense by tearing our limbs off."

"I'm in earnest. I think we should go."

"I agree that I'd like our wealth returned to us. But we cannot risk the lady's safety, Elric."

"I am to be Elric's wife, Moonglum. Therefore if he visits the King of Org, I shall come too."

Moonglum lifted an eyebrow. "A quick courtship."

"She speaks the truth, however. We shall all go to Org—and sorcery will protect us from the King's uncalled-for wrath."

"And still you wish for death and vengeance, Elric," shrugged Moonglum mounting. "Well, it's all the same to me, since your roads, whatever else, are profitable ones. You may be the Lord of Bad Luck by your own reckoning, but you bring good luck to me, I'll say that."

"No more courting death," smiled Elric, "but we'll have some revenge, I hope."

"Dawn will be with us soon," Moonglum said. "The Orgian citadel lies six hours' ride from here by my working, south-southeast by the Ancient Star, if the map I memorised in Nadsokor was correct."

"You have an instinct for direction that never fails, Moonglum. Every caravan should have such a man as you."

"We base an entire philosophy on the stars in Elwher," Moonglum replied. "We regard them as the master plan for everything that happens on Earth. As they revolve around the planet they see all things, past, present, and future. They are our gods."

"Predictable gods, at least," said Elric, and they rode off towards Org with light hearts, considering the enormity of their risk.

2.

Little was known of the tiny kingdom of Org, save that the Forest of Troos lay within its boundaries; and to that, other nations felt, it was welcome. The people were unpleasant to look upon, for the most part, and their bodies were stunted and strangely altered. Legend had it that they were the descendants of the Doomed Folk who had wrought such destruction upon the Earth an entire Time Cycle before. Their rulers, it was said, were shaped like normal men insofar as their outward bodily appearance went, but their minds were warped more horribly than the limbs of their subjects.

The inhabitants were few and were generally scattered, ruled by their king from his citadel, which was also called Org.

It was for this citadel that Elric and his companions rode; and, as they did so, Elric explained how he planned to protect them all from the Orgians.

In the forest he had found a particular leaf which, when used with certain invocations (which were harmless in that the invoker was in little danger of being harmed by the spirits he marshalled), would invest that person, and anyone else to whom he gave the drug distilled from the leaf, temporary invulnerability.

The spell somehow reknitted the skin and flesh structure so that it would withstand any edge and almost any blow. Elric explained, in a rare garrulous mood, how the drug and spell combined to achieve the effect, but his archaicisms and esoteric words meant little to the other two.

They stopped an hour's ride from where Moonglum expected to find the citadel so that Elric could prepare the drug and invoke the spell.

He worked swiftly over a small fire, using an alchemist's pestle and mortar, mixing the shredded leaf with a little water. As the brew bubbled on the fire, he drew peculiar runes on the ground, some of which were twisted into such alien forms that they seemed to disappear into a different dimension and reappear beyond it.

> "Bone and blood and flesh and sinew,
> Spell and spirit bind anew;
> Potent potion work the life charm,
> Keep its takers safe from harm."

So Elric chanted as a small pink cloud formed in the air over the fire, wavered, reformed into a spiral shape which curled downwards into the bowl. The brew spluttered and then was still. The albino sorcerer said: "An old boyhood spell, so simple that I'd near forgotten it. The leaf for the potion grows only in Troos, and therefore it is rarely possible to perform."

The brew, which had been liquid, had now solidified, and Elric broke it into small pellets. "Too much," he warned, "taken at one time is poison, and yet the effect can last for several hours. Not always, though, but we must accept that small risk." He handed both of them a pellet, which they received dubiously. "Swallow them just before we reach the citadel," he told them, "or in the event of the Orgians finding us first."

Then they mounted and rode on again.

Some miles to the southeast of Troos, a blind man sang a grim song in his sleep and so woke himself. . . .

They reached the brooding citadel of Org at dusk. Guttural, drooling voices shouted at them from the battlements of the square-cut ancient dwelling place of the Kings of Org. The thick rock oozed moisture and was corroded by lichen and sickly, mottled moss. The only entrance large enough for a mounted man to pass through was reached by a path almost a foot deep in evil-smelling black mud.

"What's your business at the Royal Court of Gutheran the Mighty?"

They could not see who asked the question.

"We seek hospitality and an audience with your liege," called Moonglum cheerfully, successfully hiding his nervousness. "We bring important news to Org."

A twisted face peered down from the battlements. "Enter, strangers, and be welcome," it said unwelcomingly.

The heavy wooden drawgate shifted upwards to allow them entrance, and the horses pushed their way slowly through the mud and so into the courtyard of the citadel.

Overhead, the grey sky was a racing field of black tattered clouds, which streamed towards the horizon as if to escape the horrid boundaries of Org and the disgusting Forest of Troos.

The courtyard was covered, though not so deeply, with the same foul mud as had impaired their progress to the citadel. It was full of heavy, unmoving shadow. On Elric's right, a flight of steps went up to an arched entrance which was hung, partially, with the same unhealthy lichen he had seen on the outer walls and, also, in the Forest of Troos.

Through this archway, brushing at the lichen with a pale, beringed hand, a tall man came and stood on the top step, regarding the visitors through heavy-lidded eyes. He was, in contrast to the other Orgians, handsome, with a massive, leonine head and long hair as white as Elric's; although the hair on the head of this great, solid man was somewhat dirty, tangled, unbrushed. He was dressed in a heavy jerkin of quilted, embossed leather, a yellow kilt which reached to his ankles; and he carried a wide-bladed dagger, naked in his belt. He was older than Elric, aged between forty and fifty, and his powerful if somewhat decadent face was seamed and pock-marked.

He stared at them in silence and did not welcome them; instead, he signed to one of the battlement guards, who caused the drawgate to be lowered. It came down with a crash, blocking off their way of escape.

"Kill the men and keep the woman," said the massive man in a low monotone. Elric had heard dead men speak in that manner.

As planned, Elric and Moonglum stood either side of Zarozinia and remained where they were, arms folded.

Puzzled, shambling Orgians came warily at them, their loose trousers dragging in the mud, their hands hidden by the long shapeless sleeves of their filthy garments. They swung their cleavers. Elric felt a faint shock as the blade thudded on to his arm, but that was all. Moonglum's experience was similar.

The Orgians fell back, amazement and confusion on their bestial faces.

The tall man's eyes widened. He put one ring-covered hand to his thick lips, chewing at a nail.

"Our swords have no effect upon them, King! They do not cut and they do not bleed. What are these folk?"

Elric laughed theatrically. "We are not common folk, little human, be assured. We are the messengers of the gods and come to your king with a message from our great masters. Do not worry, we shall not harm you, since we are in no danger of being harmed. Stand aside and make us welcome."

Elric could see that King Gutheran was puzzled and not absolutely taken in by his words. Elric cursed to himself. He had measured the Orgian's intelligence by those he had seen. This king, mad or not, was much more intelligent, was going to be harder to deceive. He led the way up the steps towards glowering Gutheran.

"Greetings, King Gutheran. The gods have, at last, returned to Org and wish you to know this."

"Org has had no gods to worship for an eternity," said Gutheran hollowly, turning back into the citadel. "Why should we accept them now?"

"You are impertinent, King."

"And you are audacious. How do I know you come from the gods?" He walked ahead of them, leading them through the low-roofed halls.

"You saw that the swords of your subjects had no effect upon us."

"True. I'll take that incident as proof for the moment. I suppose there must be a banquet in your—honour—I shall order it. Be welcome, messengers." His words were ungracious, but it was virtually impossible to detect anything from Gutheran's tone, since the man's voice stayed at the same pitch.

Elric pushed his heavy riding cloak back from his shoulders and said lightly: "We shall mention your kindness to our masters."

The Court was a place of gloomy halls and false laughter; and, although Elric put many questions to Gutheran, the king would not answer them, or did so by means of ambiguous phrases which meant nothing. They were not given chambers wherein they could refresh themselves but instead stood about for several hours in the main hall of the citadel; and Gutheran, while he was with them and not giving orders for the banquet, sat slumped on his throne and chewed at his nails, ignoring them.

"Pleasant hospitality," whispered Moonglum.

"Elric—how long will the effects of the drug last?" Zarozinia had remained close to him. He put his arm around her shoulders. "I do not know. Not much longer. But it has served its purpose. I doubt if they will try to attack us a second time. However, beware of other attempts, subtler ones, upon our lives."

The main hall, which had a higher roof than the others and was completely surrounded by a gallery, which ran around it well above the floor, fairly close to the roof, was chilly and unwarmed. No fires burned in the several hearths, which were open and let into the floor, and the walls dripped moisture and were undecorated; damp, solid stone, timeworn and gaunt. There were not even rushes upon the floor, which was strewn with old bones and pieces of decaying food.

"Hardly house-proud, are they?" commented Moonglum, looking around him with distaste and glancing at brooding Gutheran, who was seemingly oblivious of their presence.

A servitor shambled into the hall and whispered a few words to the king. He nodded and arose, leaving the Great Hall.

Soon men came in, carrying benches and tables, and began to place them about the hall.

The banquet was, at last, due to commence. And the air had menace in it.

The three visitors sat together on the right of the king, who had donned a richly jeweled chain of kingship, whilst his son and several pale-faced female members of the royal line sat on the left, unspeaking even among themselves.

Prince Hurd, a sullen-faced youth who seemed to bear a resentment against his father, picked at the unappetising food which was served them all.

He drank heavily of the wine, which had little flavour but was strong, fiery stuff, and this seemed to warm the company a little.

"And what do the gods want of us poor Orgians?" Hurd said, staring hard at Zarozinia with more than friendly interest.

Elric answered: "They ask nothing of you but your recognition. In return they will, on occasions, help you."

"That is all?" Hurd laughed. "That is more than those from the Hill can offer, eh, father?"

Gutheran turned his great head slowly to regard his son.

"Yes," he murmured, and the word seemed to carry warning.

Moonglum said: "The Hill—what is that?"

He got no reply. Instead, a high-pitched laugh came from the entrance to the Great Hall. A thin, gaunt man stood there staring ahead with a fixed gaze. His features, though emaciated, strongly resembled Gutheran's. He carried a stringed instrument and plucked at the gut so that it wailed and moaned with melancholy insistence.

Hurd said savagely: "Look, father, 'tis blind Veerkad, the minstrel, your brother. Shall he sing for us?"

"Sing?"

"Shall he sing his songs, father?"

Gutheran's mouth trembled and twisted, and he said after a moment: "He may entertain our guests with an heroic ballad if he wishes, but. . . ."

"But certain other songs he shall not sing . . ." Hurd grinned maliciously. He seemed to be tormenting his father deliberately in some way which Elric could not guess. Hurd shouted at the blind man: "Come, Uncle Veerkad—sing!"

"There are strangers present," said Veerkad hollowly above the wail of his own music. "Strangers in Org?"

Hurd giggled and drank more wine. Gutheran scowled and continued to tremble, gnawing at his nails.

Elric called: "We'd appreciate a song, minstrel."

"Then you'll have the song of the Three Kings in Darkness, strangers, and hear the ghastly story of the Kings of Org."

"No!" shouted Gutheran, leaping from his place, but Veerkad was already singing:

> "Three Kings in darkness lie,
> Gutheran of Org, and I,
> Under a bleak and sunless sky—
> The third beneath the Hill.
> When shall the third arise?
> Only when another dies. . . ."

"Stop!" Gutheran got up in an obviously insane rage and stumbled across the table, trembling in terror, his face blanched, striking at the blind man, his brother. Two blows and the minstrel fell, slumping to the floor and not moving. "Take him out! Do not let him enter again." The king shrieked and foam flecked his lips.

Hurd, sober for a moment, jumped across the table, scattering dishes and cups and took his father's arm.

"Be calm, father. I have a new plan for our entertainment."

"You! You seek my throne. 'Twas you who goaded Veerkad to sing his dreadful song. You know I cannot listen without. . . ." He stared at the door. "One day the legend shall be realised and the Hill-King shall come. Then shall I, you, and Org perish."

"Father," Hurd was smiling horribly, "let the female visitor dance for us a dance of the gods."

"What?"

"Let the woman dance for us, father."

Elric heard him. By now the drug must have worn off. He could not afford to show his hand by offering his companions further doses. He got to his feet.

"What sacrilege do you speak, Prince?"

"We have given you entertainment. It is the custom in Org for our visitors to give us entertainment also."

The hall was electric with menace. Elric regretted his plan to trick the Orgians, now. But there was nothing he could do. He had intended to exact tribute from them in the name of the gods, but obviously these madmen feared more immediate and tangible dangers than any the gods might represent.

He had made a mistake, put the lives of his friends in danger as well as his own, What should he do? Zarozinia murmured:

"I have learned dances in Ilmiora, where all ladies are taught the art. Let me dance for them. It might placate them and bedazzle them to make our work easier."

"Arioch knows our work is hard enough now. I was a fool to have conceived this plan. Very well, Zarozinia, dance for them, but with caution." He shouted at Hurd: "Our companion will dance for you, to show you the beauty that the gods create. Then you must pay the tribute, for our masters grow impatient."

"The tribute?" Gutheran looked up. "You mentioned nothing of tribute."

"Your recognition of the gods must take the form of precious stones and metals, King Gutheran. I thought you to understand that."

"You seem more like common thieves than uncommon messengers, my friends. We are poor in Org and have nothing to give away to charlatans."

"Beware of your words, King!" Elric's clear voice echoed warningly through the hall.

"We'll see the dance and then judge the truth of what you've told us."

Elric seated himself, grasped Zarozinia's hand beneath the table as she arose, giving her comfort.

She walked gracefully and confidently into the centre of the hall and there began to dance. Elric, who loved her, was amazed at her splendid grace and artistry. She danced the old, beautiful dances of Ilmiora, entrancing even the thick-skulled Orgians; and, as she danced, a great golden Guest Cup was brought in.

Hurd leaned across his father and said to Elric: "The Guest Cup, Lord. It is our custom that our guests drink from it in friendship."

Elric nodded, annoyed at being disturbed in his watching of the wonderful dance, his eyes fixed on Zarozinia as she postured and glided. There was silence in the hall.

Hurd handed him the cup and absently he put it to his lips. Seeing this Zarozinia danced on to the table and began to weave along it to where Elric sat. As he took the first sip, Zarozinia cried out and, with her foot, knocked the cup from his hand. The wine splashed on to Gutheran and Hurd who half rose, startled. "It was drugged, Elric. They drugged it!"

Hurd lashed at her with his hand, striking her across the face. She fell from the table and lay moaning slightly on the filthy floor. "Bitch! Would the messengers of the gods be harmed by a little drugged wine?"

Enraged, Elric pushed aside Gutheran and struck savagely at Hurd so that the young man's mouth gushed blood. But the drug was already having effect. Gutheran shouted something and Moonglum drew his sabre, glancing upwards. Elric was swaying; his senses were jumbled, and the scene had an unreal quality. He saw servants grasp Zarozinia but could not see how Moonglum was faring. He felt sick and dizzy, could hardly control his limbs.

Summoning up his last remaining strength, Elric clubbed Hurd down with one tremendous blow. Then he collapsed into unconsciousness.

3.

There was the cold clutch of chains about his wrists, and a thin drizzle was falling directly on to his face, which stung where Hurd's nails had ripped it.

He looked about him. He was chained between two stone menhirs upon an obvious burial barrow of gigantic

size. It was night, and a pale moon hovered in the heavens
above him. He looked down at the group of men below.
Hurd and Gutheran were among them. They grinned at
him mockingly.

"Farewell, messenger. You will serve us a good purpose
and placate the Ones from the Hill!" Hurd called as he and
the others scurried back towards the citadel, which lay, silhouetted, a short distance away.

Where was he? What had happened to Zarozinia—and
Moonglum? Why had he been chained thus upon—realisa-
tion and remembrance came—*the Hill!*

He shuddered, helpless in the strong chains which held
him. Desperately he began to tug at them, but they would
not yield. He searched his brain for a plan, but he was
confused by torment and worry for his friends' safety. He
heard a dreadful scuttling sound from below and saw a
ghastly white shape dart into the gloom. Wildly he struggled in the rattling iron which held him.

In the Great Hall of the citadel, a riotous celebration was
now reaching the state of an ecstatic orgy. Gutheran and
Hurd were totally drunk, laughing insanely at their victory.

Outside the Hall, Veerkad listened and hated. Particularly he hated his brother, the man who had deposed and
blinded him to prevent his study of sorcery, by means of
which he had planned to raise the King from Beneath the
Hill.

"The time has come, at last," he whispered to himself
and stopped a passing servant.

"Tell me—where is the girl kept?"

"In Gutheran's chamber, master."

Veerkad released the man and began to grope his way
through the gloomy corridors up twisting steps, until he
reached the room he sought. Here he produced a key, one
of many he'd had made without Gutheran's knowing, and
unlocked the door.

Zarozinia saw the blind man enter and could do nothing. She was gagged and bound with her own dress and
still dazed from the blow Hurd had given her. They had
told her of Elric's fate, but Moonglum had so far escaped
them; guards hunted him even now in the stinking corridors of Org.

"I've come to take you to your companion, lady," smiled blind Veerkad. Grasping her roughly with strength that his insanity had given him, he picked her up and fumbled his way towards the door. He knew the passages of Org perfectly, for he had been born and grown up among them.

But two men were in the corridor outside Gutheran's chamber. One of them was Hurd, Prince of Org, who resented his father's appropriation of the girl and desired her for himself. He saw Veerkad bearing the girl away and stood silent while his uncle passed.

The other man was Moonglum, who observed what was happening from the shadows where he had hidden from the searching guards. As Hurd followed Veerkad, on cautious feet, Moonglum followed him.

Veerkad went out of the citadel by a small side door and carried his living burden towards the looming Burial Hill.

All about the foot of the monstrous barrow swarmed the leprous-white ghouls who sensed the presence of Elric, the Orgians' sacrifice to them.

Now Elric understood.

These were the things the Orgians feared more than the gods. These were the living-dead ancestors of those who now revelled in the Great Hall. Perhaps these were actually the Doomed Folk. Was that their doom? Never to rest? Never to die? Just to degenerate into mindless ghouls? Elric shuddered.

Now desperation brought back his memory.

He cried to Arioch, the Demon God of Melniboné, and his voice was an agonised wail to the brooding sky and the pulsing earth.

"Arioch! Destroy the stones. Save your servant! Arioch—master—aid me!"

It was not enough. The ghouls gathered together and began to scuttle, gibbering, up the barrow towards the helpless albino.

"*Arioch! These are the things that would forsake your memory! Aid me to destroy them!*"

The earth trembled and the sky became overcast, hiding the moon but not the white-faced, bloodless ghouls, who were now almost upon him.

And then a ball of fire formed in the sky above him and

the very sky seemed to shake and sway around it. Then, with a roaring crash, two bolts of lightning slashed down, pulverising the stones and releasing Elric.

He got to his feet, knowing that Arioch would demand his price, as the first ghouls reached him.

He did not retreat, but in his rage and desperation leapt among them, smashing and flailing with the lengths of chain. The ghouls fell back and fled, gibbering in fear and anger, down the hill and into the barrow.

Elric could now see that there was a gaping entrance to the barrow below him; black against the blackness. Breathing heavily, he found that his belt pouch had been left him. From it he took a length of slim, gold wire and began frantically to pick at the locks of the manacles.

Veerkad chuckled to himself, and Zarozinia, hearing him, was almost mad with terror. He kept drooling the words into her ear: "When shall the third arise? Only when another dies. When that other's blood flows red—we'll hear the footfalls of the dead. You and I, we shall resurrect him and such vengeance will he wreak upon my cursed brother. Your blood, my dear, it will be that released him." He felt that the ghouls were gone and judged them placated by their feast. "Your lover has been useful to me," he laughed as he began to enter the barrow. The smell of death almost overpowered the girl as the blind madman bore her downwards into the heart of the Hill.

Hurd, sobered after his walk in the colder air, was horrified when he saw where Veerkad was going; the barrow, the Hill of the King, was the most feared spot in the land of Org. Hurd paused before the black entrance and turned to run. Then, suddenly, he saw the form of Elric, looming huge and bloody, descending the barrow slope, cutting off his escape.

With a wild yell he fled into the Hill passage.

Elric had not previously noticed the prince, but the yell startled him, and he tried to see who had given it but was too late. He began to run down the steep incline towards the entrance of the barrow. Another figure came scampering out of the darkness.

"Elric! Thank the stars and all the Gods of Earth! You live!"

"Thank Arioch, Moonglum. Where's Zarozinia?"

"In there—the mad minstrel took her with him and Hurd followed. They are all insane, these kings and princes; I see no sense to their actions."

"I have an idea that the minstrel means Zarozinia no good. Quickly, we must follow."

"By the stars, the stench of death! I have breathed nothing like it—not even at the great battle of the Eshmir Valley where the armies of Elwher met those of Tararn Gashtek, Lord of the Mounted Hordes, and half-a-million corpses strewed the valley from end to end."

"If you've no stomach. . . ."

"I wish I had none. It would not be so bad. Come. . . ."

They rushed into the passage, led by the far-away sounds of Veerkad's maniacal laughter and the somewhat nearer movements of a fear-maddened Hurd, who was now trapped between two enemies and yet more afraid of a third.

Hurd blundered along in the blackness, sobbing to himself in his terror.

In the weirdly phosphorescent Central Tomb, surrounded by the mummified corpses of his ancestors, Veerkad chanted the resurrection ritual before the great coffin of the Hill-King—a giant thing, half as tall again as Veerkad, who was tall enough. Veerkad was forgetful for his own safety and thinking only of vengeance upon his brother Gutheran. He held a long dagger over Zarozinia, who lay huddled and terrified upon the ground near the coffin.

The spilling of Zarozinia's blood would be the culmination of the ritual and then—

Then Hell would, quite literally, be let loose. Or so Veerkad planned. He finished his chanting and raised the knife just as Hurd came screeching into the Central Tomb with his own sword drawn. Veerkad swung round, his blind face working in thwarted rage.

Savagely, without stopping for a moment, Hurd ran his sword into Veerkad's body, plunging the blade in up to the hilt so that its bloody point appeared sticking from his back. But the other, in his groaning death spasms, locked his hands about the prince's throat. Locked them immovably.

Somehow, the two men retained a semblance of life and, struggling with each other in a macabre death-dance, swayed about the glowing chamber. The coffin of the Hill-King began to tremble and shake slightly, the movement hardly perceptible.

So Elric and Moonglum found Veerkad and Hurd. Seeing that both were near dead, Elric raced across the Central Tomb to where Zarozinia lay, unconscious, mercifully, from her ordeal. Elric picked her up and made to return.

He glanced at the throbbing coffin.

"Quickly, Moonglum. That blind fool has invoked the dead, I can tell. Hurry, my friend, before the hosts of Hell are upon us."

Moonglum gasped and followed Elric as he ran back towards the cleaner air of night.

"Where to now, Elric?"

"We'll have to risk going back to the citadel. Our horses are there and our goods. We need the horses to take us quickly away, for I fear there's going to be a terrible bloodletting soon if my instinct is right."

"There should not be too much opposition, Elric. They were all drunk when I left. That was how I managed to evade them so easily. By now, if they continued drinking as heavily as when last I saw them, they'll be unable to move at all."

"Then let's make haste."

They left the Hill behind them and began to run towards the citadel.

4.

Moonglum had spoken truth. Everyone was lying about the Great Hall in drunken sleep. Open fires had been lit in the hearths, and they blazed, sending shadows skipping around the Hall. Elric said softly:

"Moonglum, go with Zarozinia to the stables and prepare our horses. I will settle our debt with Gutheran first." He pointed. "See, they have heaped their booty upon the table, gloating in their apparent victory."

Stormbringer lay upon a pile of burst sacks and saddle-bags, which contained the loot stolen from Zarozinia's uncle and cousins and from Elric and Moonglum.

Zarozinia, now conscious but confused, left with Moonglum to locate the stables; and Elric picked his way towards the table, across the sprawled shapes of drunken Orgians, around the blazing fires, and caught up, thankfully, his hell-forged runeblade.

Then he leaped over the table and was about to grasp Gutheran, who still had his fabulously gemmed chain of kingship around his neck, when the great doors of the Hall crashed open and a howling blast of icy air sent the torches dancing and leaping. Elric turned, Gutheran forgotten, and his eyes widened.

Framed in the doorway stood the King from beneath the Hill.

The long-dead monarch had been raised by Veerkad, whose own blood had completed the work of resurrection. He stood in rotting robes, his fleshless bones covered by tight, tattered skin. His heart did not beat, for he had none; he drew no breath, for his lungs had been eaten by the creatures which feasted on such things. But, horribly, he lived. . . .

The King from the Hill. He had been the last great ruler of the Doomed Folk who had, in their fury, destroyed half the Earth and created the Forest of Troos. Behind the dead King crowded the ghastly hosts who had been buried with him in a legendary past.

The massacre began!

What secret vengeance was being reaped, Elric could only guess at—but whatever the reason, the danger was still very real.

Elric pulled out *Stormbringer* as the awakened horde vented their anger upon the living. The Hall became filled with the shrieking, horrified screams of the unfortunate Orgians. Elric remained, half-paralysed in his horror, beside the throne. Aroused, Gutheran woke up and saw the King from the Hill and his host. He screamed, almost thankfully:

"At last I can rest!"

And fell dying in a seizure, robbing Elric of his vengeance.

Veerkad's grim song echoed in Elric's memory. The Three Kings in Darkness—Gutheran, Veerkad, and the King from beneath the Hill. Now only the last lived—and he had been dead for millennia.

The King's cold, dead eyes roved the Hall and saw Gutheran sprawled upon his throne, the ancient chain of office still about his throat. Elric wrenched it off the body and backed away as the King from beneath the Hill advanced. And then his back was against a pillar and there were feasting ghouls everywhere else.

The dead King came nearer and then, with a whistling moan which came from the depths of his decaying body, launched himself at Elric, who found himself fighting desperately against the Hill-King's clawing, abnormal strength, cutting at flesh that neither bled nor suffered pain. Even the sorcerous runeblade could do nothing against this horror that had no soul to take and no blood to let.

Frantically, Elric slashed and hacked at the Hill-King, but ragged nails raked his flesh and teeth snapped at his throat. And above everything came the almost overpowering stench of death as the ghouls, packing the Great Hall with their horrible shapes, feasted on the living and the dead.

Then Elric heard Moonglum's voice calling and saw him upon the gallery which ran around the Hall. He held a great oil jar.

"Lure him close to the central fire, Elric. There may be a way to vanquish him. Quickly, man, or you're finished!"

In a frantic burst of energy, the Melnibonéan forced the giant king towards the flames. Around them, the ghouls fed off the remains of their victims, some of whom still lived, their screams calling hopelessly over the sound of carnage.

The Hill-King now stood, unfeeling, with his back to the leaping central fire. He still slashed at Elric. Moonglum hurled the jar.

It shattered upon the stone hearth, spraying the King with blazing oil. He staggered, and Elric struck with his full power, the man and the blade combining to push the Hill-King backwards. Down went the King into the flames and the flames began to devour him.

A dreadful, lost howling came from the burning giant as he perished.

Flames licked everywhere throughout the Great Hall, and soon the place was like Hell itself, an inferno of licking fire through which the ghouls ran about, still feasting, unaware of their destruction. The way to the door was blocked.

Elric stared around him and saw no way of escape—save one.

Sheathing *Stormbringer*, he ran a few paces and leaped upwards, just grasping the rail of the gallery as flames engulfed the spot where he had been standing.

Moonglum reached down and helped him to clamber across the rail.

"I'm disappointed, Elric," he grinned, "you forgot to bring the treasure."

Elric showed him what he grasped in his left hand—the jewel-encrusted chain of kingship.

"This bauble is some reward for our hardships," he smiled, holding up the glittering chain. "I stole nothing, by Arioch! There are no kings left in Org to wear it! Come, let's join Zarozinia and get our horses."

They ran from the gallery as masonry began to crash downwards into the Great Hall.

They rode fast away from the halls of Org and, looking back, saw great fissures appear in the walls and heard the roar of destruction as the flames consumed everything that had been Org. They destroyed the seat of the monarchy, the remains of the Three Kings in Darkness, the present and the past. Nothing would be left of Org save an empty burial mound and two corpses, locked together, lying where their ancestors had lain for centuries in the Central Tomb. They destroyed the last link with the previous Time Cycle and cleansed the Earth of an ancient evil. Only the dreadful Forest of Troos remained to mark the coming and the passing of the legendary Doomed Folk.

And the Forest of Troos was a warning.

Weary and yet relieved, the three saw the outlines of Troos in the distance, behind the blazing funeral pyre.

And yet, in his happiness, Elric had a fresh problem on his mind now that danger was past.

"Why do you frown now, love?" asked Zarozinia.

"Because I think you spoke the truth. Remember you said I placed too much reliance on my runeblade here?"

"Yes—and I said I would not dispute with you."

"Agreed. But I have a feeling that you were partially right. On the burial mound and in it I did not have *Stormbringer* with me—and yet I fought and won, because I feared for your safety." His voice was quiet. "Perhaps, in time, I can keep my strength by means of certain herbs I found in Troos and dispense with the blade forever?"

Moonglum shouted with laughter hearing these words. "Elric—I never thought I'd witness this. You daring to think of dispensing with that foul weapon of yours! I don't know if you ever shall, but the thought is comforting."

"It is, my friend, it is." He leaned in his saddle and grasped Zarozinia's shoulders, pulling her dangerously towards him as they galloped without slackening speed. And as they rode he kissed her, heedless of their pace.

"A new beginning!" he shouted above the wind. "A new beginning, my love!"

And then they all rode laughing towards Karlaak by the Weeping Waste, to present themselves, to enrich themselves, and to attend the strangest wedding the Northern Lands had ever witnessed. For it would be more than a marriage between the awful evil-bringer of legends and a senator's youthful daughter—it would be a marriage between the dark wisdom of the Ancient World and the bright hope of the New.

And who could tell what such a combination would bring about?

The Earth would soon know, for Elric of Melniboné was the maker of legends and there were legends yet to make!

IN THE OLD age of the earth, the moon was an almost forgotten memory. The dull-red sun drifted towards the gray horizon like an old man creeping to his death bed. The earth itself was falling into decay. In the crumbling cities, the remnants of humanity gave themselves up to music, merriment, and revelry. In the encroaching forests, weirdly mutated creatures lurked. Sorcery was the only knowledge worth pursuing—and it was pursued, with dire effects. The only limitation on a sorcerer's power was the fact that spells were very difficult to memorize—an ordinary mind could encompass two or three at a time; a trained mind, five or six—and, once a spell was used, all recollection of it vanished until the magician committed it once more to memory.

The greatest of all empires of that age was Grand Motham, whose four kingdoms stretched inland from the Melantine Gulf almost to the unnamed ocean to the east, beyond the Maurenon Mountains. Largest of these four kingdoms was Ascolais, bounded to the north and east by the Land of the Falling Wall, to the south by Almery, and to the southeast by the Ide of Kauchique. The chief city of Ascolais was Kaiin, the White City, half in ruins, lying at the foot of the Porphiron Scar where the swift Derna emptied into the Melantine Gulf. Here in these days of the dying earth, the subjects of Prince Kandive the Golden cruised in their flower-laden barges, feasted in echoing halls whose frescoes and bas-reliefs had been almost obliterated by time, and wandered off to make love in the shadows of endless, torchlit gardens. But outside the cities was life of another kind: swift, brutal, and deadly. . . .

Jack Vance, a Californian, has for many years been a leading writer of science and mystery fiction. He practices a formidable array of avocations, including ceramics, cornet playing, and (with two colleagues) building and sailing a houseboat. As a young man serving a four-year hitch in the merchant marine, he wrote a series of loosely-linked novelettes in the setting I have just described. In 1950 these tales were published in a paperbacked book, The Dying Earth. This edition appeared but briefly on the stands and was long the subject of a desperate search by connoisseurs. More recently The Dying Earth has been reprinted by Lancer Books. "Mazirian the Magician" is one of the first two stories in the collection. Vance hopes eventually to write more tales in this setting.

139

MAZIRIAN
THE MAGICIAN

• JACK VANCE

DEEP in thought, Mazirian the Magician walked his garden. Trees fruited with many intoxications overhung his path, and flowers bowed obsequiously as he passed. An inch above the ground, dull as agates, the eyes of mandrakes followed the tread of his black-slippered feet. Such was Mazirian's garden—three terraces growing with strange and wonderful vegetations. Certain plants swam with changing iridescences; others held up blooms pulsing like sea-anemones, purple, green, lilac, pink, yellow. Here grew trees like feather parasols, trees with transparent trunks threaded with red and yellow veins, trees with foliage like metal foil, each leaf a different metal—copper, silver, blue tantalum, bronze, green iridium. Here blooms like bubbles tugged gently upward from glazed green leaves, there a shrub bore a thousand pipe-shaped blossoms, each whistling softly to make music of the ancient Earth, of the ruby-red sunlight, water seeping through black soil, the languid winds. And beyond the roqual hedge the trees of the forest made a tall wall of mystery. In this waning hour of Earth's life no man could count himself familiar with the glens, the glades, the dells and deeps, the secluded clearings, the ruined pavilions, the sun-dappled pleasaunces, the gullies and heights, the various brooks, freshets, ponds, the meadows, thickets, brakes, and rocky outcrops.

Mazirian paced his garden with a brow frowning in thought. His step was slow and his arms were clenched be-

141

hind his back. There was one who had brought him puzzlement, doubt, and a great desire: a delightful woman-creature who dwelt in the woods. She came to his garden half-laughing and always wary, riding a black horse with eyes like golden crystals. Many times had Mazirian tried to take her; always her horse had borne her from his varied enticements, threats, and subterfuges.

Agonized screaming jarred the garden. Mazirian, hastening his step, found a mole chewing the stalk of a plant-animal hybrid. He killed the marauder, and the screams subsided to a dull gasping. Mazirian stroked a furry leaf and the red mouth hissed in pleasure.

Then: "K-k-k-k-k-k-k," spoke the plant. Mazirian stooped, held the rodent to the red mouth. The mouth sucked, the small body slid into the stomach-bladder underground. The plant gurgled, eructated, and Mazirian watched with satisfaction.

The sun had swung low in the sky, so dim and red that the stars could be seen. And now Mazirian felt a watching presence. It would be the woman of the forest, for thus had she disturbed him before. He paused in his stride, feeling for the direction of the gaze.

He shouted a spell of immobilization. Behind him the plant-animal froze to rigidity and a great green moth wafted to the ground. He whirled around. There she was, at the edge of the forest, closer than ever she had approached before. Nor did she move as he advanced. Mazirian's young-old eyes shone. He would take her to his manse and keep her in a prison of green glass. He would test her brain with fire, with cold, with pain, and with joy. She should serve him with wine and make the eighteen motions of allurement by yellow lamp-light. Perhaps she was spying on him; if so, the Magician would discover immediately, for he could call no man friend and had forever to guard his garden.

She was but twenty paces distant—then there was a thud and pound of black hooves as she wheeled her mount and fled into the forest.

The Magician flung down his cloak in rage. She held a guard—a counter-spell, a rune of protection—and always she came when he was ill-prepared to follow. He peered into the murky depths, glimpsed the wanness of her body flitting through a shaft of red light, then black shade and she was gone. . . . Was she a witch? Did she come of her own volition, or—more likely—had an enemy sent her to deal him inquietude? If so, who might be guiding her? There was Prince Kandive the Golden, of Kaiin, whom Mazirian had bilked of his secret of renewed youth. There was Azvan the Astronomer, there was Turjan—hardly Turjan, and here Mazirian's face lit in a pleasing recollection. . . . He put the thought aside. Azvan, at least, he could test. He turned his steps to his workshop, went to a table where rested a cube of clear crystal, shimmering with a red and blue aureole. From a cabinet he brought a bronze gong and a silver hammer. He tapped on the gong and the mellow tone sang through the room and out, away and beyond. He tapped again and again. Suddenly Azvan's face shone from the crystal, beaded with pain and great terror.

"Stay the strokes, Mazirian!" cried Azvan. "Strike no more on the gong of my life!"

Mazirian paused, his hand poised over the gong.

"Do you spy on me, Azvan? Do you send a woman to regain the gong?"

"Not I, Master, not I. I fear you too well."

"You must deliver me the woman, Azvan; I insist."

"Impossible, Master! I know not who or what she is!"

Mazirian made as if to strike. Azvan poured forth such a torrent of supplication that Mazirian with a gesture of disgust threw down the hammer and restored the gong to its place. Azvan's face drifted slowly away, and the fine cube of crystal shone blank as before.

Mazirian stroked his chin. Apparently he must capture the girl himself. Later, when black night lay across the forest, he would seek through his books for spells to guard him through the unpredictable glades. They would be poignant corrosive spells, of such a nature that one would daunt the brain of an ordinary man and two render him mad. Mazirian, by dint of stringent exercise, could encompass four of the most formidable, or six of the lesser spells.

He put the project from his mind and went to a long vat bathed in a flood of green light. Under a wash of clear fluid lay the body of a man, ghastly below the green glare, but of great physical beauty. His torso tapered from wide shoulders through lean flanks to long strong legs and arched feet; his face was clean and cold with hard flat features. Dusty golden hair clung about his head.

Mazirian stared at the thing, which he had cultivated from a single cell. It needed only intelligence, and this he knew not how to provide. Turjan of Miir held the knowledge, and Turjan—Mazirian glanced with a grim narrowing of the eyes at a trap in the floor—refused to part with his secret.

Mazirian pondered the creature in the vat. It was a perfect body; therefore might not the brain be ordered and pliant? He would discover. He set in motion a device to draw off the liquid, and presently the body lay stark to the direct rays. Mazirian injected a minim of drug into the neck. The body twitched. The eyes opened, winced in the glare. Mazirian turned away the projector.

Feebly the creature in the vat moved its arms and feet, as if unaware of their use. Mazirian watched intently: perhaps he had stumbled on the right synthesis for the brain.

"Sit up!" commanded the Magician.

The creature fixed its eyes upon him, and reflexes joined muscle to muscle. It gave a throaty roar and sprang from the vat at Mazirian's throat. In spite of Mazirian's strength it caught him and shook him like a doll.

For all Mazirian's magic he was helpless. The mesmeric spell had been expended, and he had none other in his brain. In any event he could not have uttered the space-twisting syllables with that mindless clutch at his throat.

His hand closed on the neck of a leaden carboy. He swung and struck the head of his creature, which slumped to the floor.

Mazirian, not entirely dissatisfied, studied the glistening body at his feet. The spinal coordination had functioned well. At his table he mixed a white potion, and, lifting the golden head, poured the fluid into the lax mouth. The creature stirred, opened its eyes, propped itself on its elbows. The madness had left its face—but Mazirian sought in vain for the glimmer of intelligence. The eyes were as vacant as those of a lizard.

The Magician shook his head in annoyance. He went to the window, and his brooding profile was cut black against the oval panes. . . . Turjan once more? Under the most dire inquiry Turjan had kept his secret close. Mazirian's thin mouth curved wryly. Perhaps if he inserted another angle in the passage. . . .

The sun had gone from the sky and there was dimness in Mazirian's garden. His white night-blossoms opened and their captive gray moths fluttered from bloom to bloom. Mazirian pulled open the trap in the floor and descended stone stairs. Down, down, down. . . . At last a passage intercepted at right angles, lit with the yellow light of eternal lamps. To the left were his fungus beds, to the right a stout oak and iron door, locked with three locks. Down and ahead the stone steps continued, dropping into blackness. Mazirian unlocked the three locks, flung wide the door. The room within was bare except for a stone pedestal supporting a glass-topped box. The box measured a yard on a side and was four or five inches high. Within the box— actually a squared passageway, a run with four right angles—moved two small creatures, one seeking, the other evading. The predator was a small dragon with furious red eyes and a monstrous fanged mouth. It waddled along the passage on six splayed legs, twitching its tail as it went. The other stood only half the size of the dragon—a strong-featured man, stark naked, with a copper fillet binding his long black hair. He moved slightly faster than his pursuer, which still kept relentless chase, using a measure of craft, speeding, doubling back, lurking at the angle in case the man should unwarily step around. By holding himself continually alert, the man was able to stay beyond the reach of the fangs. The man was Turjan, whom Mazirian by trickery had captured several weeks before, reduced in size, and thus imprisoned.

Mazirian watched with pleasure as the reptile sprang upon the momentarily relaxing man, who jerked himself clear by the thickness of his skin. It was time, Mazirian thought, to give both rest and nourishment. He dropped panels across the passage, separating it into halves, isolating man from beast. To both he gave meat and pannikins of water.

Turjan slumped in the passage.

"Ah," said Mazirian, "you are fatigued. You desire rest?"

Turjan remained silent, his eyes closed. Time and the world had lost meaning for him. The only realities were the gray passage and the interminable flight. At unknown intervals came food and a few hours rest.

"Think of the blue sky," said Mazirian, "the white stars, your castle Miir by the river Derna; think of wandering free in the meadows."

The muscles at Turjan's mouth twitched.

"Consider, you might crush the little dragon under your heel."

Turjan looked up. "I would prefer to crush your neck, Mazirian."

Mazirian was unperturbed. "Tell me, how do you invest your vat creatures with intelligence? Speak, and you go free."

Turjan laughed, and there was madness in his laughter.

"Tell you? And then? You would kill me with hot oil in a moment."

Mazirian's thin mouth drooped petulantly.

"Wretched man, I know how to make you speak. If your mouth were stuffed, waxed and sealed, you would speak! Tomorrow I take a nerve from your arm and draw coarse cloth along its length."

The small Turjan, sitting with his legs across the passageway, drank his water and said nothing.

"Tonight," said Mazirian with studied malevolence, "I add an angle and change your run to a pentagon."

Turjan paused and looked up through the glass cover at his enemy. Then he slowly sipped his water. With five angles there would be less time to evade the charge of the monster, less of the hall in view from one angle.

"Tomorrow," said Mazirian, "you will need all your agility." But another matter occurred to him. He eyed Turjan speculatively. "Yet even this I spare you if you assist me with another problem."

"What is your difficulty, febrile Magician?"

"The image of a woman-creature haunts my brain, and I would capture her." Mazirian's eyes went misty at the thought. "Late afternoon she comes to the edge of my garden riding a great black horse—you know her, Turjan?"

"Not I, Mazirian." Turjan sipped his water.

Mazirian continued. "She has sorcery enough to ward away Felojun's Second Hypnotic Spell—or perhaps she has some protective rune. When I approach, she flees into the forest."

"So then?" asked Turjan, nibbling the meat Mazirian had provided.

"Who may this woman be?" demanded Mazirian, peering down his long nose at the tiny captive.

"How can I say?"

"I must capture her," said Mazirian abstractedly: "What spells, what spells?"

Turjan looked up, although he could see the Magician only indistinctly through the cover of glass.

"Release me, Mazirian, and on my word as a Chosen Hierarch of the Maram-Or, I will deliver you this girl."

"How would you do this?" asked the suspicious Mazirian.

"Pursue her into the forest with my best Live Boots and a headful of spells."

"You would fare no better than I," retorted the Magician. "I give you freedom when I know the synthesis of your vat-things. I myself will pursue the woman."

Turjan lowered his head that the Magician might not read his eyes.

"And as for me, Mazirian?" he inquired after a moment.

"I will treat with you when I return."

"And if you do not return?"

Mazirian stroked his chin and smiled, revealing fine white teeth. "The dragon could devour you now, if it were not for your cursed secret."

The Magician climbed the stairs. Midnight found him in his study, poring through leather-bound tomes and untidy portfolios. . . . At one time a thousand or more runes, spells, incantations, curses, and sorceries had been known. The reach of Grand Motholam—Ascolais, the Ide of Kauchique, Almery to the South, the Land of the Falling Wall to the East—swarmed with sorcerers of every description, of whom the chief was the Arch-Necromancer Phandaal. A hundred spells Phandaal personally had formulated—though rumor said that demons whispered at his ear when he wrought magic. Pontecilla the Pious, then ruler of Grand Motholam, put Phandaal to torment, and after a terrible night, he killed Phandaal and outlawed sorcery throughout the land. The wizards of Grand Motholam fled like beetles under a strong light; the lore was dispersed and forgotten, until now, at this dim time, with the sun dark, wilderness obscuring Ascolais, and the white city Kaiin half in ruins, only a few more than a hundred spells remained to the knowledge of man. Of these, Mazirian had access to seventy-three, and gradually, by stratagem and negotiation, was securing the others.

Mazirian made a selection from his books and with great effort forced five spells upon his brain: Phandaal's Gyrator, Felojun's Second Hypnotic Spell, The Excellent Prismatic Spray, The Charm of Untiring Nourishment, and The Spell of the Omnipotent Sphere. This accomplished, Mazirian drank wine and retired to his couch.

The following day, when the sun hung low, Mazirian went to walk in his garden. He had but short time to wait. As he loosened the earth at the roots of his moon-geraniums a soft rustle and stamp told that the object of his desire had appeared.

She sat upright in the saddle, a young woman of exquisite configuration. Mazirian slowly stooped, as not to startle her, put his feet into the Live Boots and secured them above the knee.

He stood up. "Ho, girl," he cried, "you have come again. Why are you here of evenings? Do you admire the roses? They are vividly red because live red blood flows in their petals. If today you do not flee, I will make you the gift of one."

Mazirian plucked a rose from the shuddering bush and advanced toward her, fighting the surge of the Live Boots. He had taken but four steps when the woman dug her knees into the ribs of her mount and so plunged off through the trees.

Mazirian allowed full scope to the life in his boots. They gave a great bound, and another, and another, and he was off in full chase.

So Mazirian entered the forest of fable. On all sides mossy boles twisted up to support the high panoply of leaves. At intervals shafts of sunshine drifted through to lay carmine blots on the turf. In the shade long-stemmed flowers and fragile fungi sprang from the humus; in this ebbing hour of Earth nature was mild and relaxed.

Mazirian in his Live Boots bounded with great speed through the forest; yet the black horse, running with no strain, stayed easily ahead.

For several leagues the woman rode, her hair flying behind like a pennon. She looked back and Mazirian saw the face over her shoulder as a face in a dream. Then she bent forward; the golden-eyed horse thundered ahead and soon was lost to sight. Mazirian followed by tracing the trail in the sod.

The spring and drive began to leave the Live Boots, for they had come far and at great speed. The monstrous leaps became shorter and heavier, but the strides of the horse, shown by the tracks, were also shorter and slower. Presently Mazirian entered a meadow and saw the horse, riderless, cropping grass. He stopped short. The entire expanse of tender herbiage lay before him. The trail of the horse leading into the glade was clear, but there was no trail leaving. The woman therefore had dismounted somewhere behind—how far he had no means of knowing. He walked toward the horse, but the creature shied and bolted through the trees. Mazirian made one effort to follow, and discovered that his Boots hung lax and flaccid—dead.

He kicked them away, cursing the day and his ill-fortune. Shaking the cloak free behind him, a baleful tension shining on his face, he started back along the trail.

In this section of the forest, outcroppings of black and green rock, basalt and serpentine, were frequent—forerunners of the crags over the River Derna. On one of these rocks Mazirian saw a tiny man-thing mounted on a dragonfly. He had skin of a greenish cast; he wore a gauzy smock and carried a lance twice his own length.

Mazirian stopped. The Twk-man looked down stolidly.

"Have you seen a woman of my race passing by, Twk-man?"

"I have seen such a woman," responded the Twk-man after a moment of deliberation.

"Where may she be found?"

"What may I expect for the information?"

"Salt—as much as you can bear away."

The Twk-man flourished his lance. "Salt? No. Liane the Wayfarer provides the chieftain Dandanflores salt for all the tribe."

Mazirian could surmise the services for which the bandit-troubadour paid salt. The Twk-men, flying fast on their dragon-flies, saw all that happened in the forest.

"A vial of oil from my telanxis blooms?"

"Good," said the Twk-man. "Show me the vial."

Mazirian did so.

"She left the trail at the lightning-blasted oak lying a little before you. She made directly for the river valley, the shortest route to the lake."

Mazirian laid the vial beside the dragon-fly and went off toward the river oak. The Twk-man watched him go, then dismounted and lashed the vial to the underside of the dragon-fly, next to the skein of fine harl the woman had given him thus to direct Mazirian.

The Magician turned at the oak and soon discovered the trail over the dead leaves. A long open glade lay before him, sloping gently to the river. Trees towered to either side, and the long sundown rays steeped one side in blood, left the other deep in black shadow. So deep was the shade that Mazirian did not see the creature seated on a fallen tree; and he sensed it only as it prepared to leap on his back.

Mazirian sprang about to face the thing, which subsided again to sitting posture. It was a Deodand, formed and featured like a handsome man, finely muscled, but with a dead black lusterless skin and long slit eyes.

"Ah, Mazirian, you roam the woods far from home," the black thing's soft voice rose through the glade.

The Deodand, Mazirian knew, craved his body for meat. How had the girl escaped? Her trail led directly past.

"I come seeking, Deodand. Answer my questions, and I undertake to feed you much flesh."

The Deodand's eyes glinted, flitting over Mazirian's body. "You may in any event, Mazirian. Are you with powerful spells today?"

"I am. Tell me, how long has it been since the girl passed? Went she fast, slow, alone or in company? Answer, and I give you meat at such time as you desire."

The Deodand's lips curled mockingly. "Blind Magician! She has not left the glade." He pointed, and Mazirian followed the direction of the dead black arm. But he jumped back as the Deodand sprang. From his mouth gushed the syllables of Phandaal's Gyrator Spell. The Deodand was jerked off his feet and flung high in the air, where he hung whirling, high and low, faster and slower, up to the tree-tops, low to the ground. Mazirian watched with a half-smile. After a moment he brought the Deodand low and caused the rotations to slacken.

"Will you die quickly or slow?" asked Mazirian. "Help me and I kill you at once. Otherwise you shall rise high where the pelgrane fly."

Fury and fear choked the Deodand.

"May dark Thial spike your eyes! May Kraan hold your living brain in acid!" And it added such charges that Mazirian felt forced to mutter countercurses.

"Up then," said Mazirian at last, with a wave of his hand. The black sprawling body jerked high above the treetops to revolve slowly in the crimson bask of setting sun. In a moment a mottled bat-shaped thing with hooked snout swept close and its beak tore the black leg before the crying Deodand could kick it away. Another and another of the shapes flitted across the sun.

"Down, Mazirian!" came the faint call. "I tell what I know."

Mazirian brought him close to earth.

"She passed alone before you came. I made to attack her but she repelled me with a handful of thyle-dust. She went to the end of the glade and took the trail to the river. This trail leads also past the lair of Thrang. So is she lost, for he will sate himself on her till she dies."

Mazirian rubbed his chin. "Had she spells with her?"

"I know not. She will need strong magic to escape the demon Thrang."

"Is there anything else to tell?"

"Nothing."

"Then you may die." And Mazirian caused the creature to revolve at ever greater speed, faster and faster, until there was only a blur. A strangled wailing came and presently the Deodand's frame parted. The head shot like a bullet far down the glade; arms, legs, viscera flew in all directions.

Mazirian went his way. At the end of the glade the trail led steeply down ledges of dark green serpentine to the River Derna. The sun had set and shade filled the valley. Mazirian gained the riverside and set off downstream toward a far shimmer known as Sanra Water, the Lake of Dreams.

An evil odor came to the air, a stink of putrescence and filth. Mazirian went ahead more cautiously, for the lair of Thrang the ghoul-bear was near, and in the air was the feel of magic—strong brutal sorcery his own more subtle spells might not contain.

The sound of voices reached him, the throaty tones of Thrang and gasping cries of terror. Mazirian stepped around a shoulder of rock, inspected the origin of the sounds.

Thrang's lair was an alcove in the rock, where a fetid pile of grass and skins served him for a couch. He had built a rude pen to cage three women, these wearing many bruises on their bodies and the effects of much horror on their faces. Thrang had taken them from the tribe that dwelt in silk-hung barges along the lake-shore. Now they watched as he struggled to subdue the woman he had just captured. His round gray man's face was contorted, and he tore away her jerkin with his human hands. But she held away the great sweating body with an amazing dexterity. Mazirian's eyes narrowed. Magic, magic!

So he stood watching, considering how to destroy Thrang with no harm to the woman. But she spied him over Thrang's shoulder.

"See," she panted, "Mazirian has come to kill you."

Thrang twisted about. He saw Mazirian and came charging on all fours, venting roars of wild passion. Mazirian later wondered if the ghoul had cast some sort of spell, for a strange paralysis strove to bind his brain. Perhaps the spell lay in the sight of Thrang's raging gray-white face, the great arms thrust out to grasp.

Mazirian shook off the spell, if such it were, and uttered a spell of his own, and all the valley was lit by streaming darts of fire, lashing in from all directions to spit Thrang's blundering body in a thousand places. This was the Excellent Prismatic Spray—many-colored stabbing lines. Thrang was dead almost at once, purple blood flowing from countless holes where the radiant rain had pierced him.

But Mazirian heeded little. The girl had fled. Mazirian saw her white form running along the river toward the lake and took up the chase, heedless of the piteous cries of the three women in the pen.

The lake presently lay before him, a great sheet of water whose further rim was but dimly visible. Mazirian came down to the sandy shore and stood seeking across the dark face of Sanra Water, the Lake of Dreams. Deep night with only a verge of afterglow ruled the sky, and stars glistened on the smooth surface. The water lay cool and still, tideless as all Earth's waters had been since the moon had departed the sky.

Where was the woman? There, a pale white form, quiet in the shadow across the river. Mazirian stood on the riverbank, tall and commanding, a light breeze ruffling the cloak around his legs.

"Ho, girl," he called. "It is I, Mazirian, who saved you from Thrang. Come close, that I may speak to you."

"At this distance I hear you well, Magician," she replied. "The closer I approach the farther I must flee."

"Why then do you flee? Return with me and you shall be mistress of many secrets and hold much power."

She laughed. "If I wanted these, Mazirian, would I have fled so far?"

"Who are you then that you desire not the secrets of magic?"

"To you, Mazirian, I am nameless, lest you curse me. Now I go where you may not come." She ran down the shore, waded slowly out till the water circled her waist, then sank out of sight. She was gone.

Mazirian paused indecisively. It was not good to use so many spells and thus shear himself of power. What might exist below the lake? The sense of quiet magic was there, and though he was not at enmity with the Lake Lord, other beings might resent a trespass. However, when the figure of the girl did not break the surface, he uttered the Charm of Untiring Nourishment and entered the cool waters.

He plunged deep through the Lake of Dreams, and as he stood on the bottom, his lungs at ease by virtue of the charm, he marveled at the fey place he had come upon. Instead of blackness a green light glowed everywhere, and the water was but little less clear than air. Plants undulated to the current, and with them moved the lake flowers, soft with blossoms of red, blue and yellow. In and out swam large-eyed fish of many shapes.

The bottom dropped by rocky steps to a wide plain where trees of the underlake floated up from slender stalks to elaborate fronds and purple water-fruits, and so till the misty wet distance veiled all. He saw the woman, a white water nymph now, her hair like dark fog. She half-swam, half-ran across the sandy floor of the water-world, occasionally looking back over her shoulder. Mazirian came after, his cloak streaming out behind.

He drew nearer to her, exulting. He must punish her for leading him so far. . . . The ancient stone stairs below his work-room led deep and at last opened into chambers that grew ever vaster as one went deeper. Mazirian had found a rusted cage in one of these chambers. A week or two locked in the blackness would curb her willfulness. And once he had dwindled a woman small as his thumb and kept her in a little glass bottle with two buzzing flies. . . .

A ruined white temple showed through the green. There were many columns, some toppled, some still upholding the pediment. The woman entered the great portico under the shadow of the architrave. Perhaps she was attempting to elude him; he must follow closely. The white body glimmered at the far end of the nave, swimming now over the rostrum and into a semi-circular alcove behind.

Mazirian followed as fast as he was able, half-swimming, half-walking through the solemn dimness. He peered across the murk. Smaller columns here precariously upheld a dome from which the keystone had dropped. A sudden fear smote him, then realization as he saw the flash of movement from above. On all sides the columns toppled in, and an avalanche of marble blocks tumbled at his head. He jumped frantically back.

The commotion ceased, the white dust of the ancient mortar drifted away. On the pediment of the main temple the woman kneeled on slender knees, staring down to see how well she had killed Mazirian.

She had failed. Two columns, by sheerest luck, had crashed to either side of him, and a slab had protected his body from the blocks. He moved his head painfully. Through a chink in the tumbled marble he could see the woman, leaning to discern his body. So she would kill him? He, Mazirian, who had already lived more years than he could easily reckon? So much more would she hate and fear him later. He called his charm, the Spell of the Omnipotent Sphere. A film of force formed around his body, expanding to push aside all that resisted. When the marble ruins had been thrust back, he destroyed the sphere, regained his feet, and glared about for the woman. She was almost out of sight, behind a brake of long purple kelp, climbing the slope to the shore. With all his power he set out in pursuit.

T'sain dragged herself up on the beach. Still behind her came Mazirian the Magician, whose power had defeated each of her plans. The memory of his face passed before her and she shivered. He must not take her now.

Fatigue and despair slowed her feet. She had set out with but two spells, the Charm of Untiring Nourishment and a spell affording strength to her arms—the last permitting her to hold off Thrang and tumble the temple upon Mazirian. These were exhausted; she was bare of protection; but, on the other hand, Mazirian could have nothing left.

Perhaps he was ignorant of the vampire-weed. She ran up the slope and stood behind a patch of pale, wind-beaten grass. And now Mazirian came from the lake, a spare form visible against the shimmer of the water.

She retreated, keeping the innocent patch of grass between them. If the grass failed—her mind quailed at the thought of what she must do.

Mazirian strode into the grass. The sickly blades became sinewy fingers. They twined about his ankles, holding him in an unbreakable grip, while others sought to find his skin.

So Mazirian chanted his last spell—the incantation of paralysis, and the vampire grass grew lax and slid limply to earth. T'sain watched with dead hope. He was now close upon her, his cloak flapping behind. Had he no weakness? Did not his fibers ache, did not his breath come short? She whirled and fled across the meadow, toward a grove of black trees. Her skin chilled at the deep shadows, the somber frames. But the thud of the Magician's feet was loud. She plunged into the dread shade. Before all in the grove awoke she must go as far as possible.

Snap! A thong lashed at her. She continued to run. Another and another—she fell. Another great whip and another beat at her. She staggered up, and on, holding her arms before her face. Snap! The flails whistled through the air, and the last blow twisted her around. So she saw Mazirian.

He fought. As the blows rained on him, he tried to seize the whips and break them. But they were supple and springy beyond his powers, and jerked away to beat at him again. Infuriated by his resistance, they concentrated on the unfortunate Magician, who foamed and fought with transcendent fury, and T'sain was permitted to crawl to the edge of the grove with her life.

She looked back in awe at the expression of Mazirian's lust for life. He staggered about in a cloud of whips, his furious obstinate figure dimly silhouetted. He weakened and tried to flee, and then he fell. The blows pelted at him —on his head, shoulders, the long legs. He tried to rise but fell back.

T'sain closed her eyes in lassitude. She felt the blood oozing from her broken flesh. But the most vital mission yet remained. She reached her feet, and reelingly set forth. For a long time the thunder of many blows reached her ears.

Mazirian's garden was surpassingly beautiful by night. The star-blossoms spread wide, each of magic perfection, and the captive half-vegetable moths flew back and forth. Phosphorescent water-lilies floated like charming faces on the pond, and the bush which Mazirian had brought from far Almery in the south tinctured the air with sweet fruity perfume.

T'sain, weaving and gasping, now came groping through the garden. Certain of the flowers awoke and regarded her curiously. The half-animal hybrid sleepily chittered at her, thinking to recognize Mazirian's step. Faintly to be heard was the witsful music of the blue-cupped flowers singing of ancient nights when a white moon swam the sky, and great storms and clouds and thunder ruled the seasons.

T'sain passed unheeding. She entered Mazirian's house, found the workroom where glowed the eternal yellow lamps. Mazirian's golden-haired vat-thing sat up suddenly and stared at her with his beautiful vacant eyes.

She found Mazirian's keys in the cabinet, and managed to claw open the trap door. Here she slumped to rest and let the pink gloom pass from her eyes. Visions began to come—Mazirian, tall and arrogant, stepping out to kill Thrang; the strange-hued flowers under the lake; Mazirian, his magic lost, fighting the whips. . . . She was brought from the half-trance by the vat-thing timidly fumbling with her hair.

She shook herself awake and half-walked, half-fell down the stairs. She unlocked the thrice-bound door, thrust it open with almost the last desperate urge of her body. She wandered in to clutch at the pedestal where the glass-topped box stood and Turjan and the dragon were playing their desperate game. She flung the glass crashing to the floor, gently lifted Turjan out and set him down.

The spell was disrupted by the touch of the rune at her wrist, and Turjan became a man again. He looked aghast at the nearly unrecognizable T'sain.

She tried to smile up at him.

"Turjan—you are free—"

"And Mazirian?"

"He is dead." She slumped wearily to the stone floor and lay limp. Turjan surveyed her with an odd emotion in his eyes.

"T'sain, dear creature of my mind," he whispered, "more noble are you than I, who used the only life you knew for my freedom."

He lifted her body in his arms.

"But I shall restore you to the vats. With your brain I build another T'sain, as lovely as you. We go."

He bore her up the stone stairs.

BETWEEN the years when the oceans drank Atlantis and the gleaming cities, and the years of the rise of the sons of the Aryas, there was an Age undreamed-of, when shining kingdoms lay spread across the world like blue mantles beneath the stars—Nemedia, Ophir, Brythunia, Hyperborea, Zamora with its dark-haired women and towers of spider-haunted mystery, Zingara with its chivalry, Koth that bordered on the pastoral lands of Shem, Stygia with its shadow-guarded tombs, Hykrania whose riders wore steel and silk and gold. But the proudest kingdom of the world was Aquilonia, reigning supreme in the dreaming West. Hither came Conan the Cimmerian, black-haired, sullen-eyed, sword in hand, a thief, a reaver, a slayer, of gigantic melancholics and gigantic mirth, to tread the jeweled thrones of the earth under his sandaled feet.

Three thousand years before, the sinister empire of Acheron and its capital, purple-towered Python, had fallen before the onrush of northern barbarians, the Hyborian tribes. These tribes in turn had built up their own brilliant civilization, embodied in the kingdoms of Aquilonia, Nemedia, Corinthia, Argos, and their neighbors. Hence this period is called the Hyborian Age. Its greatest hero was Conan, a barbarian from the northern land of Cimmeria, who waded through rivers of blood to become, at last, king of Aquilonia.

Once, early in his career, Conan's enemies captured and crucified him. When a vulture flew down to try to peck his eyes out, Conan bit the bird's head off. You just can't have a tougher hero than that. That is why the club of admirers of heroic fantasy calls itself the Hyborian Legion, and its fan magazine is called Amra, a name used by Conan when he was a pirate among the black corsairs of Kush.

Robert E. Howard, the creator of Conan, was a Texan and a prolific writer of pulp-magazine fiction in the early 1930s. Despite certain literary faults, Howard was one of the greatest natural story-tellers the genre has produced. Nobody has excelled him in constructing a fast-moving, smoothly-flowing tale of headlong, violent, gripping action. His stories are not only readable but also endlessly rereadable.

Unfortunately, Howard was also maladjusted to the point of psychosis. In 1936, at the age of thirty, he ended a promising literary career by suicide.

Seventeen Conan stories were published in Weird Tales in the 1930s. Three more, discovered among his manuscripts, appeared in various magazines in 1952-53. All twenty tales were published by Gnome Press in five clothbound volumes—The Coming of Conan, Conan the Barbarian, etc.—in 1950-54; these are all out of print. There were also two volumes of pastiches: Tales of Conan, which

I rewrote from other Howard manuscripts, and The Return of Conan, on which I collaborated with Björn Nyberg. Many of these and other Howard stories have been reprinted in magazines, collections, and anthologies. Plans are on foot to reprint the entire Conan saga in paperback form.

SHADOWS IN ZAMBOULA

• ROBERT E. HOWARD

1. A Drum Begins

"**P**ERIL hides in the house of Aram Baksh!"

The speaker's voice quivered with earnestness and his lean, black-nailed fingers clawed at Conan's mightily-muscled arm as he croaked his warning. He was a wiry, sun-burnt man with a straggling black beard, and his ragged garments proclaimed him a nomad. He looked smaller and meaner than ever in contrast to the giant Cimmerian with his black brows, broad chest, and powerful limbs. They stood in a corner of the Sword-Makers' Bazaar, and on either side of them flowed past the many-tongued, many-colored stream of the Zamboula streets, which is exotic, hybrid, flamboyant, and clamorous.

Conan pulled his eyes back from following a bold-eyed, red-lipped Ghanara, whose short slit skirt bared her brown thigh at each insolent step, and frowned down at his importunate companion.

"What do you mean by peril?" he demanded.

The desert man glanced furtively over his shoulder before replying, and lowered his voice.

"Who can say? But desert men and travelers *have* slept in the house of Aram Baksh, and never been seen or heard of again. What became of them? *He* swore they rose and went their way—and it is true that no citizen of the city has ever disappeared from his house. But no one saw the

161

travelers again, and men say that goods and equipment recognized as theirs have been seen in the bazaars. If Aram did not sell them, after doing away with their owners, how came they there?"

"I have no goods," growled the Cimmerian, touching the shagreen-bound hilt of the broadsword that hung at his hip. "I have even sold my horse."

"But it is not always rich strangers who vanish by night from the house of Aram Baksh!" chattered the Zuagir. "Nay, poor desert men have slept there—because his score is less than that of the other taverns—and have been seen no more. Once a chief of the Zuagirs whose son had thus vanished complained to the satrap, Jungir Khan, who ordered the house searched by soldiers."

"And they found a cellar full of corpses?" asked Conan in good-humored derision.

"Nay! They found naught! And drove the chief from the city with threats and curses! But"—he drew closer to Conan and shivered—"something else was found! At the edge of the desert, beyond the houses, there is a clump of palm-trees, and within that grove there is a pit. And within that pit have been found human bones, charred and blackened! Not once, but many times!"

"Which proves what?" grunted the Cimmerian.

"Aram Baksh is a demon! Nay, in this accursed city which Stygians built and which Hyrkanians rule—where white, brown, and black folk mingle together to produce hybrids of all unholy hues and breeds—who can tell who is a man? At night he assumes his true guise and carries his guests off into the desert where his fellow demons from the waste meet in conclave."

"Why does he always carry off strangers?" asked Conan skeptically.

"The people of the city would not suffer him to slay their people, but they care naught for the strangers who fall into his hands. Conan, you are of the West, and know not the secrets of his ancient land. But, since the beginning of happenings, the demons of the desert have worshipped Yog, the Lord of the Empty Abodes, with fire—fire that devours human victims.

"Be warned! You have dwelt for many moons in the tents of the Zuagirs, and you are our brother! Go not to the house of Aram Baksh!"

"Get out of sight!" Conan said suddenly. "Yonder comes a squad of the city-watch. If they see you they may remember a horse that was stolen from the satrap's stable—"

The Zuagir gasped and moved convulsively. He ducked between a booth and a stone horse-trough, pausing only long enough to chatter: "Be warned, my brother! There are demons in the house of Aram Baksh!" Then he darted down a narrow alley and was gone.

Conan shifted his broad sword-belt to his liking and calmly returned the searching stares directed at him by the squad of watchmen as they swung past. They eyed him curiously and suspiciously, for he was a man who stood out even in such a motley throng as crowded the winding streets of Zamboula. His blue eyes and alien features distinguished him from the Eastern swarms, and the straight sword at his hip added point to the racial difference.

The watchmen did not accost him, but swung on down the street, while the crowd opened a lane for them. They were Pelishtim, squat, hook-nosed, with blue-black beards sweeping their mailed breasts—mercenaries hired for work the ruling Turanians considered beneath themselves, and no less hated by the mongrel population for that reason.

Conan glanced at the sun, just beginning to dip behind the flat-topped houses on the western side of the bazaar, and hitching once more at his belt, moved off in the direction of Aram Baksh's tavern.

With a hillman's stride he moved through the ever-shifting colors of the streets, where the ragged tunics of whining beggars brushed against the ermine-trimmed khalats of lordly merchants and the pearl-sewn satin of rich courtezans. Giant black slaves slouched along, jostling blue-bearded wanderers from the Shemitish cities, ragged nomads from the surrounding deserts, traders and adventurers from all the lands of the East.

The native population was no less heterogeneous. Here, centuries ago, the armies of Stygia had come, carving an empire out of the eastern desert. Zamboula was but a small trading-town then, lying amidst a ring of oases, and inhabited by descendants of nomads. The Stygians built it into a city and settled it with their own people, and with Shemite and Kushite slaves. The ceaseless caravans, threading the desert from east to west and back again, brought riches and more mingling of races. Then came the conquering Turanians, riding out of the East to thrust back the boundaries of Stygia, and now for a generation Zamboula had been Turan's westernmost outpost, ruled by a Turanian satrap.

The babel of a myriad tongues smote on the Cimmerian's ears as the restless pattern of the Zamboula streets weaved about him—cleft now and then by a squad of clattering horsemen, the tall, supple warriors of Turan, with dark hawk-faces, clinking metal and curved swords. The throng scampered from under their horses' hoofs, for they were the lords of Zamboula. But tall, somber Stygians, standing back in the shadows, glowered darkly, remembering their ancient glories. The hybrid population cared little whether the king who controlled their destinies dwelt in dark Khemi or gleaming Aghrapur. Jungir Khan ruled Zamboula, and men whispered that Nafertari, the satrap's mistress, ruled Jungir Khan; but the people went their way, flaunting their myriad colors in the streets, bargaining, disputing, gambling, swilling, loving, as the people of Zamboula have done for all the centuries its towers and minarets have lifted over the sands of the Kharamun.

Bronze lanterns, carved with leering dragons, had been lighted in the streets before Conan reached the house of Aram Baksh. The tavern was the last occupied house on the street, which ran west. A wide garden, enclosed by a wall, where date-palms grew thick, separated it from the houses farther east. To the west of the inn stood another grove of palms, through which the street, now become a road, wound out into the desert. Across the road from the tavern stood a row of deserted huts, shaded by straggling palm-trees and occupied only by bats and jackals. As Conan came down the road he wondered why the beggars, so plentiful in Zamboula, had not appropriated these empty houses for sleeping-quarters. The lights ceased some distance behind him. Here were no lanterns, except the one hanging before the tavern gate: only the stars, the soft dust of the road underfoot, and the rustle of the palm-leaves in the desert breeze.

Aram's gate did not open upon the road, but upon the alley which ran between the tavern and the garden of the date-palms. Conan jerked lustily at the rope which depended from the bell beside the lantern, augmenting its

clamor by hammering on the iron-bound teakwood gate
with the hilt of his sword. A wicket opened in the gate
and a black face peered through.

"Open, blast you," requested Conan. "I'm a guest. I've
paid Aram for a room, and a room I'll have, by Crom!"

The black craned his neck to stare into the starlit road
behind Conan; but he opened the gate without comment,
and closed it again behind the Cimmerian, locking it and
bolting it. The wall was unusually high; but there were
many thieves in Zamboula, and a house on the edge of the
desert might have to be defended against a nocturnal
nomad raid. Conan strode through a garden where great
pale blossoms nodded in the starlight, and entered the taproom, where a Stygian with the shaven head of a student
sat at a table brooding over nameless mysteries, and some
nondescripts wrangled over a game of dice in a corner.

Aram Baksh came forward, walking softly, a portly man,
with a black beard that swept his breast, a jutting hook-
nose, and small black eyes which were never still.

"You wish food?" he asked. "Drink?"

"I ate a joint of beef and a loaf of bread in the *suk*,"
grunted Conan. "Bring me a tankard of Ghazan wine—I've
got just enough left to pay for it." He tossed a copper coin
on the wine-splashed board.

"You did not win at the gaming-tables?"

"How could I, with only a handful of silver to begin
with? I paid you for the room this morning, because I
knew I'd probably lose. I wanted to be sure I had a roof
over my head tonight. I notice nobody sleeps in the streets
in Zamboula. The very beggars hunt a niche they can
barricade before dark. The city must be full of a particularly bloodthirsty brand of thieves."

He gulped the cheap wine with relish and then followed
Aram out of the taproom. Behind him the players halted
their game to stare after him with a cryptic speculation
in their eyes. They said nothing, but the Stygian laughed,
a ghastly laugh of inhuman cynicism and mockery. The
others lowered their eyes uneasily, avoiding one another's
glance. The arts studied by a Stygian scholar are not cal-
culated to make him share the feelings of a normal human
being.

Conan followed Aram down a corridor lighted by copper
lamps, and it did not please him to note his host's noise-

less tread. Aram's feet were clad in soft slippers, and the hallway was carpeted with thick Turanian rugs; but there was an unpleasant suggestion of stealthiness about the Zamboulan.

At the end of the winding corridor Aram halted at a door, across which a heavy iron bar rested in powerful metal brackets. This Aram lifted and showed the Cimmerian into a well-appointed chamber, the windows of which, Conan instantly noted, were small and strongly set with twisted bars of iron, tastefully gilded. There were rugs on the floor, a couch, after the eastern fashion, and ornately carven stools. It was a much more elaborate chamber than Conan could have procured for the price nearer the center of the city—a fact that had first attracted him, when, that morning, he discovered how slim a purse his roisterings for the past few days had left him. He had ridden into Zamboula from the desert a week before.

Aram had lighted a bronze lamp, and he now called Conan's attention to the two doors. Both were provided with heavy bolts.

"You may sleep safely tonight, Cimmerian," said Aram, blinking over his bushy beard from the inner doorway.

Conan grunted and tossed his naked broadsword on the couch.

"Your bolts and bars are strong; but I always sleep with steel by my side."

Aram made no reply; he stood fingering his thick beard for a moment as he stared at the grim weapon. Then silently he withdrew, closing the door behind him. Conan shot the bolt into place, crossed the room, opened the opposite door and looked out. The room was on the side of the house that faced the road running west from the city. The door opened into a small court that was enclosed by a wall of its own. The end-walls, which shut it off from the rest of the tavern compound, were high and without entrances; but the wall that flanked the road was low, and there was no lock on the gate.

Conan stood for a moment in the door, the glow of the bronze lamp behind him, looking down the road to where it vanished among the dense palms. Their leaves rustled together in the faint breeze; beyond them lay the naked desert. Far up the street, in the other direction, lights gleamed and the noises of the city came faintly to him.

Here was only starlight, the whispering of the palm-leaves, and beyond that low wall, the dust of the road and the deserted huts thrusting their flat roofs against the low stars. Somewhere beyond the palm groves a drum began.

The garbled warnings of the Zuagir returned to him, seeming somehow less fantastic than they had seemed in the crowded, sunlit streets. He wondered again at the riddle of those empty huts. Why did the beggars shun them? He turned back into the chamber, shut the door, and bolted it.

The light began to flicker, and he investigated, swearing when he found the palm-oil in the lamp was almost exhausted. He started to shout for Aram, then shrugged his shoulders and blew out the light. In the soft darkness he stretched himself fully clad on the couch, his sinewy hand by instinct searching for and closing on the hilt of his broadsword. Glancing idly at the stars framed in the barred windows, with the murmur of the breeze through the palms in his ears, he sank into slumber with a vague consciousness of the muttering drum, out on the desert— the low rumble and mutter of a leather-covered drum, beaten with soft, rhythmic strokes of an open black hand. . . .

2. THE NIGHT SKULKERS

It was the stealthy opening of a door which awakened the Cimmerian. He did not awake as civilized men do, drowsy and drugged and stupid. He awoke instantly, with a clear mind, recognizing the sound that had interrupted his sleep. Lying there tensely in the dark he saw the outer door slowly open. In a widening crack of starlit sky he saw framed a great black bulk, broad, stooping shoulders and a misshapen head blocked out against the stars.

Conan felt the skin crawl between his shoulders. He had bolted that door securely. How could it be opening now, save by supernatural agency? And how could a human being possess a head like that outlined against the stars? All the tales he had heard in the Zuagir tents of devils and goblins came back to bead his flesh with clammy sweat. Now the monster slid noiselessly into the room, with a crouching posture and a shambling gait; and a familiar scent assailed the Cimmerian's nostrils, but did not reassure him, since Zuagir legendry represented demons as smelling like that.

Noiselessly Conan coiled his long legs under him; his naked sword was in his right hand, and when he struck it was as suddenly and murderously as a tiger lunging out of the dark. Not even a demon could have avoided that catapulting charge. His sword met and clove through flesh and bone, and something went heavily to the floor with a strangling cry. Conan crouched in the dark above it, sword dripping in his hand. Devil or beast or man, the thing was dead there on the floor. He sensed death as any wild thing senses it. He glared through the half-open door into the starlit court beyond. The gate stood open, but the court was empty.

Conan shut the door but did not bolt it. Groping in the darkness he found the lamp and lighted it. There was enough oil in it to burn for a minute or so. An instant later he was bending over the figure that sprawled on the floor in a pool of blood.

It was a gigantic black man, naked but for a loin-cloth. One hand still grasped a knotty-headed bludgeon. The fellow's kinky wool was built up into hornlike spindles with twigs and dried mud. This barbaric coiffure had given the head its misshapen appearance in the starlight. Provided with a clue to the riddle, Conan pushed back the thick red lips, and grunted as he stared down at teeth filed to points.

He understood now the mystery of the strangers who had disappeared from the house of Aram Baksh; the riddle of the black drum thrumming out there beyond the palm groves, and of that pit of charred bones—that pit where strange meat might be roasted under the stars, while black beasts squatted about to glut a hideous hunger. The man on the floor was a cannibal slave from Darfar.

There were many of his kind in the city. Cannibalism was not tolerated openly in Zamboula. But Conan knew now why people locked themselves in so securely at night, and why even beggars shunned the open alleys and doorless ruins. He grunted in disgust as he visualized brutish black shadows skulking up and down the nighted streets, seeking human prey—and such men as Aram Baksh to open the doors to them. The innkeeper was not a demon;

he was worse. The slaves from Darfar were notorious thieves; there was no doubt that some of their pilfered loot found its way into the hands of Aram Baksh. And in return he sold them human flesh.

Conan blew out the light, stepped to the door and opened it, and ran his hand over the ornaments on the outer side. One of them was movable and worked the bolt inside. The room was a trap to catch human prey like rabbits. But this time instead of a rabbit it had caught a saber-toothed tiger.

Conan returned to the other door, lifted the bolt and pressed against it. It was immovable, and he remembered the bolt on the other side. Aram was taking no chances either with his victims or the men with whom he dealt. Buckling on his sword-belt, the Cimmerian strode out into the court, closing the door behind him. He had no intention of delaying the settlement of his reckoning with Aram Baksh. He wondered how many poor devils had been bludgeoned in their sleep and dragged out of that room and down the road that ran through the shadowed palm groves to the roasting-pit.

He halted in the court. The drum was still muttering, and he caught the reflection of a leaping red glare through the groves. Cannibalism was more than a perverted appetite with the black men of Darfar; it was an integral element of their ghastly cult. The black vultures were already in conclave. But whatever flesh filled their bellies that night, it would not be his.

To reach Aram Baksh he must climb one of the walls which separated the small enclosure from the main compound. They were high, meant to keep out the man-eaters; but Conan was no swamp-bred black man; his thews had been steeled in boyhood on the sheer cliffs of his native hills. He was standing at the foot of the nearer wall when a cry echoed under the trees.

In an instant Conan was crouching at the gate, glaring down the road. The sound had come from the shadows of the huts across the road. He heard a frantic choking and gurgling such as might result from a desperate attempt to shriek, with a black hand fastened over the victim's mouth. A close-knit clump of figures emerged from the shadows beyond the huts, and started down the road—three huge black men carrying a slender, struggling figure between them. Conan caught the glimmer of pale limbs writhing in the starlight, even as, with a convulsive wrench, the captive slipped from the grasp of the brutal fingers and came flying up the road, a supple young woman, naked as the day she was born. Conan saw her plainly before she ran out of the road and into the shadows between the huts. The blacks were at her heels, and back in the shadows the figures merged and an intolerable scream of anguish and horror rang out.

Stirred to red rage by the ghoulishness of the episode, Conan raced across the road.

Neither victim nor abductors were aware of his presence until the soft swish of the dust about his feet brought them about, and then he was almost upon them, coming with gusty fury of a hill wind. Two of the blacks turned to meet him, lifting their bludgeons. But they failed to estimate properly the speed at which he was coming. One of them was down, disemboweled, before he could strike, and wheeling cat-like, Conan evaded the stroke of the other's cudgel and lashed in a whistling counter-cut. The black's head flew into the air; the headless body took three staggering steps, spurting blood and clawing horribly at the air with groping hands, and then slumped to the dust.

The remaining cannibal gave back with a strangled yell, hurling his captive from him. She tripped and rolled in the dust, and the black fled in blind panic toward the city. Conan was at his heels. Fear winged the black feet, but before they reached the easternmost hut, he sensed death at his back, and bellowed like an ox in the slaughter-yards.

"Black dog of hell!" Conan drove his sword between the dusky shoulders with such vengeful fury that the broad blade stood out half its length from the black breast. With a choking cry the black stumbled headlong, and Conan braced his feet and dragged out his sword as his victim fell.

Only the breeze disturbed the leaves. Conan shook his head as a lion shakes its mane and growled his unsatiated blood-lust. But no more shapes slunk from the shadows, and before the huts the starlit road stretched empty. He whirled at the quick patter of feet behind him; but it was only the girl, rushing to throw herself on him and clasp his neck in a desperate grasp, frantic from terror of the abominable fate she had just escaped.

"Easy, girl," he grunted. "You're all right. How did they catch you?"

She sobbed something unintelligible. He forgot all about Aram Baksh as he scrutinized her by the light of the stars. She was white, though a very definite brunette, obviously one of Zamboula's many mixed breeds. She was tall, with a slender, supple form, as he was in a good position to observe. Admiration burned in his fierce eyes as he looked down on her splendid bosom and her lithe limbs, which still quivered from fright and exertion. He passed an arm around her flexible waist and said, reassuringly: "Stop shaking, wench; you're safe enough."

His touch seemed to restore her shaken sanity. She tossed back her thick, glossy locks and cast a fearful glance over her shoulder, while she pressed closer to the Cimmerian as if seeking security in the contact.

"They caught me in the streets," she muttered, shuddering. "Lying in wait, beneath a dark arch—black men, like great, hulking apes! Set have mercy on me! I shall dream of it!"

"What were you doing out on the streets this time of night?" he inquired, fascinated by the satiny feel of her sleek skin under his questing fingers.

She raked back her hair and stared blankly up into his face. She did not seem aware of his caresses.

"My lover," she said. "My lover drove me into the streets. He went mad and tried to kill me. As I fled from him I was seized by those beasts."

"Beauty like yours might drive a man mad," quoth Conan, running his fingers experimentally through her glossy tresses.

She shook her head, like one emerging from a daze. She no longer trembled, and her voice was steady.

"It was spite of a priest—of Totrasmek, the high priest of Hanuman, who desires me for himself—the dog!"

"No need to curse him for that," grinned Conan. "The old hyena has better taste than I thought."

She ignored the bluff compliment. She was regaining her poise swiftly.

"My lover is a—a young Turanian soldier. To spite me, Totrasmek gave him a drug that drove him mad. Tonight he snatched up a sword and came at me to slay me in his madness, but I fled from him into the streets. The Negroes seized me and brought me to this—*what was that?*"

Conan had already moved. Soundlessly as a shadow he drew her behind the nearest hut, beneath the straggling palms. They stood in tense stillness, while the low mutterings both had heard grew louder until voices were distinguishable. A group of Negroes, some nine or ten, were coming along the road from the direction of the city. The girl clutched Conan's arm, and he felt the terrified quivering of her supple body against his.

Now they could understand the gutturals of the black men.

"Our brothers are already assembled at the pit," said one. "We have had no luck. I hope they have enough for us."

"Aram promised us a man," muttered another, and Conan mentally promised Aram something.

"Aram keeps his word," grunted yet another. "Many a man we have taken from his tavern. But we pay him well. I myself have given him ten bales of silk I stole from my master. It was good silk, by Set!"

The blacks shuffled past, bare splay feet scuffing up the dust, and their voices dwindled down the road.

"Well for us those corpses are lying behind these huts," muttered Conan. "If they look in Aram's death-room they'll find another. Let's begone."

"Yes, let us hasten!" begged the girl, almost hysterical again. "My lover is wandering somewhere in the streets alone. The Negroes may take him."

"A devil of a custom this is!" growled Conan, as he led the way toward the city, paralleling the road but keeping behind the huts and straggling trees. "Why don't the citizens clean out these black dogs?"

"They are valuable slaves," murmured the girl. "There are so many of them they might revolt if they were denied the flesh for which they lust. The people of Zamboula know they skulk the streets at night, and all are careful to remain within locked doors, except when something unforeseen happens, as it did to me. The blacks prey on anything they catch, but they seldom catch anybody but strangers. The people of Zamboula are not concerned with the strangers that pass through the city.

"Such men as Aram Baksh sell these strangers to the

blacks. He would not dare attempt such a thing with a citizen."

Conan spat in disgust, and a moment later led his companion out into the road which was becoming a street, with still, unlighted houses on each side. Slinking in the shadows was not congenial to his nature.

"Where do you want to go?" he asked. The girl did not seem to object to his arm about her waist.

"To my house, to rouse my servants," she answered. "To bid them search for my lover. I do not wish the city—the priests—anyone—to know of his madness. He—he is a young officer with a promising future. Perhaps we can drive this madness from him if we can find him."

"If *we* find him?" rumbled Conan. "What makes you think I want to spend the night scouring the streets for a lunatic?"

She cast a quick glance into his face, and properly interpreted the gleam in his blue eyes. Any woman could have known that he would follow her wherever she led—for a while, at least. But being a woman, she concealed her knowledge of that fact.

"Please," she began with a hint of tears in her voice, "I have no one else to ask for help—you have been kind—"

"All right!" he grunted. "All right! What's the young reprobate's name?"

"Why—Alafdhal. I am Zabibi, a dancing-girl. I have danced often before the satrap, Jungir Khan, and his mistress Nafertari, and before all the lords and royal ladies of Zamboula. Totrasmek desired me, and because I repulsed him, he made me the innocent tool of his vengeance against Alafdhal. I asked a love potion of Totrasmek, not suspecting the depth of his guile and hate. He gave me a drug to mix with my lover's wine, and he swore that when Alafdhal drank it, he would love me even more madly than ever, and grant my every wish. I mixed the drug secretly with my lover's wine. But having drunk, my lover went raving mad and things came about as I have told you. Curse Totrasmek, the hybrid snake—ahhh!"

She caught his arm convulsively and both stopped short. They had come into a district of shops and stalls, all deserted and unlighted, for the hour was late. They were passing an alley, and in its mouth a man was standing, motionless and silent. His head was lowered, but Conan caught the weird gleam of eerie eyes regarding them unblinkingly. His skin crawled, not with fear of the sword in the man's hand, but because of the uncanny suggestion of his posture and silence. They suggested madness. Conan pushed the girl aside and drew his sword.

"Don't kill him!" she begged. "In the name of Set, do not slay him! You are strong—overpower him!"

"We'll see," he muttered, grasping his sword in his right hand and clenching his left into a mallet-like fist.

He took a wary step toward the alley—and with a horrible moaning laugh the Turanian charged. As he came he swung his sword, rising on his toes as he put all the power of his body behind the blows. Sparks flashed blue as Conan parried the blade, and the next instant the madman was stretched senseless in the dust from a thundering buffet of Conan's left fist.

The girl ran forward.

"Oh, he is not—he is not—"

Conan bent swiftly, turned the man on his side and ran quick fingers over him.

"He's not hurt much," he grunted. "Bleeding at the nose, but anybody's likely to do that, after a clout on the jaw. He'll come to after a bit, and maybe his mind will be right. In the meantime I'll tie his wrists with his sword-belt—so. Now where do you want me to take him?"

"Wait!" She knelt beside the senseless figure, seized the bound hands and scanned them avidly. Then, shaking her head as if in baffled disappointment, she rose. She came close to the giant Cimmerian, and laid her slender hands on his arching breast. Her dark eyes, like wet black jewels in the starlight, gazed up into his.

"You are a man! Help me! Totrasmek must die! Slay him for me!"

"And put my neck into a Turanian noose?" he grunted.

"Nay!" The slender arms, strong as pliant steel, were around his corded neck. Her supple body throbbed against his. "The Hyrkanians have no love for Totrasmek. The priests of Set fear him. He is a mongrel, who rules men by fear and superstition. I worship Set, and the Turanians bow to Erlik, but Totrasmek sacrifices to Hanuman the accursed! The Turanian lords fear his black arts and his power over the hybrid population, and they hate him. Even Jungir Khan and his mistress Nafertari fear and hate him.

If he were slain in his temple at night, they would not seek his slayer very closely."

"And what of his magic?" rumbled the Cimmerian.

"You are a fighting-man," she answered. "To risk your life is part of your profession."

"For a price," he admitted.

"There will be a price!" she breathed, rising on tiptoes, to gaze into his eyes.

The nearness of her vibrant body drove a flame through his veins. The perfume of her breath mounted to his brain. But as his arms closed about her supple figure she avoided them with a lithe movement, saying: "Wait! First serve me in this matter."

"Name your price." He spoke with some difficulty.

"Pick up my lover," she directed, and the Cimmerian stooped and swung the tall form easily to his broad shoulder. At the moment he felt as if he could have toppled over Jungir Khan's palace with equal ease. The girl murmured an endearment to the unconscious man, and there was no hypocrisy in her attitude. She obviously loved Alafdhal sincerely. Whatever business arrangement she made with Conan would have no bearing on her relationship with Alafdhal. Women are more practical about these things than men.

"Follow me!" She hurried along the street, while the Cimmerian strode easily after her, in no way discomforted by his limp burden. He kept a wary eye out for black shadows skulking under arches, but saw nothing suspicious. Doubtless the men of Darfar were all gathered at the roasting-pit. The girl turned down a narrow side street, and presently knocked cautiously at an arched door.

Almost instantly a wicket opened in the upper panel, and a black face glanced out. She bent close to the opening, whispering swiftly. Bolts creaked in their sockets, and the door opened. A giant black man stood framed against the soft glow of a copper lamp. A quick glance showed Conan the man was not from Darfar. His teeth were unfiled and his kinky hair was cropped close to his skull. He was from the Wadai.

At a word from Zabibi, Conan gave the limp body into the black's arms, and saw the young officer laid on a velvet divan. He showed no signs of returning consciousness. The blow that had rendered him senseless might have felled an ox. Zabibi bent over him for an instant, her fingers nervously twining and twisting. Then she straightened and beckoned the Cimmerian.

The door closed softly, the locks clicked behind them, and the closing wicket shut off the glow of the lamps. In the starlight of the street Zabibi took Conan's hand. Her own hand trembled a little.

"You will not fail me?"

He shook his maned head, massive against the stars.

"Then follow me to Hanuman's shrine, and the gods have mercy on our souls!"

Along the silent streets they moved like phantoms of antiquity. They went in silence. Perhaps the girl was thinking of her lover lying senseless on the divan under the copper lamps; or was shrinking with fear of what lay ahead of them in the demon-haunted shrine of Hanuman. The barbarian was thinking only of the woman moving so supplely beside him. The perfume of her scented hair was in his nostrils, the sensuous aura of her presence filled his brain and left room for no other thoughts.

Once they heard the clank of brass-shod feet, and drew into the shadows of a gloomy arch while a squad of Pelishti watchmen swung past. There were fifteen of them; they marched in close formation, pikes at the ready, and the rearmost men had their broad brass shields slung on their backs, to protect them from a knife-stroke from behind. The skulking menace of the black man-eaters was a threat even to armed men.

As soon as the clang of their sandals had receded up the street, Conan and the girl emerged from their hiding-place and hurried on. A few moments later they saw the squat, flat-topped edifice they sought looming ahead of them.

The temple of Hanuman stood alone in the midst of a broad square, which lay silent and deserted beneath the stars. A marble wall surrounded the shrine, with a broad opening directly before the portico. This opening had no gate or any sort of barrier.

"Why don't the blacks seek their prey here?" muttered Conan. "There's nothing to keep them out of the temple."

He could feel the trembling of Zabibi's body as she pressed close to him.

"They fear Totrasmek, as all in Zamboula fear him, even Jungir Khan and Nafertari. Come! Come quickly, before my courage flows from me like water!"

The girl's fear was evident, but she did not falter. Conan drew his sword and strode ahead of her as they advanced through the open gateway. He knew the hideous habits of the priests of the East, and was aware that an invader of Hanuman's shrine might expect to encounter almost any sort of nightmare horror. He knew there was a good chance that neither he nor the girl would ever leave the shrine alive, but he had risked his life too many times before to devote much thought to that consideration.

They entered a court paved with marble, which gleamed whitely in the starlight. A short flight of broad marble steps led up to the pillared portico. The great bronze doors stood wide open as they had stood for centuries. But no worshippers burnt incense within. In the day men and women might come timidly into the shrine and place offerings to the ape-god on the black altar. At night the people shunned the temple of Hanuman as hares shun the lair of the serpent.

Burning censers bathed the interior in a soft weird glow that created an illusion of unreality. Near the rear wall, behind the black stone altar, sat the god with his gaze fixed for ever on the open door, through which for centuries his victims had come, dragged by chains of roses. A faint groove ran from the sill to the altar, and when Conan's foot felt it, he stepped away as quickly as if he had trodden upon a snake. That groove had been worn by the faltering feet of the multitude of those who had died screaming on that grim altar.

Bestial in the uncertain light Hanuman leered with his carven mask. He sat, not as an ape would crouch, but cross-legged as a man would sit, but his aspect was no less simian for that reason. He was carved from black marble, but his eyes were rubies, which glowed red and lustful as the coals of hell's deepest pits. His great hands lay upon his lap, palms upward, taloned fingers spread and grasping. In the gross emphasis of his attributes, in the leer of his satyr-countenance, was reflected the abominable cynicism of the degenerate cult which deified him.

The girl moved around the image, making toward the back wall, and when her sleek flank brushed against a carven knee, she shrank aside and shuddered as if a reptile had touched her. There was a space of several feet between the broad back of the idol and the marble wall with its frieze of gold leaves. On either hand, flanking the idol, an ivory door under a gold arch was set in the wall.

"Those doors open into each end of a hairpin-shaped corridor," she said hurriedly. "Once I was in the interior of the shrine—once!" She shivered and twitched her slim shoulders at a memory both terrifying and obscene. "The corridor is bent like a horseshoe, with each horn opening into this room. Totrasmek's chambers are enclosed within the curve of the corridor and open into it. But there is a secret door in this wall which opens directly into an inner chamber—"

She began to run her hands over the smooth surface, where no crack or crevice showed. Conan stood beside her, sword in hand, glancing warily about him. The silence, the emptiness of the shrine, with imagination picturing what might lie behind that wall, made him feel like a wild beast nosing a trap.

"Ah!" The girl had found a hidden spring at last; a square opening gaped blackly in the wall. Then: "Set!" she screamed, and even as Conan leaped toward her, he saw that a great misshapen hand had fastened itself in her hair. She was snatched off her feet and jerked head-first through the opening. Conan, grabbing ineffectually at her, felt his fingers slip from a naked limb, and in an instant she had vanished and the wall showed blank as before. Only from beyond it came briefly the muffled sounds of a struggle, a scream, faintly heard, and a low laugh that made Conan's blood congeal in his veins.

3. BLACK HANDS GRIPPING

With an oath the Cimmerian smote the wall a terrific blow with the pommel of his sword, and the marble cracked and chipped. But the hidden door did not give way, and reason told him that doubtless it had been bolted on the other side of the wall. Turning, he sprang across the chamber to one of the ivory doors.

He lifted his sword to shatter the panels, but on a venture tried the door first with his left hand. It swung open

easily, and he glared into a long corridor that curved away
into dimness under the weird light of censers similar to
those in the shrine. A heavy gold bolt showed on the jamb
of the door, and he touched it lightly with his finger tips.
The faint warmness of the metal could have been detected
only by a man whose faculties were akin to those of a
wolf. That bolt had been touched—and therefore drawn—
within the last few seconds. The affair was taking on more
and more of the aspect of a baited trap. He might have
known Totrasmek would know when anyone entered the
temple.

To enter the corridor would undoubtedly be to walk into
whatever trap the priest had set for him. But Conan did
not hesitate. Somewhere in that dim-lit interior Zabibi
was a captive, and, from what he knew of the character-
istics of Hanuman's priests, he was sure that she needed
help badly. Conan stalked into the corridor with a panther-
ish tread, poised to strike right or left.

On his left, ivory, arched doors opened into the corridor,
and he tried each in turn. All were locked. He had gone
perhaps seventy-five feet when the corridor bent sharply
to the left, describing the curve the girl had mentioned.
A door opened into this curve, and it gave under his hand.

He was looking into a broad, square chamber, somewhat
more clearly lighted than the corridor. Its walls were of
white marble, the floor of ivory, the ceiling of fretted silver.
He saw divans of rich satin, gold-worked footstools of ivory,
a disk-shaped table of some massive, metal-like substance.
On one of the divans a man was reclining, looking toward
the door. He laughed as he met the Cimmerian's startled
glare.

This man was naked except for a loin-cloth and high-
strapped sandals. He was brown-skinned, with close-
cropped black hair and restless black eyes that set off a
broad, arrogant face. In girth and breadth he was enormous, with huge limbs on which the great muscles swelled
and rippled at each slightest movement. His hands were
the largest Conan had ever seen. The assurance of gigantic
physical strength colored his every action and inflection.

"Why not enter, barbarian?" he called mockingly, with
an exaggerated gesture of invitation.

Conan's eyes began to smolder ominously, but he trod
warily into the chamber, his sword ready.

"Who the devil are you?" he growled.

"I am Baal-pteor," the man answered. "Once, long ago and in another land, I had another name. But this is a good name, and why Totrasmek gave it to me, any temple wench can tell you."

"So you're his dog!" grunted Conan. "Well, curse your brown hide, Baal-pteor, where's the wench you jerked through the wall?"

"My master entertains her!" laughed Baal-pteor. "Listen!"

From beyond a door opposite the one by which Conan had entered there sounded a woman's scream, faint and muffled in the distance.

"Blast your soul!" Conan took a stride toward the door, then wheeled with his skin tingling. Baal-pteor was laughing at him, and that laugh was edged with menace that made the hackles rise on Conan's neck and sent a red wave of murder-lust driving across his vision.

He started toward Baal-pteor, the knuckles on his sword-hand showing white. With a swift motion the brown man threw something at him—a shining crystal sphere that glistened in the weird light.

Conan dodged instinctively, but, miraculously, the globe stopped short in mid-air, a few feet from his face. It did not fall to the floor. It hung suspended, as if by invisible filaments, some five feet above the floor. And as he glared in amazement, it began to rotate with growing speed. And as it revolved it grew, expanded, became nebulous. It filled the chamber. It enveloped him. It blotted out furniture, walls, the smiling countenance of Baal-pteor. He was lost in the midst of a blinding bluish blur of whirling speed. Terrific winds screamed past Conan, tugging, tearing at him, striving to wrench him from his feet, to drag him into the vortex that spun madly before him.

With a choking cry Conan lurched backward, reeled, felt the solid wall against his back. At the contact the illusion ceased to be. The whirling titanic sphere vanished like a bursting bubble. Conan reeled upright in the silver-ceil-inged room, with a gray mist coiling about his feet, and saw Baal-pteor lolling on the divan, shaking with silent laughter.

"Son of a slut!" Conan lunged at him. But the mist swirled up from the floor, blotting out that giant brown form. Groping in a rolling cloud that blinded him, Conan felt a rending sensation of dislocation—and then room and mist and brown man were gone together. He was standing alone among the high reeds of a marshy fen, and a buffalo was lunging at him, head down. He leaped aside from the ripping scimitar-curved horns, and drove his sword in behind the foreleg, through ribs and heart. And then it was not a buffalo dying there in the mud, but the brown-skinned Baal-pteor. With a curse Conan struck off his head; and the head soared from the ground and snapped beast-like tusks into his throat. For all his mighty strength he could not tear it loose—he was choking—strangling; then there was a rush and roar through space, the dislocating shock of an immeasurable impact, and he was back in the chamber with Baal-pteor, whose head was once more set firmly on his shoulders, and who laughed silently at him from the divan.

"Mesmerism!" muttered Conan, crouching and digging his toes hard against the marble.

His eyes blazed. This brown dog was playing with him, making sport of him! But this mummery, this child's play of mists and shadows of thought, it could not harm him. He had but to leap and strike and the brown acolyte would be a mangled corpse under his heel. This time he would not be fooled by shadows of illusion—but he was.

A blood-curdling snarl sounded behind him, and he wheeled and struck in a flash at the panther crouching to spring on him from the metal-colored table. Even as he struck, the apparition vanished and his blade clashed deafeningly on the adamantine surface. Instantly he sensed something abnormal. The blade stuck to the table! He wrenched at it savagely. It did not give. This was no mes-meristic trick. The table was a giant magnet. He gripped the hilt with both hands, when a voice at his shoulder brought him about, to face the brown man, who had at last risen from the divan.

Slightly taller than Conan, and much heavier, Baal-pteor loomed before him, a daunting image of muscular develop-ment. His mighty arms were unnaturally long, and his great hands opened and closed, twitching convulsively. Conan released the hilt of his imprisoned sword and fell silent, watching his enemy through slitted lids.

"Your head, Cimmerian!" taunted Baal-pteor. "I shall take

it with my bare hands, twisting it from your shoulders as the head of a fowl is twisted! Thus the sons of Kosala offer sacrifice to Yajur. Barbarian, you look upon a strangler of Yota-pong. I was chosen by the priests of Yajur in my infancy, and throughout childhood, boyhood, and youth I was trained in the art of slaying with the naked hands— for only thus are the sacrifices enacted. Yajur loves blood, and we waste not a drop from the victim's veins. When I was a child they gave me infants to throttle; when I was a boy I strangled young girls; as a youth, women, old men, and young boys. Not until I reached my full manhood was I given a strong man to slay on the altar of Yota-pong.

"For years I offered the sacrifices to Yajur. Hundreds of necks have snapped between these fingers—" he worked them before the Cimmerian's angry eyes. "Why I fled from Yota-pong to become Totrasmek's servant is no concern of yours. In a moment you will be beyond curiosity. The priests of Kosala, the stranglers of Yajur, are strong beyond the belief of men. And I was stronger than any. With my hands, barbarian, I shall break your neck!"

And like the stroke of twin cobras, the great hands closed on Conan's throat. The Cimmerian made no attempt to dodge or fend them away, but his own hands darted to the Kosalan's bull-neck. Baal-pteor's black eyes widened as he felt the thick cords of muscles that protected the barbarian's throat. With a snarl he exerted his inhuman strength, and knots and lumps and ropes of thews rose along his massive arms. And then a choking gasp burst from him as Conan's fingers locked on his throat. For an instant they stood there like statues, their faces masks of effort, veins beginning to stand out purply on their temples. Conan's thin lips drew back from his teeth in a grinning snarl. Baal-pteor's eyes were distended; in them grew an awful surprise and the glimmer of fear. Both men stood motionless as images, except for the expanding of their muscles on rigid arms and braced legs, but strength beyond common conception was warring there—strength that might have uprooted trees and crushed the skulls of bullocks.

The wind whistled suddenly from between Baal-pteor's parted teeth. His face was growing purple. Fear flooded his eyes. His thews seemed ready to burst from his arms and shoulders, yet the muscles of the Cimmerian's thick neck did not give; they felt like masses of woven iron cords under his desperate fingers. But his own flesh was giving way under the iron fingers of the Cimmerian which ground deeper and deeper into the yielding throat-muscles, crushing them in upon jugular and windpipe.

The statuesque immobility of the group gave way to sudden, frenzied motion, as the Kosalan began to wrench and heave, seeking to throw himself backward. He let go of Conan's throat and grasped his wrists, trying to tear away those inexorable fingers.

With a sudden lunge Conan bore him backward until the small of his back crashed against the table. And still farther over its edge Conan bent him, back and back, until his spine was ready to snap.

Conan's low laugh was merciless as the ring of steel.

"You fool!" he all but whispered. "I think you never saw a man from the West before. Did you deem yourself strong, because you were able to twist the heads off civilized folk, poor weaklings with muscles like rotten string? Hell! Break the neck of a wild Cimmerian bull before you call yourself strong. I did that, before I was a full-grown man—like this!"

And with a savage wrench he twisted Baal-pteor's head around until the ghastly face leered over the left shoulder, and the vertebrae snapped like a rotten branch.

Conan hurled the flopping corpse to the floor, turned to the sword again, and gripped the hilt with both hands, bracing his feet against the floor. Blood trickled down his broad breast from the wounds Baal-pteor's finger nails had torn in the skin of his neck. His black hair was damp, sweat ran down his face, and his chest heaved. For all his vocal scorn of Baal-pteor's strength, he had almost met his match in the inhuman Kosalan. But without pausing to catch his breath, he exerted all his strength in a mighty wrench that tore the sword from the magnet where it clung.

Another instant and he had pushed open the door from behind which the scream had sounded, and was looking down a long straight corridor, lined with ivory doors. The other end was masked by a rich velvet curtain, and from beyond that curtain came the devilish strains of such music as Conan had never heard, not even in nightmares.

It made the short hairs bristle on the back of his neck. Mingled with it was the panting, hysterical sobbing of a woman. Grasping his sword firmly, he glided down the corridor.

4. Dance, Girl, Dance!

When Zabibi was jerked head-first through the aperture which opened in the wall behind the idol, her first, dizzy, disconnected thought was that her time had come. She instinctively shut her eyes and waited for the blow to fall. But instead she felt herself dumped unceremoniously onto the smooth marble floor, which bruised her knees and hip. Opening her eyes she stared fearfully around her, just as a muffled impact sounded from beyond the wall. She saw a brown-skinned giant in a loin-cloth standing over her, and, across the chamber into which she had come, a man sat on a divan, with his back to a rich black velvet curtain, a broad, fleshy man, with fat white hands and snaky eyes. And her flesh crawled, for this man was Totrasmek, the priest of Hanuman, who for years had spun his slimy webs of power throughout the city of Zamboula.

"The barbarian seeks to batter his way through the wall," said Totrasmek sardonically, "but the bolt will hold."

The girl saw that a heavy golden bolt had been shot across the hidden door, which was plainly discernible from this side of the wall. The bolt and its sockets would have resisted the charge of an elephant.

"Go open one of the doors for him, Baal-pteor," ordered Totrasmek. "Slay him in the square chamber at the other end of the corridor."

The Kosalan salaamed and departed by the way of a door in the side wall of the chamber. Zabibi rose, staring fearfully at the priest, whose eyes ran avidly over her splendid figure. To this she was indifferent. A dancer of Zamboula was accustomed to nakedness. But the cruelty in his eyes started her limbs to quivering.

"Again you come to me in my retreat, beautiful one," he purred with cynical hypocrisy. "It is an unexpected honor. You seemed to enjoy your former visit so little, that I dared not hope for you to repeat it. Yet I did all in my power to provide you with an interesting experience."

For a Zamboula dancer to blush would be an impossibility, but a smolder of anger mingled with the fear in Zabibi's dilated eyes.

"Fat pig! You know I did not come here for love of you."

"No," laughed Totrasmek, "you came like a fool, creeping through the night with a stupid barbarian to cut my throat. Why should you seek my life?"

"You know why!" she cried, knowing the futility of trying to dissemble.

"You are thinking of your lover," he laughed. "The fact that you are here seeking my life shows that he quaffed the drug I gave you. Well, did you not ask for it? And did I not send what you asked for, out of the love I bear you?"

"I asked you for a drug that would make him slumber harmlessly for a few hours," she said bitterly. "And you—you sent your servant with a drug that drove him mad! I was a fool ever to trust you. I might have known your protestations of friendship were lies, to disguise your hate and spite."

"Why did you wish your lover to sleep?" he retorted. "So you could steal from him the only thing he would never give you—the ring which the jewel men call the Star of Khorala—the star stolen from the queen of Ophir, who would pay a roomful of gold for its return. He would not give it to you willingly, because he knew that it holds a magic which, when properly controlled, will enslave the hearts of any of the opposite sex. You wished to steal it from him, fearing that his magicians would discover the key to that magic and he would forget you in his conquests of the queens of the world. You would sell it back to the queen of Ophir, who understands its power and would use it to enslave men, as she did before it was stolen."

"And why did *you* want it?" she demanded sulkily.

"I understand its powers. It would increase the power of my arts."

"Well," she snapped, "you have it now!"

"I have the Star of Khorala? Nay, you err."

"Why bother to lie?" she retorted bitterly. "He had it on his finger when he drove me into the streets. He did not have it when I found him again. Your servant must have been watching the house, and have taken it from him, after I escaped him. To the devil with it! I want my lover back sane and whole. You have the ring; you have punished us both. Why do you not restore his mind to him? Can you?"

"I could," he assured her, in evident enjoyment of her distress. He drew a phial from among his robes. "This contains the juice of the golden lotus. If your lover drank it he would be sane again. Yes, I will be merciful. You have both thwarted and flouted me, not once but many times; he has constantly opposed my wishes. But I will be merciful. Come and take the phial from my hand."

She stared at Totrasmek, trembling with eagerness to seize it, but fearing it was but some cruel jest. She advanced timidly, with a hand extended, and he laughed heartlessly and drew back out of her reach. Even as her lips parted to curse him, some instinct snatched her eyes upward. From the gilded ceiling four jade-hued vessels were falling. She dodged, but they did not strike her. They crashed to the floor about her, forming the four corners of a square. And she screamed, and screamed again. For out of each ruin reared the hooded head of a cobra, and one struck at her bare leg. Her convulsive movement to evade it brought her within reach of the one on the other side and again she had to shift like lightning to avoid the flash of its hideous head.

She was caught in a frightful trap. All four serpents were swaying and striking at foot, ankle, calf, knee, thigh, hip, whatever portion of her voluptuous body chanced to be nearest to them, and she could not spring over them or pass between them to safety. She could only whirl and spring aside and twist her body to avoid the strokes, and each time she moved to dodge one snake, the motion brought her within range of another, so that she had to keep shifting with the speed of light. She could move only a short space in any direction, and the fearful hooded crests were menacing her every second. Only a dancer of Zamboula could have lived in that grisly square.

She became, herself, a blur of bewildering motion. The heads missed her by hair's breadths, but they missed, as she pitted her twinkling feet, flickering limbs, and perfect eye against the blinding speed of the scaly demons her enemy had conjured out of thin air.

Somewhere a thin whining music struck up, mingling with the hissing of the serpents, like an evil night-wind blowing through the empty sockets of a skull. Even in the flying speed of her urgent haste she realized that the darting of the serpents was no longer at random. They obeyed the grisly piping of the eerie music. They struck with a horrible rhythm, and perforce her swaying, writhing, spinning body attuned itself to their rhythm. Her frantic motions melted into the measures of a dance compared to which the most obscene tarantella of Zamora would have seemed sane and restrained. Sick with shame and terror Zabibi heard the hateful mirth of her merciless tormentor.

"The Dance of the Cobras, my lovely one!" laughed Totrasmek. "So maidens danced in the sacrifice to Hanuman centuries ago—but never with such beauty and suppleness. Dance, girl, dance! How long can you avoid the fangs of the Poison People? Minutes? Hours? You will weary at last. Your swift, sure feet will stumble, your legs falter, your hips slow in their rotations. Then the fangs will begin to sink deep into your ivory flesh—"

Behind him the curtain shook as if struck by a gust of wind, and Totrasmek screamed. His eyes dilated and his hands caught convulsively at the length of bright steel which jutted suddenly from his breast.

The music broke off short. The girl swayed dizzily in her dance, crying out in dreadful anticipation of the flickering fangs—and then only four wisps of harmless blue smoke curled up from the floor about her, as Totrasmek sprawled headlong from the divan.

Conan came from behind the curtain, wiping his broad blade. Looking through the hangings he had seen the girl dancing desperately between four swaying spirals of smoke, but he had guessed that their appearance was very different to her. He knew he had killed Totrasmek.

Zabibi sank down on the floor, panting, but even as Conan started toward her, she staggered up again, though her legs trembled with exhaustion.

"The phial!" she gasped. "The phial!"

Totrasmek still grasped it in his stiffening hand. Ruthlessly she tore it from his locked fingers, and then began frantically to ransack his garments.

"What the devil are you looking for?" Conan demanded.

"A ring—he stole it from Alafdhal. He must have, while

my lover walked in madness through the streets. Set's devils!"

She had convinced herself that it was not on the person of Totrasmek. She began to cast about the chamber, tearing up divan-covers and hangings, and upsetting vessels.

She paused and raked a damp lock of hair out of her eyes.

"I forgot Baal-pteor!"

"He's in hell with his neck broken," Conan assured her.

She expressed vindictive gratification at the news, but an instant later swore expressively.

"We can't stay here. It's not many hours until dawn. Lesser priests are likely to visit the temple at any hour of the night, and if we're discovered here with his corpse, the people will tear us to pieces. The Turanians could not save us."

She lifted the bolt on the secret door, and a few moments later they were in the streets and hurrying away from the silent square where brooded the age-old shrine of Hanuman.

In a winding street a short distance away Conan halted and checked his companion with a heavy hand on her naked shoulder.

"Don't forget there was a price—"

"I have not forgotten!" She twisted free. "But we must go to—to Alafdhal first!"

A few minutes later the black slave let them through the wicket door. The young Turanian lay upon the divan, his arms and legs bound with heavy velvet ropes. His eyes were open, but they were like those of a mad dog, and foam was thick on his lips. Zabibi shuddered.

"Force his jaws open!" she commanded, and Conan's iron fingers accomplished the task.

Zabibi emptied the phial down the maniac's gullet. The effect was like magic. Instantly he became quiet. The glare faded from his eyes; he stared up at the girl in a puzzled way, but with recognition and intelligence. Then he fell into a normal slumber.

"When he awakes he will be quite sane," she whispered, motioning to the silent slave.

With a deep bow he gave into her hands a small leathern bag, and drew about her shoulders a silken cloak. Her man-

ner had subtly changed when she beckoned Conan to follow her out of the chamber.

In an arch that opened on the street, she turned to him,
drawing herself up with a new regality.

"I must now tell you the truth," she said. "I am not Zabibi. I am Nafertari. And *he* is not Alafdhal, a poor captain
of the guardsmen. He is Jungir Khan, satrap of Zamboula."

Conan made no comment; his scarred dark countenance
was immobile.

"I lied to you because I dared not divulge the truth to
anyone," she said. "We were alone when Jungir Khan went
mad. None knew of it but myself. Had it been known that
the satrap of Zamboula was a madman, there would have
been insant revolt and rioting, even as Totrasmek planned,
who plotted our destruction.

"You see now how impossible is the reward for which
you hoped. The satrap's mistress is not—cannot be for you.
But you shall not go unrewarded. Here is a sack of gold."

She gave him the bag she had received from the slave.

"Go, now, and when the sun is up come to the palace. I
will have Jungir Khan make you captain of his guard. But
you will take your orders from me, secretly. Your first duty
will be to march a squad to the shrine of Hanuman, os-
tensibly to search for clues of the priest's slayer; in reality
to search for the Star of Khorala. It must be hidden there
somewhere. When you find it, bring it to me. You have my
leave to go now."

He nodded, still silent, and strode away. The girl, watching the swing of his broad shoulders, was piqued to note
that there was nothing in his bearing to show that he was
in any way chagrined or abashed.

When he had rounded a corner, he glanced back, and
then changed his direction and quickened his pace. A few
moments later he was in the quarter of the city containing
the Horse Market. There he smote on a door until from the
window above a bearded head was thrust to demand the
reason for the disturbance.

"A horse," demanded Conan. "The swiftest steed you
have."

"I open no gates at this time of night," grumbled the
horse-trader.

Conan rattled his coins.

"Dog's son knave! Don't you see I'm white, and alone? Come down, before I smash your door!"

Presently, on a bay stallion, Conan was riding toward the house of Aram Baksh.

He turned off the road into the alley that lay between the tavern compound and the date-palm garden, but he did not pause at the gate. He rode on to the northeast corner of the wall, then turned and rode along the north wall, to halt within a few paces of the northwest angle. No trees grew near the wall, but there were some low bushes. To one of these he tied his horse, and was about to climb into the saddle again, when he heard a low muttering of voices beyond the corner of the wall.

Drawing his foot from the stirrup he stole to the angle and peered around it. Three men were moving down the road toward the palm groves, and from their slouching gait he knew they were Negroes. They halted at his low call, bunching themselves as he strode toward them, his sword in his hand. Their eyes gleamed whitely in the starlight. Their brutish lust shone in their ebony faces, but they knew their three cudgels could not prevail against his sword, just as he knew it.

"Where are you going?" he challenged.

"To bid our brothers put out the fire in the pit beyond the groves," was the sullen, guttural reply. "Aram Baksh promised us a man, but he lied. We found one of our brothers dead in the trap-chamber. We go hungry this night."

"I think not," smiled Conan. "Aram Baksh will give you a man. Do you see that door?"

He pointed to a small, iron-bound portal set in the midst of the western wall.

"Wait there. Aram Baksh will give you a man."

Backing warily away until he was out of reach of a sudden bludgeon blow, he turned and melted around the northwest angle of the wall. Reaching his horse he paused to ascertain that the blacks were not sneaking after him, and then he climbed into the saddle and stood upright on it, quieting the uneasy steed with a low word. He reached up, grasped the coping of the wall and drew himself up and over. There he studied the grounds for an instant. The tavern was built in the southwest corner of the enclosure, the remaining space of which was occupied by groves and gardens. He saw no one in the grounds. The tavern was dark and silent, and he knew all the doors and windows were barred and bolted.

Conan knew that Aram Baksh slept in a chamber that opened into a cypress-bordered path that led to the door in the western wall. Like a shadow he glided among the trees and a few moments later he rapped lightly on the chamber door.

"What is it?" asked a rumbling voice within.

"Aram Baksh!" hissed Conan. "The blacks are stealing over the wall!"

Almost instantly the door opened, framing the tavern-keeper, naked but for his shirt, with a dagger in his hand.

He craned his neck to stare into the Cimmerian's face.

"What tale is this—*you!*"

Conan's vengeful fingers strangled the yell in his throat. They went to the floor together and Conan wrenched the dagger from his enemy's hand. The blade glinted in the starlight, and blood spurted. Aram Baksh made hideous noises, gasping and gagging on a mouthful of blood. Conan dragged him to his feet and again the dagger slashed, and most of the curly beard fell to the floor.

Still gripping his captive's throat—for a man can scream incoherently even with his tongue slit—Conan dragged him out of the dark chamber and down the cypress-shadowed path, to the iron-bound door in the outer wall. With one hand he lifted the bolt and threw the door open, disclosing the three shadowy figures which waited like black vultures outside. Into their eager arms Conan thrust the innkeeper.

A horrible, blood-choked scream rose from the Zamboulan's throat, but there was no response from the silent tavern. The people there were used to screams outside the wall. Aram Baksh fought like a wild man, his distended eyes turned frantically on the Cimmerian's face. He found no mercy there. Conan was thinking of the scores of wretches who owed their bloody doom to this man's greed.

In glee the Negroes dragged him down the road, mocking his frenzied gibberings. How could they recognize Aram Baksh in this half-naked, blood-stained figure, with the grotesquely shorn beard and unintelligible babblings? The sounds of the struggle came back to Conan, standing beside the gate, even after the clump of figures had vanished among the palms.

Closing the door behind him, Conan returned to his horse, mounted, and turned westward, toward the open desert, swinging wide to skirt the sinister belt of palm groves. As he rode, he drew from his belt a ring in which gleamed a jewel that snared the starlight in a shimmering iridescence. He held it up to admire it, turning it this way and that. The compact bag of gold pieces clinked gently at his saddle-bow, like a promise of the greater riches to come.

"I wonder what she'd say if she knew I recognized her as Nafertari and him as Jungir Khan the insant I saw them," he mused. "I knew the Star of Khorala, too. There'll be a fine scene if she ever guesses that I slipped it off his finger while I was tying him with his sword-belt. But they'll never catch me, with the start I'm getting."

He glanced back at the shadowy palm groves, among which a red glare was mounting. A chanting rose to the night, vibrating with savage exultation. And another sound mingled with it, a mad, incoherent screaming, a frenzied gibbering in which no words could be distinguished. The noise followed Conan as he rode westward beneath the paling stars